George Lacy

Pictures of Travel, Sport and Adventure

George Lacy

Pictures of Travel, Sport and Adventure

ISBN/EAN: 9783337178697

Printed in Europe, USA, Canada, Australia, Japan

Cover: Foto ©Andreas Hilbeck / pixelio.de

More available books at **www.hansebooks.com**

Yours faithfully,
The Old Pioneer

PICTURES OF TRAVEL, SPORT, AND ADVENTURE

BY

GEORGE LACY

("THE OLD PIONEER")

AUTHOR OF "LIBERTY AND LAW," "PIONEER HUNTERS, TRADERS AND EXPLORERS
OF SOUTH AFRICA," ETC.

London
C. ARTHUR PEARSON LIMITED
HENRIETTA STREET W.C.

—

1899

To

THE MEMORY OF MY COMPANIONS IN THESE

ADVENTURES, EVERY ONE OF WHOM

HAS, TO THE BEST OF MY BELIEF,

PASSED AWAY TO THE

UNKNOWN.

PREFACE

————◦◦◦————

THOSE of the "Pictures" bound together in this volume which have reference to South Africa were originally written in New Zealand, in 1876, in a book of African travels intended for publication. Pressure of journalistic work prevented me finishing this book, and the manuscript was lost for more than a dozen years. The "Pictures," therefore, do not exhaust the story of my African travels, for in 1872 and 1873 I made hunting trips to South Gazaland, in 1874 one to South Mashunaland *via* Zoutpansberg, and the same year one to the mainland opposite Zanzibar, which are not referred to. The details of these are not now sufficiently fresh in my memory to justify me in describing them. Those now presented have already been printed under the pseudonym, "The Old Pioneer," in the well-known weekly journal *South Africa*, which is the recognised authority in all matters relating to that

country.   They are now reproduced by the kind
permission of its proprietor and editor, Mr. E.
P. Mathers.   The others have not been printed
before, though a somewhat similar article to that
on the Hot Lakes of New Zealand appeared in
1880 in the long defunct *Australian Magazine*
of Sydney.

The second son of a London banker, born in
January, 1844, I was sent to the Cape in my
nineteenth year, in order to repair waste in my
constitution caused by blood-poison introduced by
vaccination, which laid me on the flat of my back
for two years.   My experience on this trip, during
which I did not travel beyond the confines of
the Cape Colony, so enamoured me of a roving
life, that for thirty years I was continually on the
move, and was rarely in one place more than a
few months at a time.   It may interest some to
hear that, without including daily hunting from a
camp of any duration, or daily journeys by rail
or coach, on foot or horseback, but only *bonâ-fide*
point-to-point journeys—that is to say, going from
one place to another without returning the same
day—I have travelled about 190,000 miles, as
follows : by mail steamer, 83,000 ; sailing vessel,
60,000 ; rail, 14,000 ; wagon, 13,000 ; horseback,
8,000 ; coach and post-cart, 7,000 ; on foot, 5,000.

Of the illustrations, those of elephant hunting
and of the Victoria Falls are from sepia drawings
of oil paintings by the famous Thomas Baines,

F.R.G.S., in my possession; those of dead game are from photos by the well-known Gazaland hunter, Mr. H. T. Glynn, and are reproduced by his kind permission; most of those of the Diamond Fields from photos kindly given to me for the purpose by Mr. E. P. Mathers; and those of New Zealand chiefly by Burton Brothers, of Dunedin. The rest are from photos I purchased in different places so many years ago that I cannot now locate them.

THE OLD PIONEER.

SANDGATE, *July*, 1899.

CONTENTS

xiii

LIST OF ILLUSTRATIONS

HUNTING IN THE AMASWAZI AND GAZA COUNTRIES

THE Amaswazi country, as most now know, lies on the East Coast of Africa, opposite Delagoa Bay, cut off from the seaboard by the Le Bombo Mountains. It is a small country, extending from the Usutu River on the south to the Umkomati on the north, a distance of about 100 miles, and from the Drakensberg Mountains on the west to the Le Bombo range on the east, something less. The Amaswazis are an amiable but warlike race, allied to the Zulus, and now much decimated by drink, small-pox, and other products of civilisation, and are practically ruled by a joint commission, representing the native, the Dutch, and the English interests, while their country is overrun by mineral seekers and concession-hunters. (The country is now taken over by the Transvaal.) The Gaza country adjoins it on the north, and has an elastic northern boundary, which at one time was supposed to extend right up to the Zambesi. The nation was founded by Sotyanjaan, one of the generals whom Chaka, the great Zulu conqueror, sent to subdue the tribes to the north; but who, like Umziligazi, the founder of the Matabili nation, re-volted from his chief, and set up for himself. It is now ruled by his grandson, Gungunyana, who has placed himself under the protection of the British South Africa Company. A considerable portion of his domain is, by the Anglo-Portuguese agreement, within the sphere of influence of the Portuguese; but Gungunyana repudiates the allegi-ance, and was only the other day with difficulty dissuaded from driving the whole of the Portuguese out of South-Eastern Africa—a feat he could easily accomplish, as his army numbers certainly not under 50,000 warriors. (This was written before the capture of Gungunyana by the Portuguese.)

At the time of which I write (1870) these countries were almost a *terra incognita* to modern travellers, and had only once before been traversed from south to north by English.

It was on the 1st of May of that year that we left the village of Grey Town, in Natal, for a six months' hunting trip in these countries. We were three in number—myself, with nearly seven years' experience of African travel, C., with nearly the same, and D., with less. The two latter both stood 6 feet 2 inches. We had all been in the Matabili country, and I had, two years before, been to the Victoria Falls of the Zambesi, then the *ultima thule* of Central African travel, and had besides been through the whole length of the Bechuana country, and in the Zulu country. We only had one wagon in Greytown, C.'s being in Harrismith, in the Orange Free State, so that we had to make a considerable *détour* to go and get it, and our single wagon was loaded almost to the roof. The wonderful road from Grey Town to Harrismith will be found described in a subsequent picture ; suffice it here to

A TYPICAL SCENE IN THE INHABITED PARTS OF SWAZILAND.

say that we reached the latter village with two or three of those mishaps inevitable to African travel, the worst of which was a stick in the Mooi River, which gave us several hours' work, and was nearly being a serious matter, as the water was so cold that both the oxen and ourselves became numbed and nearly helpless.

Let us pause awhile at the top of the Drakensberg,

10 or 12 miles before reaching Harrismith, and look back. We are in Van Reenen's Pass, 7,000 feet above the sea, and immediately beneath the fine cone of Rensberg's Kop, one of the few conical mountains in South Africa, where they are nearly all flat-topped. In front of us is spread out the whole of Fair Natal, "The Garden of South Africa," tumbling away in a marvellous jumble of startingly green rolling hills, dark bush-clothed valleys, and vast park-like expanses, all streaked and scored with lines of gleaming water. To the right frown the forbidding cliffs and precipices of Giants and Champagne Castles, 11,000 feet in altitude, and on the left, 150 miles away, but clear-cut as if within reach, another conical mountain, under which nestles the Transvaal village of Wakkerstroom. If it be a spring day, and the usual thunderstorm has passed over, and the great masses of cumuli rolled away to the south, the sea-line, 190 miles away, may be distinctly seen, and there be they who say they have seen the lighthouse on the Durban Bluff! It is a fine picture, partaking alike of the grand and the beautiful, the soft and the severe ; and so clear and crisp is the atmosphere, that little white dots of farm-houses, brown Kafir huts, and moving trains of wagons along the red roads, may be made out at distances so great that one hesitates to print them.

From Harrismith with two wagons and a level road (after Natal, that is to say) we travelled briskly

along, anxious to get to our hunting ground, 400 or
500 miles away. One after the other the giants of
Drakensberg, flat-topped and rock-faced, threw their
shadows down upon us, and were passed. Past the
great Platberg, once the haunt of droves of lions,
past the mighty Nelson's Kop, past the ill-fated
Majuba Hill, over the Vaal River, and on, on, still
among the great Krantz-crowned Table-kops, till
we reached the Chrissie Lakes. Although winter,
and bitterly cold up in these altitudes, plenty of
game was about—great herds of chocolate-coloured,
blaze-faced blesbucks awkwardly cantering away ;
herds of vicious-looking but harmless wildebeeste,
a kind of small bison, now nearly extinct; of
graceful springbuck, jumping about as though made
of watch springs, and with a snow-white line of hair
erect along their backs ; a few noble hartebeestes,
gaudy zebras, and wary ostriches ; and once a herd
of mighty elands. But we heeded them not, except
when the pot required filling ; our quarries were
mightier still.

We now turned to the east, and commenced to
descend the Drakensberg, through a wild romantic
country, strewn with enormous weather-beaten
granite boulders, some as big as the Crystal Palace,
and as smooth and flawless as an upturned basin.
There was no road now, and we had to pick our
way over the broken slopes and among the scattered
rocks as best we could. Many a charming picture
we passed—great ravines full of noble yellow-wood

trees (pines) ; crystal streams lined with lovely tree-ferns, whose bottoms were of ink-black loam, into which the wagons would sink up to the bed-planks, sometimes necessitating an off-loading, and always an aggravating loss of time and temper ; or mighty precipices, decked with green where trees could get a foot-hold, and from which great baboons grinned and swore at us.   Often it was so steep that two wheels had to be locked, and at last we came to a place like the roof of a house.   It seemed impassable, but we had to get down somehow.   Three wheels were locked, and only four oxen yoked in, instead of the usual " span " of fourteen ; the " trek-touw " (hide-rope to which the yokes are fastened) of the other wagon was made fast to the "aftertongue," and all our Kafir servants, with some volunteers from a neighbouring kraal, dragged at it to slow the wagon down.   Nevertheless, it slid down in an alarming fashion, bumping up and down like a boulder coming down a mountain-side, but reached the bottom in safety.   Nothing but a South African wagon could have done it; any English-built vehicle would have splintered into matchwood ; but these African wagons are (or were in the old days) pur-posely made loosely with very little iron about them so as to bear any amount of bending and twisting and jolting ; the only weak points about them were the iron pins connecting various parts.   The other wagon was heavier, and we were anxious about it, and not without cause, for it attained such an impetus that the "fore-loper" (oxen leader) got frightened, and threw away his "touw" (hide leading rope), and the men behind it could not keep pace with it, so that it bounded down the mountain side entirely uncontrolled at a rate that looked to us about twenty miles an hour. Every second we expected to see it dashed to atoms; but, marvellous to relate, it reached the bottom intact. Here, however, the sudden stoppage on the level ground broke the "dissel-boom" (pole), and that was all the damage done. When we looked back up that mountain slope we marvelled more than ever, and wondered how on earth we were to get up it again; while the numerous Kafirs, now assembled from all sides, gave expression to their astonishment with loud guttural "Wow's."

We were now in the valley of the Usutu, a fine river that runs into the south end of Delagoa Bay, and we shortly reached the Queen's kraal (Umbandini was then a boy). Here the expedition nearly came to grief. It is customary when asking permission to hunt in a native territory to send a present to the chief or ruler. C. and myself each sent the Amaswazi Queen a fine blanket with many coloured stripes, together with some powder and a few knick-knacks; but D., who was a Scotchman and fond of the bawbees, refused to send anything. Consequently, the Queen, with perfect justice, declined to grant us permission to hunt, and sent down a number of warriors to seize our cattle, so as to prevent us from proceeding. This was too much, for though D. was clearly in the wrong, C. and myself objected to having our property seized. We therefore armed ourselves, and D. threatened to shoot any one who approached the cattle, an act which would have been unjustifiable. I did better; I wielded an enormous African wagon-whip among them, and drove them right and left, while the rest hastily "inspanned" the oxen, and we trekked. Two or three hundred warriors followed us, rattling their assegais on their buffalo-hide shields; but we waved our revolvers, and warned them off, and eventually tired them out. It was a foolish affair, and I have no hesitation in saying that the Swazis were entirely in the right, and we entirely in the wrong. With some tribes we should have been massacred; but the Swazis are an amiable people, and fond of the English.

We were still some distance from our hunting ground; but after making a new boom, a few days' trek through very beautiful but rough and broken country, with scattered trees and thickly populated, brought us to the edge of the great forest valley lying between the Bombo Mountains and the Maschondwa Hills, which was the first goal of our enterprise.

This great bush valley, which extends, with a few breaks, up to the Limpopo, is uninhabited, being a hot-bed of malarial fever. It is also infested with the tsetse fly, whose bite is fatal to all domestic

SWAZIS AT HOME.

animals, so that hunting has to be done on foot, without dogs. In those days it swarmed with game of every description, from the elephant down. The predominant tree in it is the flat-topped mimosa ; and, looking down at it from the adjacent hills, the effect is very curious, for the tops of these trees, spreading out and touching each other, present a flat expanse, which appears to be the ground, though the latter is in reality 20 feet or 30 feet beneath.

At the last of the Kafir kraals we remained two or three days, hiring fifty boys for porters, and making arrangements for the safe care of our wagons and oxen, while we hunted in the bush below. All stores we should require for a month were then made up into convenient packages, and we started for the hunting ground. I was very unwell with a touch of fever, and could hardly walk, but we managed to struggle along for a dozen miles to a water-hole, where we camped for the night. When crossing the ridge of the Maschondwa Hills —a range now known to be full of gold reefs—we saw a herd of the true zebra, quite a different animal to the ordinary, or Burchell's, zebra one reads about in South African books. The true zebra is a much handsomer animal, and is striped all round the legs down to the hoofs. Africanders call Burchell's zebra the quagga, which, again, is a mistake, the quagga being a totally distinct animal, whose stripes only reach to the girth, and are

hardly discernible. It is now completely extinct.
At daybreak the next morning we started again in
search of another water-hole known to the Kafirs;
but somehow C. and myself got separated from the
rest, and after walking seven or eight hours we
stumbled on a pool of muddy water that tasted of
buffalo more than anything else. So C. shot a
blue wildebeeste (the brindled gnu), a larger animal
than the wildebeeste of the plains, and ash-coloured,
with black stripes, a herd of which opportunely
appeared, and we had a meal. This was the first
solid food I had eaten for four days, and I enjoyed
it very much. It looked as though we should have
to pass the night without any blankets; but a little
before sundown a couple of Kafirs appeared in
search of us, for we had fired several signal guns,
and conducted us to the camp, three miles away.
It was formed by the side of a large pool, whose
margin was thickly indented with the dried spoor of
elephants and rhinoceroses.

By this pool we had an experience which was
unique of its kind, and which no one would care to
undergo very often. It was Saturday night when
we arrived, and the next day was devoted to
making the camp ship-shape, the Kafirs building a
row of lean-to sheds for themselves, made of
branches roofed with the leaves of tree-ferns,
date-palms, and banana. In the afternoon heavy
masses of cloud came rolling up from the south-
east, and it was manifest that we were in for

serious rain—a most unusual thing at this time of the year. None of us for a moment, however, anticipated what really happened. A little after sundown drops of rain began to fall, and before we turned in a steady, quiet downpour had set in. About eleven o'clock I was awakened by a sense of

A SWAZI MASHER.

coldness, and, striking a light, found that we were lying in an inch of water. I roused the others, and we piled all the goods into a corner, and sat on them to wait for daylight. But the water rose rapidly, and was soon up to our knees, and we had to beat a retreat to the Kafir camp, which was on slightly higher ground. They had made, in front of their huts, a row of huge fires of trunks of trees thrown down by elephants, and by these we sat on logs and buckets, one having in his lap a medicine chest, another a tin box containing fifty pounds of powder, and the third a three-gallon keg of rum. (Trust him not to leave the rum under water!) The rain continued steadily all night, and, one by one, the fires were put out, and, one by one, the huts washed away, until, at daylight, we were all standing up over our knees in water, and staring blankly at each other; and there, fifty yards in front, was the upper half of a bell-tent sticking up out of the water. We looked round into the bush, and as far as could be seen through the trees there was nothing but water—water was above us, water below, and water all around. We looked at each other with dismay depicted on our dripping countenances. The situation was too ridiculous; we all burst out simultaneously into a roar of laughter. But something must be done; so the powder and medicines were wrapped up in a waterproof sheet and deposited in a tree, and we served out a peg of rum and proceeded to reconnoitre. We found that the camp had been pitched in a gentle hollow, which appeared to receive the drainage of nearly all the bush flat, and was now a roaring river three hundred yards in width, and, in some places, breast deep. We gathered a lot of logs together, and made a platform on the higher ground, where the water was only an inch or two deep, and then went to bring up the tent. It was difficult work, for the water was over a yard deep, but we got it out, with most of the goods. Of course, everything was spoilt, and the meal was half mud, the top of the sack having been left open, guns were choked, and all my papers and drawings destroyed. We pitched the tent on the platform, built up a great fire in front, gathered a huge pile of logs, and made a high and strong thorn fence round all to keep out lions, which would be sure to be on the rampage in such weather, and made ourselves as comfortable as possible to await the cessation of the rain. There was nothing to eat; there had been plenty of meat, for besides C.'s wildebeeste, another and two zebras had been killed; but all that had not been washed away had been taken by the Kafirs to their camp, which they had made under a thick clump of trees on the other side of the roaring stream. I made some porridge of the meal, which, as I have mentioned, was half mud. It did not look very inviting; but D. and myself took a plateful; C. would none of it. Directly D. tasted it an expression of pleased surprise broke over his features: "Why," he cried, "it's delicious." "So it is," I added; "it's as good as goose-liver pie," though the mess was the most damnable compound that had ever passed my lips. We went on eating with considerable apparent gusto, until C. was emboldened to try a plateful. The spoon had no sooner reached his mouth than away it went flying, spoon, plate, and porridge, out

of the tent, over the fire, and splashing into the
water beyond. " Why," he roared, spluttering the
stuff out of his mouth, "you infernal humbugs, it's
disgusting ;" which it certainly was. D. and myself threw ourselves back and roared with laughter.

At night the rain increased in intensity, and
morning showed no break in the dull level of the
clouds. And so it went on ; day after day, and
night after night, the rain fell in a maddening drip,
drip, drip, with a steadiness and persistency that
seemed to imply a second deluge. The tent had
long ceased to be waterproof, and inside it was
nearly as wet as without. Every morning anxious
faces peered out of the tent-opening, and gazed at
the leaden expanse above. But no change was
there ; heavy, dead, and dismal was all above ;
sodden, dead, and dismal all around. There was
nothing to eat but mud-porridge ; but we kept life
in us with periodical doses of rum, and assuaged the
pangs and gnawings of hunger by keeping our
stomachs distended with warm water—a wrinkle
that all travellers ought to know. On Thursday
evening the rain fell somewhat lighter. but continued steadily all day, and on Friday morning it
was still raining. But, as the day progressed, it
gradually fell lighter and lighter, and in the afternoon the clouds slowly broke, and rolled themselves
into whitened mounds and grey expanses. Later,
the whitened mounds became tinged with crimson
and pink ; purple and violet, blue and gold spread

themselves in dazzling grandeur; rays of glowing
light shot up from the west; and, as a climax, the
sun itself appeared through long lines of jewel-
capped clouds, and set in a halo of coloured glory.
Then the clouds sank, one by one, below the
horizon, and an hour afterwards the vault above
was bright and clear, the moon threw down her soft
light, and the stars twinkled with renewed brilliancy.
In the morning we were up at dawn, and the sun
rose to a cloudless sky. All nature seemed glad;
the wet trees glistened in the morning sun, and the
brilliant-plumaged birds came forth and sat on the
branches chirping merrily, and combing their
draggled feathers. The Kafirs, whom we had not
seen since Monday, turned up, looking awfully
starved and pinched. About a dozen, as we were
informed, had left, and endeavoured to reach their
kraals; we afterwards learnt that two of them had
died in the attempt. Starving as we were, it was
no use going hunting until some of the water had
run down, so the morning was spent in cleaning
and oiling guns, drying clothes and blankets, shifting the position of the tent, and making all ship-
shape. In the afternoon, we all turned out to get
something to eat. (I may here say, in parenthesis,
that in my day African hunters did not go about
with cases of tinned meats, biscuits, jams, and
champagne. Boiled meat and baked whole-meal
cakes, with coffee, was the constant fare; and when
they were tired of that baked meat and boiled meal

3

was substituted. A bottle of pickles was the only luxury ever indulged in.)

The country was fearfully muddy, but the spoor showed that game was all over the place, and I soon found a troop of five buffaloes in a dense thicket of brambly bushes, one of which I easily killed. We will draw the veil over the scene that ensued, merely remarking that neither I nor my five Kafir spoorers and gun-bearers had eaten anything since Sunday, and it was now Friday. Hunger satisfied, we carried a quantity of meat back to camp, but found that no less than four head of large game had been killed, besides my buffalo—viz., another buffalo, two blue wildebeestes, and a zebra.

This rain had extended over an immense expanse of country, for we afterwards heard that severe floods had been experienced in Natal, which carried away nearly every bridge in the Colony. It had the effect of scattering the game a good deal, as all the water-holes and gullies were filled, and game, therefore, not restricted to the neighbourhood of rivers and streams. We found by the spoor that a troop of five elephants had been close to the camp during the rains, and on the Monday morning, taking with me three Kafirs, I followed this spoor. As I travelled through the beautiful bush, the yet muddy though fast-drying ground was actually covered with buffalo spoor, like a cattle park; there must have been thousands about. Soon we saw some of the animals themselves, but I did not wait to hunt them, as I was anxious to find the elephants. Impahlas (a buck the size of a fallow-deer), too, scurried about in all directions. I also saw spoor of elands, blue wildebeeste, rhinoceros, roan antelope (a huge buck as big as a horse), waterbucks (also a large buck), kudus, sassabi (bastard hartebeeste), zebras, boars, giraffes, lions, and many others ; and it appeared as though we had got into a veritable hunter's paradise. The elephants were travelling in single file, and had beaten a perfect path through the bush, so that it was probable they were going to the north for good, and were not on the feed. For some time I had been in grass a foot high, but presently I came to a patch burnt off by some Kafir hunter, which extended for several hundred yards, and I was just at the end of this, and close to more old grass, when suddenly my boy, who was carrying my elephant gun, cried, " Nanci, nanci ! " (Look, look !) and pointing excitedly in front precipitately bolted, leaving me alone with only a Westley-Richards carbine, for the other two Kafirs had sat down somewhere behind to cut a thorn out of the foot of one of them. At first I could see nothing in particular, but presently became aware of four red animals rising slowly from the long grass. At the moment I took them for impahlas, but in a second saw that they were lions, and not more than ten yards off. My rifle was to my shoulder in an instant, but the thought flashed on me that one barrel to four lions and no climbable tree within thirty yards, was hardly good enough, so, before they had seen the movement, for their heads were turned from me, I gently lowered it, and discussed with myself whether to shoot and run, to run without shooting, or to stand my ground. The lions had now turned and faced me, and were apparently in a similar fix to myself, and did not know whether to fight or run. Their tails were working from side to side with a slow strong movement, and they were evidently growling, though, being very deaf, I did not hear them. If I made the least movement the tails lashed faster and harder, and the row of heads were lowered nearer the ground, making them look very dangerous. This lasted for some time, probably a minute, possibly five, for it is difficult to estimate time in such a position, and at last they turned and bounded away at a slow, strong, light canter. At about ten yards they stopped and again faced me, but I was still standing looking at them, and once more they bounded away. Two of them were very fine young males, much too fine to be lost, so when they were about fifty yards off, which would give me time to reach a tree, I fired at the largest, but, unfortunately, I saw my bullet deflected by a twig, and I missed him clean. I am now of opinion that had I killed the largest when they first turned towards me, the others would have been so startled at the suddenness of it that they would have made off.

Shortly afterwards I came upon D., who had also been having a queer adventure. His was with an enormous python, whose hole, where it had retired for winter quarters, had been filled with water, and it lay sunning itself when D. came across it. He was on fresh buffalo spoor (his favourite game), and did not wish to fire for fear of disturbing them ; he therefore took a knobkerrie from one of his Kafirs and commenced hammering at the brute's head. He thought he had stunned it, but the beast suddenly raised its head, opened its huge jaws, and made a dash right at D.'s face, who, in endeavouring to avoid it, fell back, and the snake scuttled over his body and made off, but was killed by the Kafirs. It was an immense snake, and when alive measured between twenty and twenty-five feet in length. Several others were killed on this and the following day ; they had probably been washed out of their winter quarters, for we saw no more during our long subsequent stay in the country.

Leaving D., I continued on the elephant spoor, which led me across the Umfelusi River to the foot of the Bombo Mountains, a range about 2,000 feet in height, and beautifully decked with scattered trees on its lower slopes. I was twenty-five miles from camp, and as the spoor continued in single file, I came to the conclusion that the elephants were on trek, and might not stop for a hundred miles. I therefore camped for the night under a tree, after successfully stalking a sassabi—a fine large chocolate-coloured buck with peculiarly shaped horns.

The next morning I clambered half-way up the Bombos to have a look at the country round. Among the trees on the lower slopes were many fine baobabs, the largest tree in the world so far as girth is concerned. The pendent fruit of this tree, like an oblong cocoanut, is full of a most agreeable acid pulp, which, if allowed to dry, gets powdery, and is then exactly like mild cream of tartar. Above the belt of trees the mountain-side was terribly rough, and great gullies and ravines of the most romantic character revealed themselves, where rocks were piled on rocks like the ruins of a massive-built city. Across one of these I saw a fine troop of elands ; but I never shot these animals unless hard up for meat. Although the largest ruminant in the world (they have been killed seven feet high at the withers), they are so gentle, so helpless, owing to their bulk, and have such large meek, supplicating eyes that it always seemed to me downright murder to slaughter them unnecessarily. Sassabis were also feeding in twos and threes, and gaudy zebras cantering about ; but I did not want them. Presently one of the Kafirs told me that there was a fine kudu bull feeding down the gully on the other side. These noble bucks are not found every day, so I determined on a stalk. Noting the direction of the wind, the best way seemed to be to descend my side of the ravine until

I was opposite the buck, which would bring me within 150 yards of it. The side was exceedingly steep and covered with boulders, large and small, with a few scattered trees. I had to go down *ventre à terre* head first; and a more fatiguing bit of stalking I never performed. I succeeded, how- ever, in getting into position without disturbing the kudu, but for a long time could not get a shot, as, in the most provoking manner, it kept its stern towards me while gingerly picking the green shoots off the bushes. But everything comes to the man who waits, and my turn came. The bullet struck it fairly in the shoulder, and, with a bound in the air, the buck rolled to the very bottom of the ravine. I was afraid the grand horns would have been broken, but, strange to say, they were uninjured. This animal has the finest horns of any in the world, grand spirals four feet and more in height, and often six along the curve. It and the sable antelope are the finest of all bucks. It was long after dark when I got back to camp. In my absence C. had performed the extraordinary feat of killing four buffaloes with four consecutive bullets. Any one who knows anything about large-game shooting will appreciate this remarkable feat. As showing that luck enters into hunting as into every- thing else, it may be said that, though he fired many shots at them, it was nearly a month before he bagged another, when he again commenced to kill them right and left.

We now sent to the wagon for another tent and fresh supplies, and shifted the camp nearer the Bombos. On his return, our major-domo, a huge Natal Kafir, informed me that the oxen had all got the so-called "bush-sickness." This was bad news, and as C., who was a splendid cattle doctor, was at the other camp, I had to send for him. During the night, as I was sleeping alone in the tent, I was awakened by something tugging at one of the tent ropes, and, looking out, saw a huge hyena. How it had got through the thorn fence I could not make out ; but, slipping on my boots, I seized one of my favourite double-barrelled Manton pistols and fired at it. The bullet only made a flesh wound, and I chased round after it and fired the other barrel with no better result. I then seized a spade that was standing up against the fence and banged that hyena about with it until it yelled with fury and tried to creep out under the fence, but I broke its back with a downward blow from the edge of the spade, and then killed it with blows on the head from a knobkerrie. It is lucky these creatures are so cowardly, for this one could easily have torn me to pieces. Soon afterwards, Jonas, one of the wagon-drivers, a regular cur, came to the tent from the Kafir camp and begged to come inside, saying there were lions prowling about. Peering out I soon made out two dusky forms about a hundred yards off, so, removing the thorn trees that closed the entrance, I took a double-barrelled rifle, reloaded my pistol, and sat on a bucket outside to watch them. With stealthy movements they came nearer and nearer to the camp, until within twenty yards, and stood out distinctly against some dark bushes behind them. This was my opportunity, and I let fly at the largest, which at once sprang into the air and came down with a dull thud, quite dead as it afterwards turned out. I then fired at the other, but apparently missed it, and it made off. Such are the night disturbances of an African hunter's camp. We dragged the dead lion inside the fence, and I turned in again.

After breakfast C. turned up, and we hastened to the wagons. Arrived there we found two of the oxen dead (of course the two best), and there was no time to be lost. We took a couple of great cooking-pots, and cutting up several bars of soap boiled them with an equal weight of salt, and gave each a bottle of the mixture, first fastening them to a wagon-wheel and then throwing them down. In bad cases we added calomel to the mixture. It was a long job, as there were forty oxen, and it took us far into the night. We returned to camp next day, after giving the strictest injunctions to the headman of the kraal not to let the oxen approach the bush, but to keep them high up on the mountain range. They all recovered, and were not attacked again.

We remained at our new camp for about two months, and though large numbers of buffaloes and smaller game were bagged, only one elephant was

killed, which fell to C., and a rhinoceros each to
D. and myself. I repeatedly advocated a move
northwards; but D. was satisfied with buffaloes,
and as he had to return in August I exacted a
promise from C. to follow me northwards when he
had gone, and subsided. Early in July a man
named Wilde, a member of a party encamped about
ten miles from us under the well-known hunter John
Clarke, was killed by a buffalo. He was inexperienced, and had rashly endeavoured to turn a
wounded buffalo out of a clump of dense thorn in
which it had ensconced itself. He was alone at the
time, but as his body was found on the top of a low
thorn tree with a big hole in the chest the rest was
easily conjectured.

But though the shooting was somewhat monotonous here, a good many adventures fell to our share.
One very nearly cost me my life. I was returning
to camp after a long tramp, during which I had
killed a buffalo and a fine waterbuck, when, just
before sundown, and when I was within a mile of
camp, I came to an open space in the bush, about
a hundred yards across, in the centre of which stood
an old dead tree-trunk with a few ghostly arms. At
the further end of the open were two old buffalo
bulls quietly feeding by themselves. They were
such huge fellows that I determined to have at least
one of them, and therefore, the wind being favourable, went down at full length to creep up, being a
firm believer in getting as near as possible to large

game. I got within thirty yards of the nearest un-
discovered, and then fired, the bullet striking fairly
behind the shoulder. The moment I fired I foolishly
sprang up to reload the barrel, the other buffalo
having dashed into the bush at the report. The
stricken one had fallen to the shot, but was on his
feet again in an instant; catching sight of me, he
made straight for me, and evidently meant business.
The second barrel failed to stop it, the bullet striking
too low in the chest. (A buffalo in charging does
not lower the head as we see in the pictures, but
throws it right back, exposing the chest ; the head
is not lowered until in the act of tossing.) I now
made for the dead tree at my best pace, and had
got within five yards of it, the buffalo being close
behind me, when down I went, " kerslap," into a big
hole, which in the long grass I had not noticed.
The hole was about three feet deep, and large
enough to hold me, and the buffalo, pounding along,
fortunately came with its fore feet just on the edge,
and took the whole thing in its stride, and continued
its way for some yards further, when it suddenly
stopped. My rifle had gone flying out of my hand
when I fell, and as I cautiously felt round for it
without showing myself, the buffalo slowly sank to
the ground. It had been an expiring effort, and
the hole had saved me, though at the moment I
thought it had lost me my life. It is never advis-
able to show oneself to a wounded buffalo, especially
when it is alone. Another day I had a nice little

adventure which might also have been fatal. I
came upon the largest herd of buffalo I ever saw ;
it must have numbered thousands, though, of course,
I could not see the whole of it through the bush.
Running alongside of the troop to pick out a big
bull, a young calf came tearing along, almost touching me. On the spur of the moment I thought I
would capture this calf, as I had had good offers
from Mr. Bates, of the Zoological Gardens, for live
specimens of African game. I therefore sprang
alongside and seized it by the tail. Calfy objected
to this, and turned into the troop, dragging me with
it, and I found myself hanging on to that calf's tail
tearing along as hard as I could split, with buffaloes
all round me, and half smothered with dust. It
was an unpleasant situation ; I dared not let go, or
I should have been trampled to death, and I did
not think I could hold on very long, while passing
buffaloes favoured me with playful digs of their
horns, one of which actually tore my shirt. Presently we passed close to a large-trunked tree, and
I instantly saw my opportunity. Letting go of the
tail I slipped behind the trunk, and the buffaloes
passed on either side without taking the least notice
of me, and soon I was alone, panting furiously,
bathed in perspiration, and coated with dust. I
did not try to capture buffalo calves that way
again.

An adventure of one of our Kafir hunters here will
serve to illustrate both the vindictiveness and the

tenacity of life of the buffalo. C. and I were returning to camp one evening, when C. heard shouts for help. We hastened in the direction of the sounds, and found this hunter up in the topmost branches of a lowish thorn tree, and reared up on its hind legs, with its fore feet over a branch, was a huge buffalo, actually trying to get at the man! When it caught sight of us it resumed its natural position, and prepared to transfer its hostile intentions to ourselves ; but a bullet in the head from C. felled it to the ground. We thought it was dead, but on approaching it it sprang up and made a furious rush, which I only avoided by a desperate spring to one side. It then turned for another charge, but another bullet in the head was a settler. This Swazi hunter had been given nine bullets in the morning ; and he said that he had hunted that buffalo from bush to bush, and fired all the nine bullets into it. On being cut up, his story was verified, for we found them all, as well as the two we had given it ; and besides these, four more, which it had apparently carried for at least a month. From their formation we knew they had been fired by one of a party of Dutchmen encamped about twenty miles to the south of us.

Lions were very numerous about this camp, and one night C. and D. declared they could not sleep for the row they made, and expressed their intention of going out "to drive the beggars off." I did not much care for the job, as the moon was young, and my deafness makes me very helpless when I cannot see ; but I could not well refuse, so we turned out, all well armed. The sounds led us to a dry watercourse without banks, but lined with large, round, dense-foliaged trees, like box trees, the foliage commencing from the ground. We took our way up the centre of this watercourse, which was about ten yards in width with a sandy bed, and suddenly C., turning his head to the right, said, "There's one." We did not see him, but challenged him with shouts ; but he refused to come out, and, reckless as we were, we did not care to go and attack him in his own fastness, so we passed on. Presently D. said, "There's another," and C., "There's another there," and then they said there was another in front and two more behind, and I thought it was getting rather warm. However, we walked up and down the bed for about an hour, with the lions growling in all directions on the other side of the line of box-like trees, which formed a complete wall on either side. But they would not come out, and we could not enter the thicket to attack them, as it was so dense that rapid locomotion would have been impossible, so that we set our faces campward, and on the way stumbled right into a lot of buffalo that were lying asleep. This enterprise was not a wise one, but in reality the lion is a much overrated animal. If there is little game in the country, and they are hungry, lions

are fairly bold and dangerous animals; and old,
toothless lions are always dangerous; but, with
plenty to eat, the lion is an arrant coward, and
a stone thrown at it will often suffice to drive it
away. This, of course, only applies to unwounded
animals; a wounded lion is always most dangerous,
as all large wounded animals are more or less.

Stalking in this, or any other African bush, is
no joke. It is hardly an exaggeration to say that
Africa is the thorniest country in the world. I
have seen thorns a foot in length on some trees,
and as hard as steel, and they run all sizes, to
the twentieth of an inch. The very grass has
spikes, which detach themselves and work through
the clothes into the flesh. The ground, too, is
scattered, often thickly, with the seed of a tree
which is armed with about a dozen spikes as sharp
as needles. When the knee or hand is placed on
one of these it is very difficult to preserve that
equanimity of temper necessary to a successful
stalk. Worse still is it when, creeping along, one
finds the spot on which the hand must be next
placed already occupied by a cobra comfortably
coiled up. I must confess that in this case I never
was able to preserve my coolness, and always
jumped up and frightened my quarry away. Once
when stalking a fine waterbuck I suddenly found
myself face to face with, and within a foot of, a
huge boar which had been asleep in the long
grass. As the gentleman commenced to sharpen

his tusks preparatory to ripping me open, I was compelled to give him a little pill, and consequently lost my waterbuck.   But the most annoying thing of all is the well-known " wacht-een-beetje " bush (wait-a-bit thorn).   This is a wretched little bush covered with thorns the size, shape, and temper of dace-hooks.   So well does it merit its name, that if one once brushes up against it one can never get away again without leaving a portion of oneself behind.   In retreating from a charge they are most dangerous, and one has not only the anxiety of keeping out of the way of the charging animal, but also keeping clear of these wretched little bushes. Poor D., who had forgotten to bring any leather gaiters, was soon in a sad way, and all his trousers were torn to rags.   He made an elegant picture in an old billycock hat, ragged shirt, trousers dragged off at the knees by the thorns, and with the ragged ends hanging down, half a yard of torn and lacerated shin, the ragged ends of a pair of socks, and boots wrapped up in the skin from the hock of a buffalo— a common hunter's dodge to preserve them.   When he came to camp in the evening he used to set a couple of Kafirs to work to pick the thorns out of his leg.   I made a large drawing of him, and ornamented the tent with it, but he took it down, nailed it to a tree, and riddled it with partridge-shot, vowing it was a libel, which it was not.   He afterwards made himself a pair of gaiters out of the gaudily-striped skin of a zebra's legs, which

gave him quite a "distangy" appearance. Poor
D.! he died of typhoid at the Diamond Fields next
year ; and Africa lost a most promising pioneer, for
he was only twenty-two.

I soon got tired of killing buffaloes, and went
back to the wagons to do a little prospecting among
the hills. I wandered about the hills for a week,
with a couple of Kafirs to carry my blankets, &c.,
and found many traces of gold ; in fact, I hit upon
several places which are now worked as gold mines,
including the well-known "Moodies." It was,
however, a good many years before the existence
of gold in this country was generally acknow-
ledged ; and letters to the Natal papers recording
discoveries were entirely disregarded. I got good
sport at the same time, for though none of the
very large game, as elephant, rhinoceros, giraffe,
or buffalo were seen, most of the great bucks were
plentiful. On my way back to the bush-camp,
with a long train of Kafirs carrying fresh supplies,
the cavalcade was suddenly put to rout by a black
rhinoceros, or pytjaan, charging into its midst.
The scene was ludicrous, as parcels, bundles, sacks,
and boxes went flying in all directions, and the
sable bearers rushed hither and thither, clambered
trees, dodged behind bushes, and tumbled over each
other in the most admired confusion. I was little
better myself, and sought shelter behind the nearest
trunk, from whence I let fly at five yards' range,
and brought the rhino to its knees. But it was

4

soon up again, charging about blindly in the most furious manner ; and it was some time before I could get another shot. However, at last I succeeded in killing it, and discipline was restored. These animals are the most dangerous in Africa, for they do not wait to be wounded before they charge, but hunt one down the moment they get wind ; and though they sometimes pass on after one wild charge, on the other hand they often stick to it, and it then becomes a life-and-death battle, and, as from the position of the horn and the shape of the head it is very difficult to get a good shot when they are charging full at one, one has to depend very much on agility in springing to one side, and taking a shoulder shot almost at the same instant. Notwithstanding the great bulk of these animals, their activity and rapidity of movement is truly astonishing, and no one who had not seen it could realise the wonderful quickness and lightness of their actions.

On my arrival at camp I found that C. had killed an elephant under the Bombos, and that they intended breaking up the camp and shifting it to that district, as we had now as many buffalo and buck hides and heads as three wagons (we had hired the dead man Wilde's) could carry, and D. had still more than a week to spare. We crossed over the Bombos and camped by a lagoon in the flat on the other side, in which there were hippopotami and alligators. The vegetation on this side was ranker, with fewer thorns, and a dense white mist usually enveloped everything after sundown. The very next day we all fell in with elephants, and each bagged one. I was spooring a troop of six or seven when I suddenly came upon two bulls standing quietly under a tree. As they had not observed me, and I could not feel any wind, I crept up among the dense undergrowth until I was within fifteen yards, and then gave the largest a conical tin-hardened bullet of five to the pound, backed by eight drachms of diamond powder. Without waiting to see the effect, I sprang up and turned and ran. This is always the best plan, for if the elephant charges one has a start, while, if he does not, no harm is done. In this case he did not, and when I returned to the spot with the Kafirs he was gone; but the copious blood-spoor told us that he had been heavily hit. We followed this for about a mile, when it led us into such a bush that I hesitated to enter it, as quick locomotion would have been impossible in case of a charge. I therefore skirted round to see if the elephant had come out on the other side. But while doing so a sudden scream and crashing of bushes caused the Kafirs to vanish precipitately from the scene. As yet I could see nothing; but soon I saw the dense bush moving not very far from me, and then the big back of the elephant loomed above the undergrowth not a dozen yards off. I fired my two barrels in quick succession in the direction I thought the shoulder would be, and again ran at my best pace. The Kafirs soon joined me, and once more we advanced and found the animal standing clear of the bush, apparently at its last gasp. At least, so we thought, for though he must have seen us he took no notice ; but there was another struggle in him, for when I raised the rifle to give him a settler, without any notice he gave a loud and shrill shriek and rushed furiously at us. I let him have the right barrel in the chest, and then springing suddenly to one side, ran for about twenty yards at right angles, and then, as the elephant stopped, gave him the other barrel in the shoulder at thirty yards. This was as much as he could carry, and the noble animal sank on his knees with his hind legs stretched back, and died in that position without falling to one side—a noble foeman indeed. The scream and trumpeting of an elephant in a rage is the most awe-inspiring sound in nature, excepting, perhaps, the awful row that goes on in the funnel of a hot geyser just before it discharges a column of water, the noise of a hurricane in the Indian Ocean, or the thunders of an African storm in the mountains. Few horses can stand it, and for this reason I have always thought foot-hunting not only the safest, but also the most likely to be successful.

The same evening I made a "scherm" by the side of a lagoon, a mile from camp, for night-hunting. A scherm is merely a hole dug in the ground and partly covered with logs. C. and myself passed the night in this ; but though we saw buffaloes and rhinos., the only result was that we were both laid up with fever for a couple of days. Scherm-shooting is most unwise, as the freshly dug ground is always redolent of malaria. On the third

A DEAD ELEPHANT, SHOWING HOW THEY OFTEN FALL,
AS DESCRIBED IN THE TEXT.

day it was agreed that I should go to Delagoa Bay for more powder and tin, and return straight to the wagons, as by that time D. would have given up hunting. I left at daylight, and walking hard through very rank country, reached Lourenço Marques on the second night. At this time this now respectable town was a miserable collection of mud huts, and the Portuguese that inhabited it passed their time in recovering from attacks of

fever, in drinking bad spirits, and in dallying with
their native women, I was not enamoured of the
place, and having finished my business next day,
started wagon-wards in the afternoon, and reached
them without adventure on the fourth evening,
living all the time on guinea-fowls, which is my
favourite food in an African bush. Buffalo meat is
first-rate if hung for a week, but terribly tough
if eaten at all fresh, and makes the teeth so sore
that one can hardly use them. The tongues and
the kidneys were the parts we usually preserved for
our own use. In lesser degree the same is true
of most of the larger bucks. An elephant's trunk
baked in a hole for not less than twenty-four hours
is first-rate; so is the foot of a young one, or of a
young hippopotamus, served in the same way; but
all the rest of its meat, except the heart and a
particular slice out of the cheek, is poor. The
rhinoceros is worthless for the table, but a hippopotamus calf is delicious, and makes splendid bacon.
The boar of the bush is coarse; but that found in
the swamps of the open grass country very tender
and good. Zebra is also good, but rather sweet.
The best of all African meats are giraffe and eland,
and they certainly ought to be reared for food.
Those who want still more variety can try a bit of
alligator, or a section of snake, or a slice of lion;
but though I have tried them all, I would not go
far to partake of them—without sauce. Iguana and
porcupine are, however, an agreeable change. It

is not to be supposed that we had nothing but meat and meal to eat in this country. Far from it. Kafirs used to come down from the hills with pumpkins, maize, ground-nuts, sweet potatoes, sorghum, and other products to exchange for meat and salt. Then there were fruits, chiefly of the strychnia family, the pulp surrounding the poisonous seeds of which is very good ; there were also a few dates and plums left from the summer. Honey was plentiful, and fish (barber fish and a sort of fresh-water mullet) was to be had for the catching in the Umfelusi, ten miles from camp. A favourite dish was a *pot-pourri*. We used to take a great cooking-pot half full of water and put in it, all cut up into pieces, say, a buffalo tongue, some pieces of buck meat, a bit of bacon, if we had any, a couple of pheasants (francolins), a hare, a guinea-fowl, some slices of pumpkin or whatever Kafir produce we had, an onion or two and a chili, if there were any left, and a few meal balls, with pepper and salt. A little fire was put under it when we went out in the morning, and the cook and camp-keeper was ordered to keep it just simmering all day. When we returned in the evening it was as delicious a mess as the veriest gourmand could desire.

Arrived at the wagons, I found C. and D. already there, and after loading up the two wagons D. returned to Natal in company with Clarke and his party, and C. and myself turned our faces northwards to the Gaza country, it being now the end of August.

Our first day's trek led us through some fearfully rough country, thinly scattered with trees. Kafir kraals were built here and there under their shade, and the girls and young men trooped out in hundreds, and accompanied us for long distances, ours being the first wagon that had ever entered this country. During the trek I noticed a long white trail behind the wagon, and on examining it found it to be meal. Friction with the side of the wagon had worked a hole in the meal-sack, and it was nearly empty. This was unfortunate, as we should be reduced to meat and what produce we could obtain from Kafirs.

Soon we crossed the Black Umfelusi (not to be confounded with one of the same name in the Zulu country), and got an awful shaking up, the bed being composed of round smooth boulders of black porphyry. Very lovely the country then became, with beautiful open glades, and long reaches under the rock-crowned hills, where the wagon passed through splendid level park-like land, and wended its way among noble trees gradually assuming their spring foliage. Sometimes we had to pass through heavy swamps and small reedy vleys, where the mud was so deep that more than once we had to off-load. Game was almost always in sight, chiefly sassibis, zebras, and rietbucks (large bucks that live in the swamps), and I also killed a fine specimen of the roan antelope, a gigantic buck with great horns thrown back to the shoulder. A sassibi I knocked over played me a nice trick. As it lay on the ground I took out my hunting knife to cut its throat, when it suddenly rose, quietly knocked me down, and cantered away! I was too astonished to give it another shot.

Six days of this work brought us to the lower end of the northernmost bend of the Umkomati, a fine river that from the apex of this bend turns south-east, and enters the north end of Delagoa Bay. The Kafirs reported the tsetse-fly on the other side of the river, so that we could go no further in that direction, and the mountains to the west looked much too forbidding to attempt a passage that way. There was, therefore, nothing for it but to leave the wagon here, and continue our way on foot. I did not much like the look of the country for the oxen ; it was too rich ; but it could not be helped. We determined, however, to go to a river a day ahead to shoot seacows (hippopotami) for ten days or a fortnight, and then return, and, if the oxen were all right, to continue our way to the north. We there-fore arranged with the headman of the kraal to look after them, and started with a dozen bearers. The Kafirs here were not so good-looking nor so amiable as the Swazis, and instead of living in the well-known beehive huts, they made low circular walls of mud and sticks, and placed conical roofs of thatch on them. Anything more beautiful than the Umkomati, where we crossed it, I never saw, and pen would fail to do justice to its loveliness. Even

C., who had a most prosaic mind, stood for some moments entranced as he gazed down the noble stream with its tree-lined banks and gems of tree-girt islets. We did not reach the Umlomati until the following afternoon, passing on the way through a marvellous forest of strychnia trees. These trees have shiny, laurel-like leaves, but smaller, and on each tree hung hundreds of great, golden, orange-like fruit, but with a hard shell like a pomegranate. We passed through miles of these, there being scarcely any other tree but the wacht-een-beetje undergrowth, which, unfortunately, is everywhere. There is enough strychnine here to poison all the world. As I have already said, the pulp surrounding the poisonous seeds of this fruit is very good, but there is one species scattered among them, and bearing a redder fruit, the pulp of which is also said to be deadly poison ; but I was not scientifically minded enough to try if this be true.

We approached the Umlomati cautiously, and thrusting the rushes that lined its banks aside, peered into the stream, and there a sight met our eyes such as I have never before or since seen. The river is but a small stream, thirty or forty yards across ; but our guide had led us to a deep reach, some three hundred yards long and of unknown depth, and in this reach the black and rugged heads of the hippos were sticking up in all directions ; not a dozen, or twenty, or fifty, but at least one hundred and fifty, of all ages and sizes, some on a level with the water, some with head and neck clear out, and many blowing. C. and myself stood astounded ; it was a bit of the world before man was. The water was smooth and glassy, studded as far as could be seen either way with the great black heads with their glistening ivory tusks, while here and there rose a jet of glittering spray. To the left the view was bounded by a group of little wooded islets, and to the right by a line of broken water and waterworn rocks, where a cloud of spray and foam indicated the existence of falls and rapids, and from the centre of which rose a number of spray-covered tree-tops, whose trunks and the islet on which they grew were hidden below the level of the water. Each side of the stream was lined with graceful reeds, over which drooped the swinging arms of luxuriant trees. For once our sporting instincts were numbed, and we sat for some time gazing at the scene conscious only of its æsthetic aspect. Soon, however, the murderous instinct reasserted itself, and when a majestic old bull raised its head and neck full out of the water, not ten yards from me, and moved slowly and easily about, the temptation became too great to be resisted, and as I pointed the rifle at the vital line in the great neck and pulled the trigger, I heard the report of C.'s rifle. A great splashing and lashing of water resounded for a second or two, and when I lowered the rifle and looked through the vapoury smoke not a head was to be seen, and, save for a few concentric rings and a ripple against the reeds, the long reach of water was as quiet and lifeless as an English canal.

As seacows sink to the bottom when dead, and do not rise for some hours, we retired from the bank and searched for a place to make a camp, and found a capital spot just above the line of rapids. We remained in this camp more than a week, and had capital sport. The hippos' heads appeared as numerous as ever before the camp was completed, and when it was ship-shape we commenced operations against them. I took up my station in a hollow among the rocks that stretched half-way across the stream, thus commanding a view right up to the islets. It has puzzled many people why so squat and clumsy-looking an animal as the hippopotamus should have been called the river-horse, but had they sat with me, then their doubts would have been at once dispelled. When these animals are much disturbed they only show the flat of their faces a few inches above the water, the nostrils being on a level with the eyes ; but when not shot at, and rarely seeing man, the whole head and the upper portion of the neck are projected. In this position the shape of the head, the angle at which it is carried, and the small and delicate ears, give it exactly the appearance of a horse swimming. The Dutch, and, for the matter of that, African, name of seacow (seekoe) has less to justify it, for, except in its plump proportions, there is no resemblance whatever. Nevertheless it is strange that nearly all the natives also call the hippopotami their cows.

The next morning, when we peered out of the tent, we saw, as we expected, a couple of round bloated masses floating about in the eddies above the fall. It was a heavy job dragging them on to

A DEAD HALF-GROWN HIPPOPOTAMUS.

the rocks for cutting up, and we could hardly have done it without the aid of a number of Kafirs, who came down from the hills to pay us a visit. The hide of a hippopotamus was in those days very valuable ; the thinner parts are made into long lashes for the great wagon-whips, and the thicker into the sjamboks (hand whips), which the wagon-drivers use to keep the after-oxen up to their work. For this purpose the hide is taken off the animal in large long slabs, which are then dried in the sun and packed. They are afterwards cut into the desired pieces and softened with grease and beating. These whips are practicably indestructible. While they were being cut up I took a long tramp down the Umkomati, into which the Umlomati ran a mile or two from our camp. There was a wide smooth path all along the river, made by the hippos; this animal making the widest path of any, as it keeps its feet apart; the elephant, on the other hand, swings one leg in front of the other as it walks, so that its track is only as wide as one of its feet. I went about ten miles down the river, seeing innumerable hippos and plenty of game such as we had been used to, together with the spoor of giraffes and rhinos, but no sign of elephants, though the Kafirs said they swarmed here in the summer. I returned to camp with my two bearers laden with ducks and guinea - fowl. A seacow calf shot by C. over-night had come to the surface, and the next day I amused myself with making a side of bacon, and rendering down a keg of lard, which is the finest cooking fat I have ever tried. In the afternoon I had a regular fight with an enormous seacow, which must have been one of the toughest old monsters that ever swam. I first gave it a long shot at 250 yards from the rocks, more to try my skill than anything else, for I really did not care for very much seacow shooting—it is too much like slaughter. From the commotion it made it was evidently struck, and when I went up stream to finish it, I judged from its refusal to put its head under water, and from its peculiar snorting, that I had broken its nose. I gave it another shot in the head, at which, to my amazement, it threw itself twice clean out of the water, and came down with a tremendous splash, receiving each time a snap-shot behind the shoulder, as well as two more from one of my Kafir hunters. A number of Kafir girls and young men who had come from the hills to see the white men, now joined us, and great was the excitement when the hippo came towards us and tried to effect a landing on the almost floating bank of reeds on which we stood. It could not, however, do so, as the water ran under their roots, so it tried to get on to a tongue of rock that jutted into the stream.; but though I shouted to them not to do so, the Kafirs drove it off with their assegais, and it turned down stream. I ran back to the rocks, and as it approached with its nose in the air I planted another bullet right in the centre of its throat, in spite of which it tried to clamber on the rocks to get at me ; but yet another shot at about a foot's range settled it, and it slipped off and sank in the deep water.

C. had been up the river and had shot a rhino-ceros and seen giraffes, and in the evening we poisoned some bits of meat with strychnine and laid them about the bush to destroy some of the numerous hyenas that the carcases had attracted.

In the morning, when returning from my bath among the rocks, I looked round for these pieces, and to my surprise saw a lion lying on the ground, which on my approach feebly raised itself on its forelegs and glared at me. As I was unarmed, I ran back to camp for my rifle, and C. and all the Kafirs returned with me. We found the lion still sitting up, and it made several abortive attempts to get on to its feet and attack us, snarling ferociously all the time. But the strychnine had done its work too well, and it rolled over in agony, and C. went up and killed it with a bullet in the eye. We were rather surprised, as lions are rather particular in their diet, and do not, as a rule, pick up offal lying about. One of the Kafirs amused us very much by going through a pantomimic performance of the whole of the actions of the lion, from the moment it first sniffed the poisoned meat until that on which it rolled over and received the bullet in the eye. The whole thing was inimitable, and when he had finished he rolled on the ground in an agony of laughter, and shouted out, "*Imbubi i itandi muti*" ("Lion does not like medicine"). Many alligators were in this stream, and C. was very nearly carried off by one. He was sitting on the bank fishing, and had got into a dozing state, when, for no particular reason that he was aware of, he suddenly became wide awake, and at once saw within two feet of his legs that innocent-looking stick-like object on the water which

he knew to be the two eyes and a piece of the forehead of an alligator. In another minute it would
have had him by the leg. No one not "in the
know" would guess these bits of stick floating
about to be alligators. Although we made no use
of them, we always waged war against these brutes;
but as they often do not rise for four days, we never
knew how many we killed.

On our last day at this camp we got giraffes.
We had gone together a long way down the
Umkomati, more intent on prospecting for gold
than on hunting, for we cared for nothing now
but elephants. We found several traces of the
precious metal, and C. again made unpleasant
acquaintance with an enormous alligator, on to
which he almost walked as it lay asleep on a
mud-bank alongside of a couple of prostrate tree-
trunks. The lash of the brute's tail was a sight to
see, and would have assuredly broken C.'s legs had
he not sprung back on realising that the animal was
not another tree. It was on another bank a little
further down that we found the fresh spoor of the
giraffes, and as we had not bagged one of these
animals this trip we followed it. It led us right
away from the river, and before we had gone a
couple of miles, we suddenly descried five long
mottled necks surmounted by graceful heads erect
above the lower line of the bush. A good stalk
brought us within thirty yards, and picking our
animals, we fired simultaneously. Mine came down

on its knees, but immediately recovered itself and made off with three of the others, C.'s going by itself in a different direction. Although putting on my best pace I soon lost sight of them, but kept along the spoor, and in about a mile came up to them again before they saw me. I stalked to within a hundred yards, and then put on a spurt, and got right alongside before they could get up steam, and with a bullet behind the shoulder brought the wounded one tottering to the ground. I let the rest go, as giraffes are among the animals I never killed wantonly, though their hides are valuable, and make whip-lashes which many prefer to those made of hippopotamus hide. C. had lost his through being over-excited. He was carrying a heavy double-barrelled elephant gun, and as he re-loaded the barrel he had fired, at the same time racing after his quarry ; in his excitement he loaded both instead of only the empty one. Consequently, one of the barrels had in it eight drachms of powder, a five-ounce bullet, and then eight more drachms and another five-ounce bullet. He fired this nice little charge at his giraffe when he came up to it, and, of course, he went flying, and, of course, into a wacht-een-beetje bush. He said that for some seconds he did not quite know what or where he was ; then he thought there must have been an earthquake, and it was some time before he realised what the matter was. When he succeeded in extricating himself from the wait-a-bit bush he decided to let the giraffe go its ways, and marched crest-fallen back to camp. I have often fired sixteen drachms of powder with one bullet, but never with another bullet in the middle of the powder. Even without this the concussion is fearful, and the blood would sometimes run down my cheek, while the shoulder felt as though it were struck with a sledge-

A DEAD GIRAFFE.

hammer. Most of the old hunters used to use these enormous charges; but I soon found it to be a mistake, for, apart from the concussion and the nervousness it caused, they disturbed the accuracy of aim. At this time eight drachms was my extreme limit, but I afterwards reduced this to five.

In all the pictures in the books of travel and hunting the giraffe is represented as galloping along with its long neck erect in the air; but in my twelve years of hunting I never saw one go in that way. The neck is thrust right forward, parallel to the line of the ground. A little consideration would show that in bush country a giraffe could not go at any pace with an erect neck ; it would cut its throat against the branches ; and in open country it follows the habit natural to it in the bush. Its pace is awkward, the two legs on the same side moving together ; but it gets over the ground at a good rate, and it takes a good horse to run them down.

On our return to the wagon we found all safe, and the oxen in perfect health. We therefore made up half a dozen light parcels of necessaries, and once more turned northwards, agreeing to hunt nothing but elephants, except for the pot. We once more crossed the Umlomati, and the next day the Ingweni (Crocodile), a larger river ; and the day after the Sabi, another fine river. Near the head-waters of this river were discovered, two or three years later, the well-known alluvial goldfields of Pilgrim's Rest ; and all the adjacent country is auriferous. So far no elephants had been seen, but a good deal of spoor only a few days old. Two days later we came to another stream, by which we determined to camp for a day or two, as the bush was getting more luxuriant and less thorny, with large numbers of the so-called elephant tree. I was, unfortunately, no botanist in those days, and do not know what family this tree belongs to. There were also numerous baobabs, with their long buds just

bursting into the great bell-like flowers, and enormous "Hottentot figs." No luck rewarded our search
here, although there was plenty of spoor; but of
other game there was more than we had ever seen
before, and lions were very numerous. So we went
on again and camped by a water-hole in the bush;
and here at last we came upon them; in fact, the
whole condition of things was reversed, for whereas
we had all these weeks been looking for elephants,
and only killing one, now we found the country full
of them, and were confronted with the problem how
we should convey all the tusks of the elephants
we intended to kill back to the wagon. But herein
we committed the common error of counting our
chickens before they were hatched. We had only
killed five, when, one evening, returning to camp
together, we found an induna (headman) and a lot
of young warriors in possession. This induna told
us that he had come from Umzila, the paramount
chief of Gazaland, the father of the present ruler,
and that he had given the strictest orders that no
elephants were to be killed in his country unless the
tusks were delivered to him (Umzila). He stated,
however, that negotiations might be made with
Umzila, under the terms of which we would be
allowed to retain one of the tusks of each animal,
but that for this purpose it would be necessary to
go to Umzila's kraal and treat with him personally.
This was a dead stop to us, as this Umzila was
reported to be the most powerful and most

bloodthirsty potentate in South Africa, not excepting Mozilikatsi, the great Matabili chieftain. So
far as was known, no white man had at this time
been to his kraal, or ever seen him, but within
a year or two several visited him, including Vincent
Erskine, Reuben Benningfield, and Robert Dubois,
a Natal trader.   His southernmost kraal was stated
to be on the Limpopo, five days to the north, and
here he was at the time living. We were, of course,
put into great difficulty, for it was out of the question that we should continue to hunt elephants for
the benefit of an African potentate; while if we
went to Umzila's we might be delayed indefinitely,
for no African has any conception of the passage
of time, and negotiations might extend over a
month. We could not afford this time, as there
were so many rivers to cross that it was imperative
that we should get on the high land before the
summer rains, now due in a month, commenced,
or we might have to abandon the wagon altogether.
However, after consultation, we determined to go to
Umzila's to try and arrange terms for a visit next
year, as, if he were inclined to procrastinate, we
could return at once, there being plenty of other
countries where we could hunt next season.   As for
the tusks we already had, the induna took possession of them ; but a judicious present to him
personally induced him to return the best pair,
which we at once sent to the wagon, and then,
with only two bearers, started northwards.

ELEPHANT CHARGING.

It is now necessary to relate an adventure with one of these five elephants which was as narrow an escape from death as I ever had. We found five bulls feeding in front of a dense piece of bush, the three hundred yards between ourselves and them being nearly open. In an undertone we arranged a plan of operations, in accordance with which C. and myself made a circuit, one to the left and one to the right, so as to get in front of the elephants, giving instructions to the two Kafir hunters we had with us to advance upon them after a certain lapse of time. When out of sight of them I bore away at right angles until I judged I was in front, when I drew up towards them and waited for some sign of movement on their part. I could not see them, but knew I was not far off, when suddenly I heard a shot, and simultaneously there was a shrill scream and a crashing of bushes, and then right in front of me, and not twelve yards off, loomed an enraged bull, advancing straight at me with outspread ears and upraised trunk. I shouted to try and turn it, but it took no notice, and when it was little more than five yards off I fired in quick succession, first at the small brain as the trunk was slightly lowered, and then at the throat. This staggered but did not stop it, and it was almost on me, when, with what presence of mind I had left, I bowed my head and dived between its forelegs. I was swept to the ground by one of the hind legs, but fortunately escaped being trodden on. As soon as I could collect myself I sprang up, and, getting behind a large tree trunk, endeavoured, with rather shaky hands, to re-load, the elephant having stopped ten or twelve yards off. The poor brute was sorely wounded ; but it stood with its stern towards me, and it was some time before I was cool enough to leave my friendly trunk and kill it with a bullet clean through the heart. This was a big bull, and as we afterwards found (its tusks were the pair we got back from the induna) one of the tusks weighed about 102 pounds, and the other about 90. An elephant killed in this district about four years afterwards by Reuben Benningfield had one tusk weighing no less than 190 pounds, the other being about 160. I saw these tusks in Durban, and as they stood against the wall, notwithstanding that they were well curved, I could not, when standing on tiptoe, reach the point of either one.

It took us only four days to reach the Limpopo, at a point opposite where Umzila's kraal was stated to be. The country through which we passed was full of game, and we were particularly surprised at the number of giraffes. We had always believed that these animals preferred the dry sandy country of the interior, rather than the moist lands and luxuriant vegetation of the coast country. We also saw a great many elephants ; but, as C. remarked, " he would see Umzila damned before he killed any elephants for him." There was a good deal of swamp in the country, and it looked very fevery.

Man proposes, &c. On arriving at the Limpopo we found all our labour had been in vain. Umzila had gone to another kraal a long way to the north, and would not return for a considerable time. It was out of the question for us to pursue him, and no one had any authority to act for him. We therefore forwarded him a double-barrelled gun, with the intimation that we should return next year and crave permission to hunt, and then turned our faces southwards again.

The Limpopo (called by the natives the Mete) where we struck it was a fine large river, apparently some 400 yards across, but not very deep. It was, in fact, fordable, although there were two channels where the water was shoulder deep. We had got near to the hill country again, and to the west could see the mountain range for a long way. The junction of the Oliphants River was a little way upstream ; but we had no time to make explorations. Although the country looked very unhealthy, there appeared to be a good many Kafirs living on the other side of the river. They were not nearly such fine specimens of humanity as the Zulus and Swazis, being neither so well-made nor with such fine countenances. Indeed, in the latter respect some of them were quite forbidding. Nevertheless they appeared to be a good-hearted people, and we met with none of the bad treatment we had been led to expect from the reports current in Natal as to the character of Umzila's people. We were rather surprised to hear that a white man had come from the interior down the Limpopo, and crossed it just above the confluence of the Oliphants River, about a month before.   We afterwards learned that this was my friend Captain Elton, afterwards Consul on the East Coast, who had made a plucky journey right down from the Tati, on the western border of the Matibili country.   He made for Delagoa Bay, and we must therefore have crossed his track.

It was very hot by this time, but we made a forced marched and reached the wagon in six days, having nothing to eat all the way but plain meat, without so much as a pinch of salt, and our drink was water—often dirty.   All was safe at the wagon, and for a couple of days we luxuriated in Kafir delicacies, while preparing for our trek south. We then bade farewell to our dusky friends with mutual expressions of good-will, and, accompanied by a number of young men who were going to civilised parts to earn money for the purchase of cows to exchange for wives, headed south.   Fortunately the rains held off, and we crossed the rivers easily, except the Usutu, whose bed being partly composed of quicksand had shifted, and we very nearly lost our wagon owing to getting into too deep water.   However, a wet cargo was the only damage, and this we soon dried.   We then had to climb the mountain ; but as the wagon was light, we did not anticipate any great difficulty in

SWAZIS BRAYING A BUCKSKIN.

this. But herein we were mistaken, for after lashing and shouting until we were tired and hoarse,
we came to a dead stick half-way up, and at length
became convinced that it was beyond the powers
of the oxen to drag it up. We therefore " off
loaded " it and sent all the things up by Kafirs,
who had assembled in considerable numbers. But
even then the oxen could, or would, not move the
wagon, and we actually had to take it to pieces
and send it up piecemeal.

We were out of the country not a moment too
soon, for the next afternoon the clouds, which had
been gathering in dense, heavy masses, began to
let fall their waters, and for three days and nights
it rained uninterruptedly. However, we got the
wagon into a cosy sheltered kloof, close to a clump
of yellow-wood trees, and made ourselves as comfortable as circumstances would permit. The Kafirs
had a bad time of it, as there was no shelter for
them but what they could find under the wagon ;
but we kept up a roaring fire and gave them the
tent at night. On the third night the oxen wandered. It is usual to fasten them up at night, but
from our sheltered position and the goodness of the
feed we thought they would not go away, and
omitted to do so. They had probably been
frightened by a leopard, and it was late the next
afternoon before we recovered them and were able
to make a fresh start.

A strange fatality now overtook us. Neither

C. nor myself were able to hit anything.   We fired time after time at all sorts of game—elands, hartebeestes, blesbucks, wildebeestes, quaggas, springbucks, oribis, pauws (great bustard), and others, but could bag nothing, and at length there was not a bite of anything to eat in the wagon.   We had had a large quantity of biltong (sun-dried meat) and a sack of mealies (maize), but the thirty Kafirs who were with us had finished the last bite of it, and for two days we were without food.   The reason of our non-success probably was that after the rains the air on the mountains was a good deal clearer than it had been in the bush below, and everything looked a great deal nearer than it really was, and we had been firing at things a quarter of a mile away under the impression that they were only two hundred yards.   At length we got our eyes in, and I bowled over a quagga (Burchell's zebra).

All our difficulties were now at an end, and we sailed gaily along, until, towards the end of November, we arrived at C.'s farm, near Harrismith, much to the surprise of his partner, who, only the previous day, had received a letter from Natal informing him that news had arrived from Delagoa Bay that we had died of fever on the Umkomati.

THE HOT LAKE DISTRICT OF NEW ZEALAND

IT was in 1878–79 that I was commissioned by the proprietor of a newspaper with which I was connected to compile a guide-book to the entire Hot Lake Districts of New Zealand. These districts are in the North Island, and extend over a line of country lying nearly north and south, and being about 110 miles in length by about 20 in breadth, and in the same direct line volcanic action appears again further north in the great active volcano on White Island, in the Bay of Plenty. The southernmost extremity is guarded by the giant mountain Ruapehu, an extinct volcano 10,000 feet in height, being the loftiest mountain in the north island of New Zealand, very near the centre of which it stands. Some 20 miles north of Ruapehu is Tongariro, an active volcano of 8,000 feet, a very handsome mountain of true conical appearance, rising isolated from the plain. At the time of which I write Ruapehu had never been ascended, and Tongariro only once or twice, both

6

mountains being *tapu*, or sacred ground, to the Maoris.

At the present day these districts are easily reached, railways approaching them from several directions, but in 1878 the nearest terminus was more than 100 miles away. I started from Tauranga, in the Bay of Plenty, a most charming little township, built on a grassy slope, and buried in weeping willows, poplars, and blue gums, and overlooking a wide landlocked harbour. This harbour is, or was, however, a *bête noir* to shipping masters, owing to its difficult bar and tortuous, shifting channel. During my year's residence in Tauranga two fine steamers, the *Taranaki* and the *Taupo*, were totally wrecked. The latter lay for months in the channel under Mount Monganui, at the heads, with her funnel out of water. Some £20,000 was spent in endeavours to raise her, and when, after many months, they were successful, and she was being towed round to Auckland, she suddenly sank in deep water.

Tauranga is about 40 miles from Ohinemutu, the village on Rotorua, and the journey was then made in one of the well-known Cobb's coaches, slung on leather "springs." Three miles out of Tauranga is the famous Gate Pah, where a handful of Maoris, in the early sixties, held at bay for many days General Cameron's force of 2,000 British troops. Some of their success was due to their strategy in planting a flag on a portion of the works that was

unoccupied, which led to this particular portion
being continuously shelled. Nevertheless, in looking over the works as they now appear, it is
difficult to acquit the British commander of very
much over-caution. As a matter of fact, all that
can now be seen is one or two mounds and a half-
filled ditch, but at the time there were extensive
underground works. Some miles further on may
be seen other *pahs* on the hilltops, and on sides of
precipices, in such positions as to be practically
impregnable. These have only been used in inter-
tribal wars among the Maoris themselves. The
position of some of them is such that the conviction
is forced upon us that if a few Maoris were able to
hold the Gate Pah against an overwhelming force,
they could, in one of these, have defied the whole
British army, if its efforts were not better directed
than on this occasion. A dozen or more miles from
Tauranga a fine belt of forest is entered, continuing
for about 20 miles ; but its chief attraction is a
gorge in the centre, caused by the passage through
the range of the Maungaroa River. The scenery
here is very fine, the road down to the stream and
up again being blasted out of the face of the perpendicular cliffs, down which it descends for about
a thousand feet, overarched the whole way with
huge pine and birch trees, among which the stream
at the bottom is completely hidden from sight. As
the sun cannot possibly penetrate this gorge the
atmosphere is exceedingly cold and clammy. In

one portion of this bush the delights of a corduroy road are experienced, and in conjunction with a springless coach can be highly recommended as a certain cure for dyspepsia.

Presently open country appears, interspersed with ranges of low bush-covered hills, and soon Rotorua breaks into view, as an uninteresting sheet of water, circular in shape, and about 20 miles across in its widest part, relieved from monotony by the high island of Mokaia in the centre. Almost ahead, and a little to the right, will be seen the first indication of boiling springs in a white column of steam which rises from the Great Geyser, Waikiti, at Whakarewarewa ; and on the further side of Rotorua other large volumes of steam will be noticed, indicating the locality of the mud-springs of Tiketere.

Ohinemutu is a small village immediately on the borders of Rotorua, and contains a few hotels, general stores, and shops, while a number of natives live on a peninsula jutting into the lake. In the immediate neighbourhood of the village are many curiosities demanding inspection. It is as well, however, here to remind readers that the terrific volcanic outbreak on Mount Tarawera in 1886 may have materially altered the aspect of many of these marvels. They are described as I saw them in 1878–79, except that I have appended to the description of Rotomahana a short account of the outbreak, and the destruction it caused.

As the visitor is about to enter the village, a

stream will be noticed running alongside the road ; this is boiling hot, and proceeds from a large pool some 20 yards across, lying close to the road, and in which the water in some places is in a state of ebullition, giving off heavy volumes of steam. A few years ago a large geyser, throwing water to the height of 30 feet, sprang from this pool, but it has since subsided. It is not safe to approach too closely, as the margin, which is covered with mineral deposit, has a very hollow sound, and must be thin. In the manuka scrub at the back of the pool are many little potholes, in which a silky saponaceous mud of a bluish slate colour is bubbling up, exactly like porridge over a quick fire. Caution is required, as some of these are completely hidden from view by the undergrowth, and a plunge into one would scarcely be agreeable. On the shore of the lake, between the water and the houses, are many boiling springs a yard or two in diameter, and steam issues from every crack in the ground. Some of these are used by the villagers as cooking places, the food to be boiled being put into a bag or kit made of the native flax, and placed in one of the boiling holes : while to boil a kettle of drinking water for tea it is placed over one of the jets of steam, which sets it boiling as quickly as a fire would. The water in the hot springs is not good to drink, being too much charged with mineral matter. One of these small springs on the margin of the lake developed into a geyser during my visit, and threw a considerable jet of water to a height of 35 feet every few hours. The little bay in the lake, formed by two small peninsulas, is a favourite bathing place for Maoris and white people, the water in it being quite warm. It is heated by two large cauldrons of boiling water a few feet away from the lake, and by numerous springs rising up under water ; but those that cannot swim had better avoid it, as the feet might be thrust into one of these.

On the longest peninsula is the Maori village, which possesses a fine *wharepuni*, or meeting-house. The great front gable of this building is completely covered with very fine carvings of the usual grotesque character affected by the Maoris. In the present case they are quite unobjectionable, but in the more remote districts they are often exceedingly gross. The scroll-work of these carvings is often very artistic and pleasing, but the figures resemble nothing in the heavens above, or in the earth beneath, or in the waters under the earth. The faces are animated tattoos, with great goggle eyes of oyster-shells, and enormous mouths set with fearful teeth. It would seem to be a moot point whether the Maoris were originally tattooed in imitation of these images, or whether the images are attempts to represent a tattooed face.

About a mile from Ohinemutu, along the shore of the lake, are a number of remarkable springs of great interest. The locality is known as Sulphur

Point, and on it will be found many large pools of filthy-looking muddy water, 20 or 30 feet across, and giving off large quantities of sulphuretted hydrogen and other gases, which escape from them in great bubbles, giving them the appearance of boiling, though they are but comfortably warm. They are all, especially one known as the White Sulphur Bath, credited with being extremely efficacious in rheumatic and kindred complaints; but at the time of which I write little was known as to the relative merits of the different springs, and, with the exception of one or two rough sheds made of scrub, no provision was made for bathers. Consequently, bathing in them was rather dangerous work, as it was often difficult to get out of the springs, owing to the mud of their banks; besides which the bathers ran the chance of being asphyxiated by poisonous gases, and a good many fatal accidents occurred. Of course all this is altered now, and fine bath-houses are erected and full information as to the properties of the different baths is posted. I believe there is also a resident medical man.

A few hundred yards inland from these baths is perhaps the most fascinating feature of the lake— a large pool of water, known there by the absurd name of Madame Rachael. The water in it is boiling hot, quiescent, and of the clearest, most transparent ultramarine blue; while the sides of the hole, which is about 15 feet across, and full to the

brim—flowing over in fact—are composed of receding slopes and pinnacles, covered with the
purest white silica and looking like coral. The
depth is tremendous, and so clear is the water that
a stone thrown in can be seen for fully forty-five
seconds before it vanishes in the blue profundity.
With the sun overhead, the charm of gazing down
into the far mysteries of these cauldrons of placid,,
pellucid, steaming water, of which there are many
in the country, is altogether indescribable. They
might well be the entrance gates to a nether world
—a world bright, beautiful, and joyous, where fairy
palaces and crystal streams glitter at every turn
beneath blue, cloudless skies.

A few hundred yards further round the lake is
a remarkable flat of hard mineral deposit, on which
are innumerable sulphur springs, varying in size
from a couple of yards to as many inches. They
discharge large quantities of sulphur of different
degrees of purity, usually in combination with some
white earthy matter. At the further end of the flat
are a number of charming little cups, two or three
inches in diameter, formed by deposits of sulphur
from tiny little springs which they surround. The
sulphur is completely enamelled, being hard,
smooth, and polished, looking exactly like prim-
rose-coloured malachite. They are all miniature
geysers, the water being jerked for some inches
out of them; but in temperature they vary considerably, some being boiling hot and others quite

THE PIPE OF THE GREAT GEYSER WAIKITI, AT WHAKAREWAREWA.

cold, springs within a couple of feet of each other being found to differ more than a hundred degrees. These charming little cups are intensely interesting, and one can watch the tiny jets of water bobbing up and down, in and out of their delicately tinted setting, for long periods. Here, also, is a horrible little hole called the Coffee Pot, full of some coffee-coloured abomination in violent action, and smelling like the plagues of Egypt.

But the chief interest of the Ohinemutu district is centred in Whakarewarewa. This is about three miles from the village, on the banks of a good-sized stream called Pueranga, emptying into Rotorua. It is a truly diabolical place, and is noted as the location of the largest true geyser in the country, known as Waikiti. The district is about a quarter or a half a mile in length, by a few hundred yards in breadth, and to attempt to describe all the wonders it contains would be almost impossible. A fresh horror meets one at every turn, and there is no end to the objects of interest. Great holes in the ground, thirty or forty or more feet in diameter, full of boiling or bubbling mud or water, some slate-coloured, some coffee-coloured, some snow-white, some sulphur-yellow, some quite green, some bright blue, and some pale pink; mud geysers jerking up quantities of bluish mud from the centre of sym-metrical cones, from six feet high, formed by the mud-spray as it falls; great deep holes full of the most transparent water, blue and boiling; holes of

clear green water; huge boiling ponds buried in
steam; streams of boiling water, now clear and
sparkling, now milk-white and opaque; flats of
pure white silica and of pale yellow sulphur;
great bubbling springs starting from the ground
in a mass of boiling water a yard thick, and
four or five feet in height; steam from every
fissure and cranny, groaning hissing, roaring, and
shrieking; ruin, dismalness, and desolation—a very
pandemonium.   And in the midst, monarch of the
weird scene, stands the great geyser-cone of Waikiti.
This very rarely played in the time of which I
write, but I was fortunate enough to witness one
of its displays.   The geyser issues from a pile of
rocks some twenty feet in height, formed from the
mineral deposit in the water, and coated with a grey
covering of silica, semi-crystallized; steam issues
from every fissure of it, and several violently boiling holes are in its sides.   The funnel in the centre
is about five feet in diameter, and of great depth.
Mysterious noises are heard to proceed from its
lowest recesses, and every few minutes these noises
will be noticed to increase in intensity, when it will
be necessary to beat a retreat, for the groaning,
shrieking, and clattering will be quickly followed
by the ejection of large volumes of steam and hot
spray, which will ascend to the height of some fifty
feet.   It is in succession to this steam and spray
that the great column of boiling water makes its
appearance.   The column, as I saw it, was ap-

MUD PONDS AT TIKETERE.

parently solid, and rose to a height of forty or fifty
feet. The rise did not appear to be of the nature
of a jerk, for the water was observed to be boiling
furiously over the hole for many seconds before
slowly attaining a height of six feet. It then shot
up rapidly, and, after standing for nearly two
minutes, slowly subsided. These displays were
then of rare occurrence, and I stayed three days
in a Maori *whare* close at hand before I was
favoured with the sight of one. Hard by there
is another geyser of similar character, but of smaller
dimensions. I have read that certain geysers in the
Yellowstone Park, in Wyoming, throw a column of
water to a height of over 300 feet, but I cannot
help thinking that these measurements are inac-
curate. If they are correct, there is nothing in
New Zealand to compare with them, although in
other respects the geyser districts of Wyoming
are nowhere in point of interest to those of New
Zealand.

Another locality of interest in the Ohinemutu district is on the opposite side of the lake, at a point
where numerous volumes of steam are continually
rising. The place is called Tiketere, and perhaps the
largest mud-springs in the whole country are to be
seen there. The distance is about a dozen miles,
and on the way is passed a large warm pond, the
water of which has a remarkably sweet, sickly taste.
The springs of Tiketere are large, powerful, and
weird-looking, boiling furiously — one especially,

which is fully thirty yards in diameter, and gives
off powerful suphurous fumes and dense clouds of
heavy, sickening steam. The water is very curative,
and many rheumatic cripples have obtained complete relief from it. Close at hand are a large
number of mud-springs, sputtering and spewing
away in hideous fashion, great bubbles of blue,
unctuous mud rising and bursting in rapid succession. Higher up the hill, after splashing up
through a waterfall of hot water, another system
of springs is to be found, and on a sort of terrace
a number of baths have been dug out, where many
invalids came and camped. About a mile further
is a charming little lake, three-quarters of a mile
in diameter, and buried far away down between
forest-clothed cliffs ; it is called Roto Kawou.

At this time the great point of attraction to
visitors to these districts was, of course, the cele-
brated terraces of Rotomahana, now, alas, no more.
In order to show them how to see some of the most
varied features of the country, I made a round trip
from Ohinemutu, going to Wairoa, on Lake Tarawera, eleven miles by coach ; across Tarawera by
canoe, nine miles ; then to Rotomahana, two miles ;
back again over Tarawera to Waitangi ; on foot to
Lake Okatina, across it in a canoe ; thence to Rotoehu
and Rotoma ; across Rotoiti, nine miles, by canoe ;
and thence across Rotorua to Ohinemutu again.

From Ohinemutu to Wairoa there was a good
coach-road, and on the way a most charming bit

IN THE BUSH—A KAURI PINE.
7

of bush was traversed, in which the great rimu
pines were smothered with the brilliant scarlet
flowers of the parasite known as the *rata*. This
bush was destroyed by the mud from the outbreak
on Mount Tarawera, although many miles away.
On leaving it the Blue Lake (Tiki Tapu) is passed,
a lovely sheet of water of cerulean hue, surrounded
by high forest-clothed hills. A narrow range of
lofty hills separates this lake from another, Kakahi,
a rhomboidal piece of water fenced in by forbidding-
looking barren mountains. The road skirts both of
these lakes, and is cut in the face of the hills that
overlook them. Soon after leaving Lake Kakahi
the Maori village of Wairoa is reached, perched
in a bush-clothed ridge, 500 feet above, and overlooking, Lake Tarawera. Close to Wairoa is a
bit of the wildest and most picturesque scenery
imaginable. Kakahi is about 300 feet higher than
Tarawera, into which its overflow waters discharge
themselves, and as the distance between the two
is only about a mile and a half, the character of
the torrent can be imagined. The stream is completely buried in heavy timber bush, and the water
rushes over the rocks at a terrific rate, leaping
down great perpendicular steps, bounding and
roaring along and lashing itself into the whitest
of foam, tearing and hissing its way among huge
scattered boulders and casting up clouds of feathery
spray, and anon completely disappearing from sight
along some mysterious underground channel, to

break again into view in streaks of burnished
silver among the rocks beyond. One of the cascades is 50 feet in height.

Wairoa had acquired a somewhat doubtful reputation on account of the questionable character of
the dances its people sometimes—for a consideration—got up for the delectation of male travellers,
and its destruction in the outbreak of 1866 (for
though twelve miles from Mount Tarawera it was
completely buried in mud and debris, only a few of
the inhabitants escaping) was regarded by the more
fanatical of the Maoris as a judgment of their
singular deity. I was a witness to one of these
dances, and though certainly not refined, I have
seen as bad in Paris and Vienna casinos. They
were, however, conducted according to scale, and
the more that was paid the looser they became.

The descent from the village into the bush-
clothed bay is very romantic, the whole of the
narrow gulf running far into the mountains, being
as charming a picture as one could wish to see.
The great forest trees come down completely to the
water's edge, and the noble totaras, rimus, and other
giant pines are sights in themselves. Most of the
scenery of the lake is, however, more romantic than
picturesque, the surrounding mountains being bare,
brown, and barren. Lake Tarawera is nine or ten
miles long, and the paddle along it was very enjoyable. I chose a regular Maori canoe in preference to one of the whale-boats they keep for

hire, and was paddled the whole distance by two charming damsels, who enlivened the way with

A FAIR PADDLER.

merry song and chatter, and decidedly impertinent criticisms upon some of the passengers they had paddled over, delivered with a cool *chic* that was

irresistible. We stopped half-way at a Maori village, and lunched off some of the delicious little
crayfish of the lake. At the further end, on the
left, are three mountains of about 3,000 feet in altitude. It was from the last of these, Tarawera, that
the great outbreak occurred. The traditions of the
Maoris contained no record of a previous outbreak
of this mountain, and, judging from the descriptions
of those who had ascended it, it had not been an
active volcano for ages. The first explosion, which
blew out a great crater near the top, was evidently
caused by compressed steam, and this was followed
by the ejection of vast quantities of mud, dust, and
various debris, which continued at its greatest
intensity for many hours, and with less force for
days afterwards. So vast was the quantity of mud
thrown out, that on the Rotorua road, twenty miles
away, it lay three and four feet deep, and rescue
parties had the greatest difficulty in reaching
Wairoa. Even at Tauranga, more than sixty
miles away, the dust lay for several inches, and
it was so dark that artificial light had to be used
at mid-day. ·

At the further end of the lake the canal entered
a small, deep stream of warm water, the current
of which was so swift that the paddlers could hardly
make headway against it. This ran out of Rotomahana, its course being about two miles. The first
view of Rotomahana was decidedly disappointing,
for it was in truth nothing more than an exag-

NATURAL HOT BATHS NEAR THE TOP OF THE WHITE TERRACE.

gerated horse-pond, less than a mile across, partly
covered with sedges, and surrounded by low, dismal-
looking hills of dark-red earth, which were seen to
be steaming and smoking in many different points.
On the left, rising from the top of the hill immediately overlooking the lake, was a dense column
of steam of the most delicate turquoise blue, and
a similar column rose on the other side, springing
respectively from the great cauldrons which had
formed the Pink and White Terraces.   Te Tarata,
the far-famed White Terrace, directly after broke
into view, and in no way belied its fame, although
a good deal of exaggerated nonsense has been
written about it.   It was most unquestionably one
of Nature's most marvellous productions, and one so
unique in character, and so dissimilar to all that we
have been accustomed to look upon as the result
of her handiwork, that it was difficult at first to
persuade oneself that it really was a work of nature
and not of art.   "Nature's above Art," says the
Bard, and those who have quarrelled with the
epigram would have found in Te Tarata and its
companion Otukapuarangi, the Pink Terrace, works,
apparently in her own line, which Art would have
found it difficult to improve upon.

These terraces were (*then !*) perhaps over one
hundred feet in height, the white being slightly the
higher, and were arranged in innumerable steps of all
sizes and depths, from six or eight feet to an inch or
two, each step being the segment of a circle, and each

forming, by means of its upper rim, a bath of warm water from the size of a saucer to that of a small swimming bath. Though called White and Pink respectively, neither of them was strictly of the colour indicated, the "snow-white alabaster," about which so many poetical and imaginative individuals have raved, being neither more nor less than a decided pearl-grey; and the "delicate rose-pink" partaking a good deal more of brick colour. These remarks will be understood to refer to the general effect, for in places both plaster-of-Paris white and decided reddish-pink prevailed. Neither have writers been very happy in describing the nature of the mineral deposits of which they were formed. "Marble-like," "delicate tracery," "lace work," "arabesque work," "tattooing" and similar expressions have been employed, but none of them give the faintest indication of what character the deposit really took. As a matter of fact, it differed materially in the two terraces. Te Tarata was rough and covered with *scales*, less than an inch in length and semi-erect, each scale in its turn being similarly marked. Otukapuarangi, on the other hand, was perfectly smooth, but uneven and worked into rounded surfaces like chalcedony. The White Terrace was the more imposing in appearance, being fan-like in shape, and spreading out from the top until its lower rim extended for perhaps two hundred yards; while the Pink was not more than a third of this, but widened out

above. Each had an immense cauldron of tur-
quoise-blue water at the top, enclosed on three
sides in a crater of red earth, and it was from the
overflow of the water that the mineral deposit was
derived. That appertaining to the White Terrace
was the larger, and exceeded perhaps twenty-five
yards in width. It was also hotter and was continually in a state of most violent ebullition, every
now and again throwing up an immense body of
water, ten or twelve feet thick, to a height of more
than twenty feet, while the heat near it was quite
unbearable.

All who have written on these terraces have
compared them to something in this world or the
next, but none, to my mind, have been at all
successful in their comparisons. The world of
fairy-folk and kelpies has been the favourite one
to draw upon, but I can scarcely conceive anything
more incongruous than fairyland and Rotomahana.
The terraces were themselves most fascinating to
behold, but the accessories were—as far as mere
ocular effect goes — dismal in the extreme, and
neither the fairy-folk people nor those who plunged
into yet other worlds could point to any genuine
comparison. The imaginative beholder might,
however, by keeping his eyes fixed on the
terraces, and excluding the surroundings, have hit
upon some conception having some plausibility
about it. He might, for instance, have supposed
himself to have wandered into some Brobdignagian

land, and to have come upon the place where mysterious religious rites were conducted. The terraces would have seemed to him gigantic altars, approached by noble flights of marble steps, and the great clouds of turquoise steam would have been the smoke from incense burning on the top. Such an illusion would have been easy, and the shadow of the beholder, cast upon the steam by the setting sun, might well have been a spectre-priest about to invoke some dread and mystic power.

Though at Rotomahana everything was overshadowed by the majesty of the terraces, yet there were other strange things of exceeding interest to be seen. In the hills overlooking the lake were dismal ravines, in which were many violently boiling springs, great pools of boiling mud, spluttering mud-cones, ponds of blue, green, and white water, and huge steaming holes giving forth deafening noises, diabolical as the cries and groans of the denizens of Tartarus.

All these marvels are now, alas! no more. Rotomahana no longer exists. The lovely terraces, the eighth wonder of the world, are buried deep in many feet of mud, and in all probability shattered to atoms. Where was the lake is now a deep crater, said by some to be 200 feet in depth, at the bottom of which are numerous great mud-volcanoes. This crater of itself is said to be of surpassing interest, but it cannot be mentioned in the same breath with the terraces. Those marvel-

THE PINK TERRACE, ROTOMAHANA.

lous structures, which had taken ages to build up, were absolutely unique. The world had nothing like them to show. Terraces of mineral deposit there are in Wyoming, in Iceland, in Japan, in Queensland, and in other places, but compared to those of Rotomahana they were as the work of a pavement-artist compared to that of a Millais. And after decorating this world for æons, in one short night the work of ages is destroyed. Truly Nature is cruel! The practical mind might, however, find some consolation for the loss of these terraces in the fact that the mud ejected from Tarawera has fertilised a circle of country a hundred miles in diameter, which before was worthless pumice-sand.

From Rotomahana I paddled once more across Lake Tarawera to Waitangi, a Maori village destroyed, with all its inhabitants, by the eruption. A rough walk of half an hour or so brought me to another lake, called Okatina, set in high, bold cliffs, timber-clothed to the water, though in some places quite bare, hundreds of acres of great forest trees, with the soil in which they grew, having slipped down into the lake and disappeared in the profound depths of its waters, Close at hand is another pretty lake called Okarika. I crossed Okatina in a canoe in about an hour. It was a charming passage; the lake is so small, and the cliffs are so high, that one felt low down in a cañon cut by some river, and practically separated from the rest of the world. From Okatina a rough bush-track through a forest of magnificent trees and tree-ferns leads, in about three hours, to the western arm of Rotoiti, where I passed the night in a Maori *whare*. The next morning I visited two of the most lovely little lakes imaginable—Rotoehu and Rotoma, charming sheets of blue water far down among forest-clothed cliffs. These two lakes are perfect gems, and are in character, I should imagine, peculiar to New Zealand. Canoeing on either of them is simply the poetry of living. Waterfowl is plentiful, delicious little crayfish are to be netted in their waters; and with a small tent to sleep in, one could dream away the hours for weeks in these sylvan and lacustrine solitudes. On the eastern shore of Rotoehu are some interesting hot springs, and a large one highly charged with gas, the water of which contains some salt of soda.

Rotoiti is a long, narrow lake, and very beautiful, some of its bays being exquisitely picturesque. Several hot springs are on its shores, some about the centre having effected many remarkable cures in rheumatic complaints. The outlet of the lake, the river Kaituna, is well worth a visit, the scenery in the neighbourhood being very pleasing and romantic. A nine-mile direct paddle from the starting-point, but much further if Kaituna or any of the bays are visited, brings the tourist to the Ohau, which connects Rotorua with Rotoiti, and over which is a bridge. From this point it is six miles to the island of Mokaia, in the centre of

Rotorua, where there are many interesting hot springs and the ruins of a mansion built by Sir George Grey. At the time of my visit the original stone god brought by the first Maori immigrants to New Zealand from the island of Hawaiki, in the Pacific (for the Maoris have only inhabited New Zealand for about five hundred years), was lying buried on Mokaia. It was subsequently dug up and presented to Sir George Grey, who placed it in the Auckland Museum. Those with a taste for legendary lore will find voluminous stores of it among the natives living in the island. The well-known legend of Hinemoa and her lover, which was turned into verse by Mr. Alfred Domett, the poet-premier of New Zealand, had its location here. Six miles' more paddling lands the tourist once again at Ohinemutu.

At this time few tourists saw more than the springs and geysers about Rotorua and the terraces of Rotomahana, but my instructions were to find out all that was worth visiting, and the result of my ramblings was the discovery that, with the exception of the Terraces and Whakarewarewa, hardly any visitor ever saw the real wonders of these hot-spring districts. As a guide I engaged the well-known Jack Lofly, a runaway man-of-wars-man who had lived more than twenty years among the Maoris of these districts. He then owned a sort of hotel and baths he had made himself near Lake Taupo. Men of this kind are to be found

8

among almost all aboriginal tribes, the tendency to revert to type being clearly not yet outgrown.

We left Ohinemutu on horseback, proceeding in a southerly direction, and in a dozen or fifteen miles reached a range of hills known as the Paeroa Mountains, and standing about 1,500 feet above a long, flat valley. This valley had rarely been visited, but was full of extraordinary things. The first wonder was a narrow, deep stream, flowing with immense rapidity, and of a temperature almost at the boiling-point ; it is perhaps the most copious supply of water at so high a temperature in the whole country. Owing to the marshy nature of the valley, the many mud-craters about, and the burning, dangerous hills above, we were not able to reach its source, and I believe no one has seen it. On its course are several strange deep wells, round and even as if made by human hands, and with boiling water far away down in them. These were evidently once large geysers, but they cannot have played for long, as their sides are clothed with ferns, some of which are said to be natives of the tropic archipelago, and to be found nowhere else within 2,000 miles. A little further under the range is one of the most effective natural pictures I ever saw. A large mass of bare, smooth rock that must be at least 500 feet in height stands sheer out of the range, about a third of its height from the foot, and this great rock is set all round in a deep fringe of enormous totara trees, each a perfect

picture in itself, so grand in growth are they. I
do not think I ever saw an isolated bit of scenery
so unique and taking. Soon, however, the eye is
assailed with scenery of quite another character.
" Horrors upon horrors accumulate," and a wilder
spectacle need not be desired. The whole range
is burning from top to bottom. Chemical action,
apparently similar to the slaking of lime, is going
on, and the mountain stands sheer above one,
gradually slipping away so that pointed peaks are
left, bare, smoking, and whitey-grey in colour.
Not a sign of vegetation is to be seen, only a
vast mountain of white mud. Anything more
dreary could scarcely be conceived ; yet the fascination of looking up at the great grey peaks,—so
close that every crack and cranny can be distinctly
seen—burning and steaming, is extreme. It is a
portion of the world in its chaotic age, still in a
state of fusion. At the foot of these peaks are
numerous weird and curious sights, but the ground
is excessively dangerous, chemical action going on
fiercely underground within a few feet of the surface. Some of the mud-geysers are very large,
and one of them in particular is (if it now exists,
which is improbable) probably the largest in the
world. There are also some very symmetrical
mud-cones from two to fifteen feet in height, and
many strange-looking pools of chalk-white, pale
pink, and sulphur-coloured mud, giving off great
quantities of gas. Exploration at the foot of these

peaks is attended with great danger, and Lofly said that every time he had been there the place presented a different aspect, on account of the surface continually falling in and forming fresh mud-ponds.

Further along the range are many fierce emissions of steam on the hillside, and near the summit, a mile or two from the peaks, a dense cloud of heavy steam is continually forced upwards with great violence, apparently indicating the presence of one of the largest boiling pools in the country. Lofly said that no one had ever seen it, and he refused to go up with me, declaring that it was *tapu*, and that the Maoris would kill us ; but my private opinion was that he did not care for a fifteen hundred feet climb, as he was stout and scant of breath.

A few miles further, a scramble over some very broken country partly covered with fine forest trees brought us suddenly on to the Waikato River, running very rapidly through a cañon it has formed for itself, the hills on either side varying from 400 to 1,000 feet. The scenery is very fine and romantic. On the opposite side of the river is the Maori village of Oraki-Korako, and on both sides are innumerable fumaroles, solfataras, geysers, mud-geysers, and wonders of all sorts. In fact, although there are more mud-springs and boiling holes at Tokano, at the foot of Tongariro, it is here at Oraki-Korako that the most columns of steam are to be seen. On a cold morning before the sun

has risen the spectacle is positively extraordinary.
On the right bank of the river the hills are very
high, and rise at a very steep incline from the
water; on the other side they recede a few hundred
yards; but on both sides, for a distance of about a
mile of the river's course, jets of steam, large and
small, are rising, and from one position over a
hundred may be counted in sight together. Nor
is it steam alone that Oraki-Korako has to show;
indeed, I think there is more variety there than
anywhere else, and it is certainly one of the most
interesting spots in the Hot Lake districts, but in
1878 very few people had visited it. There are
five or six terraces, and though they bear no
comparison whatever to those of Rotomahana,
either in extent or in arrangement, yet they are
not without beauty, and are of much interest.
Three or four on the right bank, extending for a
third of the height of the hills to the water's edge,
are perfectly snow-white, and viewed from the
opposite side are very attractive, but will not bear
that close inspection which enhances the beauties of
those of Rotomahana. Another on the left bank is
of brick colour, much wider than the white ones,
but very shallow. The most extraordinary of all is
formed of a totally different substance to any other.
It is on the right bank, and is about thirty yards in
width, by perhaps a couple of hundred in height.
Its colour is bright green and vivid pink, the latter
predominating, with occasional admixtures of bright

yellow and dull blue. From a height of about twenty or twenty-five feet hangs down to the water's edge a strange and exceedingly graceful fringe of these colours, in separate symmetrical festoons, the width of which is fully thirty yards. This is surely one of the most curious of Nature's freaks. The substance of which it is formed is equally remarkable, and seems, when examined, to be more of vegetable than mineral nature. In fact, it is like fungus, being spongy and very slippery to the touch. When these stalactites, so to speak, are broken, they are as a rule found to be in three layers or strata, the inmost being a thick pale pink, then a thin bright green one, and then another pink one brighter than the first. Sometimes, however, the green is outside, and sometimes these colours are varied with yellow and blue. The stalactites averaged about two inches in thickness. The source of this curious stuff is a small warm stream which makes its way down the hill, first by the side of a large white terrace, on to which it then runs, covering .it with this remarkable formation, and forming the extraordinary fringe described. It is strange that Hochstetter, who, under instructions from the New Zealand Government, wrote an elaborate description of these districts, makes no mention of this terrace and fringe, although he alludes to many of the other wonders of Oraki-Korako, of which it is by far the most striking feature. As it is hardly conceivable that it can have been formed since the period of his explorations, the only inference is that he did not personally visit Oraki-Korako, but relied upon the descriptions of Maoris, who omitted mention of this particular feature.

The upper portion of this terrace, before the stream turns on it, is very symmetrical, two or three steps, 6 or 7 feet in height and 30 yards in width, being perfectly formed, and it is not easy to understand how Nature could have made walls of such plumb-line exactness. On the flat places there are also many boiling pools of large size, one of which acts intermittently, being quiescent for some minutes and then commencing to boil violently, and again subsiding. There is also a large hole from whence proceeds a most terrible noise. From this terrace up the river the scrub is 20 feet in height and very dense, and locomotion was difficult, the rotten, dangerous nature of the ground and the number of boiling mud-holes no whit improving it. A few hundred yards from the last terrace a dismal-looking spot at the summit of the hill and nearly 500 feet above the river, is reached, which has all the appearance of having been once the crater of an active volcano, although now covered with thick vegetation.

Here my Maori guide (Lofly having again declined to do any climbing, and had never been up here) suddenly disappeared into the bowels of the earth, calling on me to follow him. I did so, and making a perpendicular descent of about 25 feet by a ladder cut in the soil, found myself landed in a charming grove of tree-ferns, one of the prettiest nooks imaginable, and in strange contrast to the wild surroundings. From these ferns opens out a great arched cave, sloping down into the earth at an angle of 45 degrees. The length of the cave is about 200 feet, the height of the arch about 150 feet, and the width about 45 feet. The descent is over great boulders of limestone, covered with a slight incrustation of alum. At the bottom is a pool of blue water, pleasantly warm and strongly impregnated with alum, lumps of which lie about. Looking up from the pool, through the arch towards the sky, and through the clump of magnificent tree-ferns which shut it in, one sees a wonderfully pleasing picture, quite different to the dull, gloomy manuka scrub that prevails through this district.

From the Alum Cave to the other terraces was real hard work, the manuka scrub being extremely dense and strong, and in some places almost impenetrable. I did not find anything of very special interest, but the ground had never been explored, and not a twentieth part of the springs have ever been looked upon by human beings. The third terrace is very white and beautiful, and is fed by three boiling springs, but until the manuka is cleared off by fire or otherwise, the wonders of these hills can never be known. At one place a most diabolical noise was heard, but owing to the steepness and the density of the scrub we could not get at it.

The left bank of the river also has its interesting features. The stream is extremely rapid, and great exertions have to be made by the paddlers to keep the canoe from being carried past the landing-place. Immediately on landing one sees a number of mud-springs, mostly pink, white, and grey, but one of them is quite a bright red. There is a strange fascination about these mud-springs bubbling away like boiling porridge ; the colours are very soft and pure, and often of shades that could hardly be produced artificially ; but coloured mud, even in a boiling state, can hardly be called beautiful. Never-theless, one never tires of watching them, and each fresh group is welcomed with new delight. Perhaps the dominant sensation is wonder rather than admiration ; but whatever it be, it is irresistible.

A little way up the river is a large terrace of pink or brick-colour deposit, which is full of interest. Near the water's edge is a great geyser, which in 1878 had not played for some years, but which the Maoris declared used to throw a jet of water right across the river at an angle of some 60 degrees. If this be the case, the jet must have been from 250 feet to 300 feet in height, and have rivalled the Excelsior, the largest of those of the Yellowstone district. Hochstetter says he witnessed a display straight up to a height of 60 feet ; but the Maori chief who had lived here all his life declared that it always threw in a slanting direction. There are also some very remarkable holes on this terrace, which form perfect natural baths. One of these has a natural seat, on which the bather can sit up to his neck in water, and as the water is soft and smooth as glycerine, and pleasantly warm, a greater luxury can scarcely be conceived than dallying in this bath. If the bather be not bashful he will perhaps not be incommoded by the presence of half a dozen Maori belles in the bath at the same time, for such is the primitive custom. But the most curious thing here is a small and pretty geyser originating in the centre of the hot pool from which this bath is supplied with water. This charming little geyser plays at regular intervals of about five minutes, and throws a thin jet of water to a distance of about 50 feet—not straight up in the air, but in a perfect arc. The duration of the display is about half a minute, and though the volume of water ejected is not greater than that thrown by a small fire-engine, the effect, nevertheless, is very pleasing. Close at hand is another bath, coated, like the last, with incrustations exactly similar to those of Otuka-puarangi, into which run two streams of water, one almost at boiling-point and the other ice-cold, and as the distance between them is not more than a yard, one foot can be scalded and the other frozen should such sensations be desired. Further up the river are some immense mud-cones, continually spluttering up little pats of bluish mud, and more

mud-springs of large size. It is a curious fact that
all the Maoris of these districts eat the mud thrown
up by these mud-cones. This is not from want of
food, for they have plenty, nor is it taken medi-
cinally, but from mere habit, first perhaps formed in

MAORI GIRLS IN THE "KING COUNTRY" IN THEIR FLAX MANTLES.

some famine. I tried it several times, and though
I could swallow it without repugnance I preferred a
mutton-chop. I stayed three days in Oraki-Korako,
and should have stopped longer but the fleas in the
Maori *whares* fairly drove me away. I tried two or
three, but they were all alive, and at last I had to
roll myself up in my rug outside. Even Lofty's
seasoned hide could not stand them, and he declared

he had not had a wink of sleep all the time he was there. I have seen larger and more numerous specimens in many places, but none so vicious as these. As for the Maoris, they seem to be able to do without sleep, and keep up a chatter all night.

From Oraki-Korako, a roughish ride of a dozen miles, during which some awkward climbing had to be done, brought us on to the main road from Rotorua to Lake Taupo, close to the Maori settlement of Oranui. Here I heard that Rewi Ngatimaniopoto, the paramount chief of the "King" natives, who though not actually king in name, that title being held by Tawhaio, was nevertheless king in fact, was in the village. He was there to hold a conference with a Colonial Commissioner, Major Scannel, concerning some question of boundaries, and I determined to be present. Rewi was the man who conducted the operations against us in the great war in the early sixties, and for many years he refused to see any white man. I was disappointed in his appearance, which is decidedly mean, and not to be compared to that of some of the old white-headed chiefs, with their faces a maze of tattooed scroll-work. Rewi was only tattooed on the nose, with a few faint, hardly discernible lines on the cheeks, and though between sixty and seventy, hardly had a grey hair. Commonplace, however, as was his appearance, Rewi was a man of remarkable ability, both as a military leader and as a statesman, and for a long time he held in his

REWI NGATIMANIOPOTO.

hands the question of peace or war. On this occasion he did not appear to be in a very pliant mood, and when Major Scannel entered the meeting-house he coolly threw himself down on a rug and composed himself to slumber. As I considered this a decidedly unfriendly attitude, I at once sent off a despatch to my paper, which, carefully embellished by the editor, was given to all the papers in the colony, and produced a war scare. When I again met Rewi some weeks afterwards he expressed a desire to disembowel me, and on my inquiring why, he said that lying down was a custom of the higher-class Maoris when conferring with an inferior. I expressed my regrets, but intimated my opinion that when the unfortunate inferior was an English official, the custom would be more honoured in the breach than in the observance. He did not see it, but nevertheless invited me to dinner, and regaled me on crayfish, smoked eels, and underdone pork, washed down with gin and water, which made me ill.

A few miles from Oranui an immense fumarole or steam-hole is seen, about a quarter of a mile off the road. It is called Karapiti, and is well worth a visit, being, I think, the most powerful of its class in New Zealand. The ground in the neighbourhood is very rotten and dangerous, and is completely honeycombed with holes; but by following the brow of the hill Karapiti may be safely reached. The hole is not large, but the volume of steam ejected is immense, and so powerful that stones thrown in are cast high into the air. The ejection is not regular, but increases in intensity at intervals, like the puffing of an engine, and is accompanied by a somewhat similar but much louder noise.

Lake Taupo now breaks into view, with the snow-capped Ruapehu and the smoking Tongariro standing sentry over it at the further end, respectively some fifty and seventy miles distant, though seemingly quite close. The Waikato, which is the outlet of the lake, is once more crossed by a fine bridge and the township of Taupo, or Tapuwaiharuru, as its residents are fond of calling it, is entered. Lake Taupo, though large enough to be called an inland sea, being more than a hundred miles in circumference, is a very interesting piece of water, the shores, with the exception of the southern, being nothing more than low, rolling hills covered with dismal-looking scrub, and it has but one island, Motutaiko, chiefly remarkable for the myriads of rats on it, which, presumably, like the inhabitants of remote towns and villages, live on each other. The country at the north and south ends is, however, overflowing with interest. The first locality I inspected was Lofly's own sanatorium, two or three miles down the Waikato. He had a good little hotel, with fine orchards and gardens, and capital baths—in fact at this time they were the only ones deserving the name in the whole country. They were large enough to swim in, were constructed at the junction of two copious and rapid streams, one at a temperature little short of boiling, and the other ice-cold; and the streams were so manipulated that any temperature desired could be obtained, and they could be made to flow so that in the great bath the water would be quite cold at the bottom, and quite hot at the top. The water in the hot stream, which rushes bodily out of a hillside about half a mile from the baths, contains large quantities of chlorine and a percentage of iodine.

Numerous features of interest are to be seen in the neighbourhood of these baths, mostly of the usual character of boiling springs and mud-geysers, and the river scenery is in many places very fine. But the most remarkable is that known as the Crows' Nest. This is a small geyser that throws a thin jet of water every few minutes to a height of twenty or thirty feet. The peculiarity about it is that it originally broke out directly in the centre of a huge hollow tree, which has now fallen down, leaving only about eight feet of the base, and this has become petrified by the mineral matter in the water. The interior of this huge hollow piece of trunk is apparently lined with sticks, also petrified, which give it the appearance of a gigantic nest. Many speculations have been put forward as to how these sticks got there, but they are doubtless merely the remains of branches that had fallen down the hollow trunk while the tree was still living. The spring from which the geyser proceeds

9

is directly in the centre of the hollow, and care has to be exercised in looking over the top into it, as the ejection is very sudden. Another curious place close by is called the Witches' Cauldron, and is a great boiling hole of intensely blue water, situated in a crater the sides of which are covered with a mineral deposit of all the colours of the rainbow.

Two or three miles down the river is a very charming waterfall called Te Huku. The stream suddenly becomes enclosed in a narrow chasm in the volcanic rock, about 250 yards long, and in some places not more than 10 feet wide; it lashes furiously through this, and then plunges bodily into a wide, still, tree-lined bay or pool. The height of the fall is not more than 30 feet, but the volume of water is very great. The old bed of the river was very much larger in past ages than at present.

The volcanic action in these regions must at one time have been terrific, for the whole country, far and wide, is a mass of pumice sand of unknown depth; but, as shown by some of the cuttings on the roads, certainly over 50 feet.

The eruptions took place subsequently to the island being covered with vegetable, and probably with animal life. This is shown by the existence of great charred trunks of trees far down in the pumice, many of which may be seen on the Napier road 20 and 30 feet from the surface. Perfect trunks of great trees, that have not borne leaves for ten thousand years, may in this way be seen, completely preserved from decay by the pumice.

Eight miles from the village of Taupo is a small lake known as Roto Kawa, which emphatically

TE HUKU FALLS.

demands a visit. Previous to my visit, ·hardly a dozen people had seen it, and only the strong-nerved people should visit it, as it is excessively dangerous, much of the ground being so thin that a step forward might be fatal. The road passes close under the cone of the extinct volcano Tauhara, 3,400 feet above the sea and 1,300 feet above Lake Taupo. This is a very picturesque, isolated mountain, standing solitary out of the plain; its northern side is clothed from summit to base with fine forest trees, its south side bare. Roto Kawa is not more than three miles in circumference, and is adjoined by a marsh of flax bushes and raupo of about the same size, a famous breeding place for wildfowl. The volcanic remains are at the further end, where steam rises in every direction from an expanse of the ground partly surrounded by low hills of bare red earth, probably the crater of a volcano not long extinct. The largest volume of steam arises from an extraordinary little pond, or lake, of 120 yards by 20, which is separate from Roto Kawa by a scrub-covered neck, a few yards in width. This pond is boiling in dozens of places with different degrees of violence, and is remarkable for being of three distinct colours. In the centre, where there are two large boiling places, it is bright pea-green; in some other boiling places, clear bright blue; and in the rest, dull whitish blue. The water in the main lake is a dirty bay-green, and tastes strongly of sulphuric acid. The shore on one side of this small lake is covered with crystallised sulphur, and is very hollow in many places. The ground round the rest of it is most dangerous, and in attempting to make my way one of my feet went through the surface, revealing beneath a horrid mess of boiling mud only a foot or two below the ground on which we were walking. Lofly, who had the rubicund face of a Falstaff, turned as white as a corpse, and we gave up the attempt.

Stretching from this boiling pond to the low hills is a vast expanse of ash, completely hot to the feet, and sounding very hollow—so hollow that it was in fear and trembling that we ventured to cross it; indeed, in one place Lofly, who was of a portly build, threw himself full length upon the ground and proceeded in the manner of a wily serpent. In many places it has fallen in, and ghastly valleys full of great boiling mud-ponds and mud-cones have been formed. Great blocks of pure sulphur of the richest colour and beautifully crystallised lie about this wildest of regions. The entire absence of life, the dangerous character of the ground, the bare steaming hills, coated in many places with brilliant-coloured mineral deposit, the extent and number of the sunken valleys full of hideous mud-springs, the vast masses of hot ash, and the great boiling pond combine to make it mystic and uncanny in the extreme.

The last hot springs of the northern Taupo districts are at the south base of Tauhara, where, in what may be called caves, are a couple of large ponds, one of which is boiling; the overflow from them forms the hot stream Waipahihi, which, after a course of a few hundred yards, discharges into Lake Taupo.

The village of Taupo itself is built upon hollow ground, and as one walks along the street the footsteps sound and feel as though walking on a floor that had begun to give way. A steamer plied across the lake to Tokano, touching at various Maori settlements, but unfortunately at this time it had somehow sunk at its anchorage in a little bay. Consequently, I had to ride about thirty miles through a number of dismal and dangerous swamps. I might as well have stayed away, for throughout the two days I could spare for Tokano it rained incessantly, and with a volume that put extensive exploration out of the question. I only saw innumerable springs and mud-geysers of the usual character. Hochstetter says that there are upwards of five hundred of them, but they are of no special interest. Close to the lake a portion of the Kakaramen range, a spur of the great Kaimanawa chain of which Tongariro is the extremity, is undergoing precisely the same kind of chemical action that has already been noticed as occurring to Paeroa, and the hill in consequence appears to be on fire.

Some years ago a complete avalanche of hot mud slid off this hill, and buried a Maori settlement established at its foot. Among those who lost their lives by this catastrophe was the famous Te Heu Heu, one of the most able and restless of the chiefs who fought against us in the early wars.

Tongariro is nearly twenty miles from Tokano, and in its sides hot springs break out in many places, and about two-thirds of the way up, on the north-west side, there is evidently a very large body of water indeed, as the steam rising from it is visible sixty or seventy miles off. At the time of

which I write several people said they had been
to the summit, but the Maoris at Tokano stoutly
maintained that it was *tapu*, and that no one would
be allowed to ascend it. At the top is a crater
from which showers of ashes are occasionally
thrown, and streams of lava poured ; but the

THE ACTIVE VOLCANO, MOUNT TONGARIRO, IN THE NORTH ISLAND
OF NEW ZEALAND, 8,000 FEET HIGH.

eruptions only take place at very long intervals,
often of many months, if not years. Ruapehu is
extinct, and is usually snow-capped. Notwithstanding the model of its summit in the Sydney
Exhibition of 1879, it had then never been
ascended by white men.

Tongariro is the south limit of the volcanic

action of New Zealand, the northern limit being on White Island. This is an active volcano in the Bay of Plenty, about 80 miles from Tauranga. It rises about 1,000 feet above the sea, and on it is a great boiling lake, to which those on the mainland are but duck-ponds. From this lake rises an immense column of steam to a height of at least 2,000 feet. It is difficult to get near this lake on account of the intolerable stench, but large quantities of sulphur are brought from it by a private company. The island is quite out of the path of the ordinary traveller, and is difficult to get at. On the occasion of my visit in a steamer belonging to the sulphur company, we were unable to land owing to bad weather.

Dr. (now Sir J.) Hector, the Colonial Geologist of New Zealand, says that all these wonders are merely the results of chemical action, without any connection with volcanic fires ; but this is virtually disproved by the fact that they all lie between the two volcanoes, Tongariro and White Island, by the hot ashes of Roto Kawa, and by the outbreak of Tarawera. We must remember that Dr. Hector long declared that it was impossible that gold could be found in New Zealand. That the visible effects of boiling mud and water, and steaming mountains, and exhalations of gas and steam result from simple chemical action is highly probable, but it is certain that the chemical action itself is set up by the heat of internal fires. To deny to these phenomena any connection whatever with volcanic action seems absurd ; and while we can accept without prejudice Dr. Tyndall's explanation of the mechanism, so to speak, of geysers, we do not thereby renounce the volcanic theory, but only begin to understand a little how the heat of volcanic fires is applied.

From Tokano I cut across country so as to strike the Taupo-Napier road at the foot of the Kaimanawa ranges, and catch the Napier coach. This drive of a hundred miles is, I think, one of the most romantic in the world, for though it lacks the great heights of the Rockies, the Andes, and other ranges, it is full of interest and beauty from beginning to end. The road ascends to a height of 4,000 feet, and the gorges, ravines, and valleys it crosses are very fine and grand. A cañon fenced in by high mountains is at length reached, and is followed at the bottom, the Petane River which formed it being crossed no less than fifty-four times in some twenty miles. Page after page could be written on the wild and romantic beauty of this road, though the effort to award to one particular spot the palm in interest is vain, and the magnificent bush gorges on both sides of Tarawera—far away from the lake and mountain of that name—the glorious views overlooking the valley of the Waipanga, to which a descent of 2,500 feet is made and risen again on the other side, the wild barrenness of the Mohako.

and the bare volcanic hills of the country between that river and the Petane flit before the mind in assertion of their claims, and linger in the memory as sights never to be forgotten. The view from the highest point attained above the Waipanga on the south side will probably be deemed by most to be the grandest ; and it certainly is very fine, whether looking down into the valley of the river babbling over its stony bed, and to the grand forests which clothe the wonderfully broken hills beyond, or to the wild-looking volcanic cones and the deep ravines between them on the other side of the divide. Not the least interesting feature of the journey was the driving of the coachman, George Jones. This man was about the best whip I ever saw, and the way in which he came down at full speed to the valley of the Waipangi, with a sheer precipice of 1,500 feet within a few inches of his wheels, turning the sharp V-shaped corners with hardly any lessening of his speed, was something to be remembered.

QUEER EXPERIENCES OF A REMIT-
TANCE MAN

PERHAPS of all forms of adventure which beset those who find their pleasure in wandering abroad, the deprivation of food or water for prolonged periods is most dreaded by those who have been forced to submit to it. In the case of water, of course, the period can never be very prolonged, for the human system will not work without it, and I doubt if any authenticated case could be found of a human being existing in a conscious or active state without it, or some substitute for it, for more than ten days. Three days in the Zambesi desert was quite enough for me. Joseph McCabe, the South African traveller and explorer back in the fifties, was nineteen days in the Kalahari without a drop of water for himself or oxen, but then melons grew profusely and formed an excellent substitute.

But it is really astonishing how long one can subsist with little or no food. Five days without a mouthful of anything but water I found to have no appreciable effect, either at the time or subsequently.

In fact, I believe I was all the better for it. But a month's starvation, or what practically amounted to starvation, had a lasting effect upon me which I have never shaken off.

It was in New Zealand, twenty-two years ago. I was there for my sins. Fifteen years of rolling about the world had resulted in a crop of moss that would not have fetched a brass farthing in the open market. It was suggested to me that I should retire to the solitudes of New Zealand as a hopeless failure, and there hide my abashed head. I had been enjoying myself to the top of my bent, and as the process emptied my pockets, why, I felt no humiliation in accepting the fifty pounds per quarter which my father, a fairly wealthy man, intimated that he would forward to me.

But man proposes, and the New Zealand Government disposes. The Post Office in that delightful colony was, in those days, apparently conducted on the assumption that letters were an unwholesome luxury, and that the colonists would be much better employed in tilling the soil than in corresponding with their friends. Any way, every obstacle was put in the way of receiving letters, especially English ones, with punctuality and regularity, and the post-office clerk was superciliousness crystallised, whose ignorance of everything connected with his office was complete.

And so it came about that my very first fifty pounds went astray. With my usual craving for

seeing everything that was to be seen, I had
devoted the cash in my pockets on landing to taking
a trip round the Middle Island, and eventually I
found myself in Nelson without so much as the
conventional half-crown, which has formed the
basis of so many colossal fortunes.

Now, I never was a traveller of the new school,
but belonged distinctly to the old. The new school
carries about indiarubber baths, scented soap, cara-
mels, chocolates, champagne, evening suits, and all
sorts of mysterious things that we of the old school
hardly knew the use of. In all my travels my
impedimenta for personal use never consisted of
more than one small portmanteau, often not even
that. On the present occasion it embraced nothing
but a razor and a tooth-brush. In the interests of
economy, so striking a feature in my constitution, I
had adopted the plan of wearing a flannel shirt for
a fortnight or so, and then throwing it away and
buying a new one. By this means I avoided the
cost of washing, and the destructive attentions of
the colonial laundress. A paper collar was in those
days the height of the mode. I had not even a
watch; for when last in London it had gone on a
visit to my " uncle," and had never returned, in pro-
test no doubt against the rough usage to which it
had for so many years been subjected.

And so, when the post-office clerk informed me,
with the air of a grand duke instructing his boot-
black, that no letters had arrived for me by the

mail, I felt a qualm in my inside which almost made me, like Mark Twain's steamship passenger, place my hand on the spot and say, " Oh my ! " For I knew no one, and I never carried a letter of intro- duction in my life, always preferring to find my own friends. However, after consigning the Post Office and all its works to perdition, I went out and stood in the road a penniless outcast.

The view outside was not without its features of interest. To the left the gloomy heights of the Collingwood district, scored with white lines of water-cascades, stood frowning over the troubled waters of the great bay ; to the right the huge hump of the Dunn Mountain towered aloft, and the wooded range of the Whakapuaka country followed the line of the bay far into the distance ; while in front the Great Boulder Bank showed its dull greys parallel to it, rising sheer out of the seething greens of the bay waters.

I did not make these observations at the time and transfer them to my note-book. What I said was, " Well, I'm damned ! " which summed up the situation succinctly enough for the time being. The shock had the rather curious effect of making me exceedingly hungry, so I strolled up Trafalgar Street, and feasted myself upon the displays made in the windows of bakers' shops and restaurants. Thus refreshed, I sat down upon the end of the jetty, and took counsel with the restless waters. They told me that if I went to an hotel and frankly

explained matters, I could easily get board and
lodging for a few weeks on credit. But I was
proud. To have been refused would have been
worse than starving, and there were many un-
principled loafers in the colony in those days, so
that hotel-keepers were not unnaturally suspicious.
So I sat there till dusk, and then strolled up to
what was called the Botanical Gardens. These
"gardens" were nothing more than a rounded,
steeply sloping hill, some 200 or 300 feet high,
planted with scattered trees, and with a winding
path cut up to its summit, where several seats were
placed.

At the foot of the hill I found a large piece of old
sacking hanging on a fence, and this I sequestered.
Taking my way up the path until I got above the
line of the rising night mists, I sought for a soft
place protected from the cold airs that came sough-
ing down from the mountains. There I spread my
sacking, and, rolling myself up in it, lay watching
the lights of the town below, which through the
thin white mist looked like firedrakes in a marsh.
Then I tucked my head under the sacking, and fell
into a troubled sleep. Presently I woke up with
that strange sensation that conveys to the highly
strung the knowledge of the presence of human
beings, though unseen and unheard. I turned my
head round, and saw on the path a little above me
a pair of ghostly shapes that the faint light of the
now risen moon showed me to be a man and

10

a woman clinging to each other, apparently in terror.

I rose and bade them pass without fear. It was an amorous young couple who had prolonged their endearments on the summit to an unseemly hour, and as they passed, looking fearfully at the lion in the path which had caused them so much terror, I thought to myself that so pretty a young girl had far better have been at home with her mother than up there with a wanton young man. A few paces past me they stopped, and whispered together, and then the girl returned towards me holding out her hand, and said in a pleasant voice, " Please take this." I drew back. I had not come to this yet ; so, finding me persistent, they pursued their way.

Next morning, after a breakfast of watercresses, and a toilet in the little pool fed by a trickle in the hillside in which they grew, I descended to the town, and, in pursuance of my determination come to under the sacking in the small hours when it became too cold to sleep, sought for some temporary employment. But in Nelson, the Sleepy Hollow of New Zealand, as it was known, no one ever did anything except on the days when the weekly steamer came in. The shops opened, and their proprietors leaned against their door-sills smoking and expectorating ; the half-dozen cabmen dozed on their boxes at the top of the steep and picturesque street ; the policemen supported the burden of existence against the soft sides of the lamp-posts ; the lawyers exchanged the latest *équivoques* at the nearest bar; the doctors sat moodily in their surgeries waiting for patients that never came, and helping themselves to surreptitious pegs out of bottles labelled *Ex. Copaib.;* the parsons foregathered under the trees by the church and bemoaned the materialism of the age; and even the hop-growers in the outskirts sat on wheelbarrows and sleepily watched the bines twisting round their poles. I had no chance in such a community. My accomplishments were not negotiable. I wrote an atrocious hand, and though quick at figures had small knowledge of the mysteries of book-keeping; there was no demand for elephant-hunters; there was no race meeting, and jockeys and horse-trainers were superfluous; there were said to be a score of billiard-markers unemployed — the Nelsonites regarded billiard-playing as too much like hard work; the *rôle* of professional cricketer was not understood; an expert in rough diamonds and diamond-mining could not earn a Chinese "cash" in a decade; and a knowledge of coffee-growing was as unsaleable as one of the etiology of mummies. Even spade-work was not to be had, it was not the season. I offered my services to a baker, explaining that I could make splendid pastry with hippopotamus fat, much better than the sticky bath-buns and jam-puffs in his window, but he told me in a cold-blooded way that he didn't keep no "hippopotamuses" on his estate.

So I gave it up, and retired once more to my eyrie on the hill, and, wrapping myself up in my sacking, shut out the affronts of a cold and heartless world. In the morning I took up my bed and walked—walked along the slopes of the Whaka-puaka hills until I came to a little flat platform, surrounded by a semicircle of hawthorn trees in full berry, through which ran a trickling crystal streamlet fringed with watercress. There I pitched my camp, and after a repast of the berries and cresses leaned back against a rock and sunned myself.

The old formula to live on a penny a day ran, " A penn'orth of dried apples for breakfast ; for dinner a quart of water to swell 'em ; take tea with a friend." But if in this *menu* hawthorn berries are substituted for dried apples, a penny would feed one for a month. They are the most absolutely satisfying provender I have ever tried, and few have sampled more varieties. When well swelled out with water they cause such a cloying colic, that if a nicely roasted pheasant were set before one it would be spurned with disgust. In consistency and character I can only liken them to spunyarn powdered with grated bath-brick. Watercress, on the other hand, is a windy diet, which leaves one the emptier the more one consumes. But by judiciously combining the two I did fairly well, and occupied the little grassy plateau for three or four days. Fortunately no rain fell, and I basked in the sun by day, watching the farmers' carts on the road far below, and the ever changing lights and shadows of the great bay, and at night peacefully snoring in my sack.

It was an idyllic existence—peaceful, temperate, and healthy; but soon its monotony began to pall on me. I was of a restless disposition, for ever on the move, and the peace, and quiet, and stagnation of that little bower, with its fringe of crimson berries, began to get on my nerves, and I felt that I must go out again into the world. If it had not been for a tiny wren-like bird, that sat on a stone and chirped at me for half the day, I could not have stayed so long. So I made a careful toilet with the aid of my pocket-comb and the little pool for a looking-glass. I tried to remove the stubble from my face, but having no soap, the first movement of the razor gave me such a thrill that I desisted. Then I took up the sacking, but do what I would I could not fold it so as to make it look like a railway rug, or anything a gentleman need be ashamed to be seen carrying! Even a starving man is not above the littlenesses of his fuller brethren. So I reluctantly thrust it into one of the hawthorn bushes, and whistling a cheery goodbye to the little wren, returned to Nelson.

The lordly post-office clerk regarded me more haughtily than ever when he once more informed me that there was nothing for me, and this time with a look of suspicion, as though he thought that perhaps he had better hand me over to the police.

Did not Burgess and Kelly and Sullivan, but a few years before, walk into that same office and jocosely demand remittances, what time they were sticking up and murdering every solitary gold-digger and traveller in the mountains round about ?

Then I walked up the Waimea Valley to the village of Richmond, some six or seven miles up. A melancholy sight was this rich alluvial valley at that time. Some crazy enthusiast, to remind him of home, had imported thistle seed, and it had spread over the entire valley, so that it looked as though it were under an enormous crop of wool, for the heads were now dry and white. The air was full of the floating seed, as if huge flakes of snow were for ever falling from a blue sky.

At Richmond I obtained two days' employment, my pay being board and lodging at the inn, clearing brambles out of a gentleman's garden. In my weak state it was hard work, and I made but slow progress, and considerably damaged my hands and clothes with the thorns. I was allowed for supper at the inn some bread and cheese and a pint of colonial beer, and under the influence of this I borrowed some sheets of foolscap and wrote a screamingly funny account of the adventures of a young man in search of a future in New Zealand, which afterwards appeared in the *Cape Monthly Magazine.* But when my work was finished, and no more could be obtained, and I wandered about a starving vagrant again, reaction set in, and I was plunged into a mood of gloomy foreboding. The hawthorn berries in this district were smaller and drier than those of Whakapuaka, and the cresses more stringy. The ditches in which I had to sleep were damp, and I missed my old friend the piece of sacking.

I wandered about here for several days, vainly trying for an odd job at the farms. One day I saw through a tall gate a fine walled-in orchard, where the crimson and gold apples and the russet-red pears hung in thousands. Memories of my youthful escapades, in which enraged farmers and snarling dogs figured, arose in my mind; but I went away from that orchard without purloining a single apple! Had adversity made me virtuous? No. Do all I would, I could not scale that wall. Joshua is said to have overthrown walls by means of trumpet-blasts. I do not believe it. I am confident that a string of invectives concocted from the vocabularies of elephant-hunters, gold and diamond diggers, sea-faring sinners, mess-room soakers, and back-block lost sheep would far exceed in blighting properties the blasts of Joshua's trumpets. But that orchard wall did not fall. Judging from relative explosive properties, I do not think a ton of dynamite would have had any effect on it.

Making my way back towards Nelson, I walked along the railway line, and about half-way a thing so strange happened to me that I hesitate to write it. The spirit of scepticism is abroad, and the tales of the traveller are scoffed at by young men whose experiences are confined to the glades of Fleet Street and the wilds of Brighton. The Bishop of Nelson resides in the neighbourhood, and he has a private railway station, at which trains stop by signal. It is, or was, a lean-to shed, open for the centre third of its frontage, and boarded in at each end, but without windows. It seemed to me a nice place to pass the night in, so after foraging round for some supper, which took the form of a couple of raw potatoes I found on a refuse heap, I lay down in a corner on the seat which ran round the interior.

In the early morning as I lay in a dozing state I heard an approaching train. I did not move, and I ·heard it stop. Then suddenly a man loomed above me, said hurriedly, " You're Mr. Lane ; take this," and thrust something into my inert hand which was lying beside me. Then he disappeared, and I heard a door bang and the train move off. I had not moved, being hardly awake, and for the moment I thought it was an illusion caused by disordered nerves consequent on my starved condition. But when I looked into my hand, four half-crowns were lying there ! The illusion theory would not hold water, as I demonstrated by biting the coins. Spectral half-crowns will not stand teeth trained on buffalo meat. Who that man was, and how he could know that I was inside the shed, I have never to this day found out.

At Nelson I went to a restaurant and feasted royally on a pound of steak, a great hunk of crusty bread, and a "long colonial." Then I bought a stick of tobacco, and after paying my respects to the honourable and exalted post-clerk, sat on the jetty smoking my pipe, and musing how beautiful and excellent a world it was. Adversity had not yet taught me prudence, and in the evening I repeated the steak and the beer, and then lay down between a pair of sheets, with a warm blanket over me! How I did sleep! Indeed, I should not have awoke the whole day had not the chambermaid pulled my hair. And then I found I had a splitting headache, and wanted no breakfast. I drank a long beer, after which my appetite returned, when, seeing that three of my half-crowns had gone, I spent the rest in a knuckle of cold boiled ham and a loaf of. bread, and took them up to my bower on the hill-side. My self-respect was all gone now, or I could not have walked down the street with a greasy ham-bone but half-concealed by a scrap of paper. Indeed, I felt, as I certainly looked, like a first-class loafer.

But in my bower all that went for nothing. I drew out my sacking, spread it in the sun, and casting myself upon it, reclined with all the luxury of an Oriental on his divan. I had meat and bread and vegetables and water; what more could a 'man want? And then my little friend the wren came and chirped to me from his stone, and I cast him

crumbs from my loaf, which after eyeing sus-
piciously for a while, and then critically turning
about with his beak, he eventually swallowed with
gusto.

For several more sunny days—I was never quite
sure how many—I sat up there talking to my wren,
and dreaming of days in Paris and Vienna, of
moving accidents by flood and field, of past
triumphs and failures, and of sweet faces smiling
at me. When I first thought of these I laughed
aloud. " As though any pretty face could smile at
such a scarecrow," I said to myself. I went to the
little pool and looked at my reflection on its lucid
surface, and laughed louder than before. I finished
my ham and most of my bread on the second day,
reserving a piece of the latter for the wren, and
then I returned to berries and cresses. But once
more I wearied of the restfulness ; wearied of the
solemn silence ; wearied of the glinting of the sea,
and of the sombre blues and purples of the mountains beyond ; wearied even of the sun in its lonely,
sovereign daily march. I could endure it no longer.
What remained of the piece of bread I put upon a
flat rock for the wren, replaced my sack in the bush,
and scrambled down the mountain-side.

This time I went in the other direction. The
marine cable was being laid, and the shore end was
to be landed at a place christened Cable Bay, about
fifteen miles distant, and I thought that perhaps I
might get something to do at the works and build-

ings being carried on there. Fifteen miles of newly cut New Zealand bush-road is not child's play, even for a robust and healthy man ; but to one in my condition it was a sickener. There are no haw-thorns and no cresses in the virgin bush, for both are exotics, and it does not contain any edible pro-duct that ever I could discover ; so that after nine hours of dragging my reluctant limbs along the awful ruts and asperities of that direful road, I arrived at the bay in a condition of collapse. The workmen were just beginning their evening meal in the great room of an unfinished building, and the boiled mutton and rice which I was invited to share soon put new life into me. But the next morning I was set to work carrying buckets of water to make mortar, two at a time, from a stream in the hollow to the works on a rounded rise three hundred yards away. I struggled manfully at this for two or three hours, and then I gave it up. Nature refused to do any more.

There was nothing else they could give me to do, so I retraced my steps towards Nelson through the towering pines and over the neck-breaking corduroys laid across the road in the soft places. About three miles from Nelson was a wayside inn, with strawberry and fruit gardens, and it was nearly dusk when I arrived there. I slowed down in my walk, trying to muster up courage to go in and ask for a meal and bed. Then I stopped, and as I did so I seemed to feel something pushing at the back of my head, as though to force it down. I turned it, but there was no one there, and again thinking it to be a nervous affection, I was about to pass on when the pushing was repeated, and bending my head to it I saw lying in the dust at my feet a half-crown!

Does a providence look after us in our times of trial; or do the spirits of departed friends hover about us in our wanderings? I could not argue the point; all I could do was to pick up the coin and order some bread and cheese and beer. A bed was given to me as well, and the next morning I returned to Nelson and found my remittance awaiting me!

All this time—three weeks and more—it had been lying at a country village, the very Richmond in whose ditches I had slept! When I was at the inn there, eating my bread and cheese to the order of a local storekeeper, next door there was lying for me a draft for fifty pounds whenever I was pleased to call for it! Why it should have gone to Richmond, when no such name was on the envelope, was a secret known only to the post-office officials. When I put the question to the worshipful clerk, he loftily told me that I did not understand the post-office business. He was right; I did not.

DESERTED ALLUVIAL GOLDFIELDS
OF VICTORIA

IT was in 1881 that the ill-fated P. & O. steamer *Bokhara* conveyed me along the smooth reaches of "Our Beautiful Harbour," and out into the restless ocean, through the noble gates of Sydney Heads. Although the Sydneyites a little too aggressively insist on its unapproachable attractiveness, they have good reason for this. Few scenes on the world's surface can surpass in loveliness Sydney Harbour as seen in the spring, when the eucalypti that cover, or used to cover, the enclosing hills put forth their young shoots, and make the whole hillsides glow with rosy red, shading off into sage-green. Every few hundred yards opens up a fresh bay of surpassing loveliness, where the trees, so different in their tints to any others in the world, come down to the water's edge, and contrast so well with the symmetrical Norfolk pines which surround the white houses on the crest.

But while Port Jackson may claim to be the loveliest landlocked sea in the world, surely Port

Philip is the ugliest. Not even the presence of Melbourne, the Queen City of the South, can redeem it from dreariness, for (be it said with bated breath if there is any Melbournite around) the Queen City herself appears at a distance but a dull, dirty, and uninviting realm. As we steam up to the wharf we pass under the stern of the Victoria navy, and exchange compliments with a gallant greaser who is leaning over the taffrail in an attitude of melancholy dejection, doubtless meditating on what they would do when they all became admirals of the fleet.

At the time of which I write there was great bitterness between Sydney and Melbourne on the subject of tariffs, and I was warned in the former place that the custom-house jacks-in-office of Melbourne would pull my belongings to pieces in their zeal in search of contraband. When I remembered that in landing at Sydney from New Zealand the officials there were proceeding to search for cheeses among my Sunday-go-to-meetings, and only desisted when I insinuated that I was a pressman commissioned to describe the Exhibition, I wondered what on earth the Melbourners would do. Conceive my astonishment when, as I stood twirling my keys round my finger while waiting for the myrmidons to begin, a couple of ragged galloots seized my portmanteau, crying, "Just in time to catch the train, sir; carry your things for a shilling." Not a sign of a gold-laced cap anywhere. Only as

we passed up the wharf to the station did a
deliberate individual in a fusty uniform, sitting
reading a newspaper in a sentry-box, call out
languidly, " Got any jewellery there ? " and receive
my reply of " No such luck " with a lazy grin.

In spite of its fine wide streets, magnificent shops,
gorgeous public buildings, and elegant churches,
Melbourne is not a cheerful-looking place. The
dull grey-blue stone of which it is chiefly built
gives it a sombre, depressing effect, and the stone
itself is so hard that little ornamentation can be
introduced. By the side of a Sydney building
of rich golden-brown Pyrmont sandstone, which
when freshly quarried is so soft that it lends itself
to the most elaborate carving, one in Melbourne
is as a prison to a palace. On the other hand,
the suburbs of Melbourne are infinitely prettier
than those of Sydney, and more tasty bungalows
and lovelier gardens could not be found anywhere.

The first impression a traveller by rail from
Melbourne receives from examining the country
through the windows is that the whole energies
of the colonists have been directed to building
fences. In the neighbourhood of the city they
are all of the same blue lava of which the houses
are built ; but the Victorians do not display the
same neatness in their erection as the Aucklanders
of New Zealand, who have a similar stone. A
Melbourne lava fence is a very slovenly affair
compared to an Auckland one ; just as a Welsh

granite fence will not compare with a Cornish. The stone fences soon give place to wooden ones, although not a vestige of a tree is to be seen for very many miles. These wooden fences are really wonderful. Besides fences made of split posts and rails, I counted no less than fourteen different methods of construction, some of them exceedingly ingenious. But perhaps the most remarkable point about them is that they enclose nothing. Mile after mile of fenced-in paddocks is passed with hardly a trace of a plough or a sign of a domestic animal. Here and there may be seen a hundred or two of sheep, or a score or so of somewhat emaciated cattle ; but the amount of work that has been done for the support of these few animals—especially as the country was once clearly covered with bush—-seems altogether out of proportion with the result. No homesteads, or farmyards, or cattlesheds, or sheepyards are visible anywhere ; nothing but a long succession of empty paddocks, fenced in various styles.

When one arrives at Geelong it is difficult to realise that such a sleepy little town should once have disputed supremacy with Melbourne. The marvellous growth of the latter is very strongly brought out by an inspection of the two places. Strange that such a miserable mud-ditch as the Yarra should have controlled such mighty destinies ! Geelong now makes wine ; Melbourne makes history.

So far the country had been open, the only growth higher than the grass—so called by courtesy —having been these fences. But as we left the bay behind and gradually crept up towards the divide, scattered ghosts of defunct gum trees stood erect in weird imbecility, and gave to the paddocks a semblance almost of ghastliness. A little further these spectres became associated with other goblins,

A BUSH VILLAGE IN VICTORIA.

little less direful in appearance than themselves. These were gum trees half dead and half alive, weather-beaten old wrecks ragged and battered as an old-fashioned three-decker after the attentions of a hostile fleet; with here a great white arm, bare and barkless, and there a sprig or two of "greenery-yallery" foliage, too mean and sickly for even a crow to perch on. And so on to Lal-lal, where we were fairly in the bush; but oh, such a wrecked and torn and dilapidated bush, looking for all the world

11

as though a solar tornado had passed over it, or a herd of Brobdignagian elephants had trodden it down. Through all this desolate country not a sign of wild-life was visible, except an occasional dejected magpie perched on a fence, and bobbing his ridiculous head up and down like an energetic park preacher demolishing all the facts of science.

Ballarat was my first objective point, and I eagerly looked out of the windows in search of the old goldfields, whose romance had so often filled my mind with longings ; but a few bare reddish hills studded with tall chimneys did not come up to my expectation. It was not until afterwards that I began to realise the marvellous amount of work done in the old alluvial days.

Ballarat is a fine town. Broad streets, splendid buildings, pretty villas and cottages, with flower gardens in the outskirts, a capital park and botanical garden, and no back slums, go to make up quite a model town. It would be difficult to beat Sturt Street anywhere. Broad enough to hold three streets of an ordinary town ; it has trees down both sides, and for part of its length in the middle as well ; and the buildings that line it are worthy of their location. Those in search of a quiet healthy residence (Ballarat is 1,400 feet above sea-level), with bright, clean, and pleasant surroundings, might do worse than pitch their tent there.

At the time of which I write its people had no occupation but watching the fluctuations of the

shares of various mines. At ten o'clock every
morning they would assemble in their hundreds
outside the exchange, and, after a glance at the
share list, stand looking at each other for the whole
of the day. They never did anything else. There
was no excitement, no life, no enthusiasm, and
apparently scarcely any interest in their own
proceedings. They looked like so many Micawbers
waiting for something to turn up; or like a mob
of friends at a funeral, waiting outside for the coffin
to come out and the procession to start. A more
demure and cheerless assemblage I never saw.
Perhaps they were all bears, and the bulls had
bettered them; I know not, for, thank Heaven, the
antics of these animals have not come within the
range of my studies. While I was there Mr. (now
Sir) Graham Berry, the democratic leader, came up
to galvanise them into life; but he met with poor
success, for the depression of the share market could
not be shaken off. I was not much impressed with
his oratory, which is too much of the cockatoo
order; and a squeaky voice did not add dignity
to it. Still less did his companion, Mr. Vale, the
temperance champion, impress me. A more in-
temperate orator I never listened to, and I found
myself wondering what, if he could feed such
ferocious malignity and acrimonious fury on a cold-
water diet, he would generate if he took to brandy
and port wine!

During my stay at Ballarat there took place the

premier sheep-show of Australia and a meeting of
the Hunt Club, so that I was able to see the best
horses and sheep this great continent can show.
They were no doubt very fine, but not so much
superior to those of South Africa and New Zealand
as I had been led to expect.

But it was the old goldfields that interested me
most. There is a fascination and romance about
doings on the goldfields of Australia and California
in the fifties that must attract any one who has any
manhood in him. About Ballarat these deserted
alluvial diggings spread in every direction, and I
was never tired of wandering over the bare red
chaotic deserts, and peering into the half-filled-up
shafts, and scrambling over the hummocks of
washed-out soil. It is a curious fact that grass and
other plants refuse to grow on these old goldfields,
and in 1881 they were as bare as when turned
over thirty years before. Perhaps the old associa-
tions are too much for them ; who can say ? The
fact remains that while a deserted stone quarry soon
becomes green, a deserted goldfield will not.

As I wandered over those dreary wastes I had
no difficulty in conjuring up the varied scenes that
were once enacted on them, for I was not a novice
in the matter. I had been one of the original
peggers-out of the great Kimberley diamond mine,
and had worked there for seven months, and had
also dug for diamonds on the Vaal River in the very
earliest days of the industry ; and I had dug for

gold on the Tugela in Natal, and in the Leydenburg
and Zoutpansberg districts of the Transvaal, and
seen the goldfields of Teremakau and the Thames,
in New Zealand. True, both men and manners
were different, but, at all events, my experience
helped me to realise more fully than I could otherwise have done all the romantic incidents one had
read about as embellishing those strangest of all

GOLD-MINING NEAR BALLARAT.

strange lives. The actual scene was easy to conjure
up. There was the confused mass of tents in all
orders of canvas architecture; and there the business
part of the camp with butchers, bakers, and general
stores and canteens, all in canvas ; and there, by the
creek, the long row of cradles and sluice-boxes ; and
over all the busy swarm of grimy, bearded diggers,
grubbing about on the surface like so many rabbits
in a warren. All this, if picturesque, was prosaic

enough; it was in the lives and manners of these
dirt-coated labourers, when they threw aside the
shovel and the pan, that the romance lay. The
lucky digger and the unfortunate could be seen side
by side; the one playing champagne ninepins the
while he refreshed himself with bank-note sandwiches and drank fiery spirit out of a bucket; the
other with bleared eyes, ragged habiliments, and
tottering frame, slowly dying of starvation. The
flaunting girls, flushed with drink and belching forth
oaths and ribald songs, reeled into their tents and
fell on their beds to dream of the days when they
were the pride of a loving father and mother, and
the adornment of a happy home. To the accom-
paniment of savage imprecations and defiant shouts
one could hear the shot of the pistol in the billiard-
room, and in the bar see the flash and gleam of
knives. Vainly would the bar-tender strive to put
a stop to the infuriate fray, for his trembling hands
betray that he is one of those unfortunates cast forth
upon the world primed to the eyes with Greek and
Latin, but innocent as a babe of any of the ordinary
helps to competence. Or perhaps, like the hollow-
eyed individual in the corner who is clearly devoured
with fever, he surveys the fray with silent apathy,
and when a lifeless body is cast outside the door,
and the turmoil quietens down, he fills the glasses
afresh with impassive indifference, and drops the
golden coins into his pocket without troubling to
give change. Down the street runs amuck a great

bearded ruffian, in the frenzy of delirium, swinging a shovel round his head, and with it attacking indiscriminately every one he falls in with. Among the tents, with dark lantern, pistol, and knife, sneaks the tent-robber, searching every empty one he comes across whose occupants are busy in the canteens, and hesitating not at murder in rifling a wretch in a drunken sleep, should the latter awake and resent his attentions. Perhaps he inadvertently puts his head into a tent where three or four diggers are playing euchre with a filthy, tobacco-spotted pack of cards, seated round a large case on which are smoking candles stuck in bottles, little piles of gold dust on bits of paper, and bottles and glasses. Then he becomes the recipient, not the deliverer, of a bullet, and if he falls lifeless at the tent-opening his epitaph is recorded with awful terseness in the words, "It's only that b——y Black Jones." Scenes such as these were common in the earliest days of the goldfields. Vulgar dissipation, coarse debauchery, and brutal crime were the characteristics of those days. The worst cannot be printed, nor could the ordinary unsophisticated imagination conceive it. A little later more romance entered into the life of the fields. The eccentricities of the lucky digger continued to the end, and vice openly advertised itself in a manner the dwellers in towns, even though they be amateur detectives, wot not of.

But coarse crime and brutal lawlessness became less common under the combined influence of the

Government and the better nature of a strong-willed section of the diggers. The bushranger took the place of the tent-sneaker, and "robbery under arms" became often quite a chivalrous business, instead of mere vulgar midnight murder. The restless souls who chafed under restraint found vent for their energies in spasmodic revolutions, and the Peter Lalors stood upon the stockades and waved their muskets, little dreaming of the knighthoods that were to descend upon their shoulders in after-days.

But surely there was a bright side to this picture as well? Perhaps so—indeed there must have been; for wherever men and women congregate there will be found tender hearts and deeds of true heroism and self-denial, and pure souls untainted by the corruption around them. But nowhere does the better side of our nature become so stunted, and nowhere does the worst so rise to the top, as under the stress of the mad race for sudden wealth in alluvial gold-digging. This was especially the case in the earliest days of this industry. When years had worn off the novelty of the thing, men could go to work in calmer moods; but when it suddenly broke upon the world as an absolutely new and unknown thing, few were the heads that could preserve their balance, when any moment might transfer them from abject poverty to undreamt-of wealth. And so, while there was a bright side, and often a very bright side, still the dark predominated.

Melbourne the gorgeous was built up from these goldfields, but who shall say what hecatombs of human victims have helped to rear it? Who shall count the broken hearts, the drunkards' deaths, the fever victims, the ruined constitutions, the vice-sapped frames, the smashed limbs, the cracked heads and bullet-pierced bodies, and all the martyrs

THE OLD BENDIGO GOLDFIELD.

to starvation, sickness, hardship, and toil? Where is to be found a record of these? Not a sign is left; all the bodies have rotted in the soil, without a stick to show that they once lived, and only the stately city remains. And yet I venture to say that if all the human suffering and anguish and passion that have helped to set up Melbourne could be raised again from the oblivion into which it has sunk, and exposed *en masse* to the public gaze, a cry of horror would ascend from the whole civilised world, and the place would be shunned as a charnel-house.

Perhaps the brightest side of the whole would be found in contemplating the enormous amount of work that was done. Truly these old deserted goldfields' are a stupendous monument of human industry. Of course I had known that an enormous amount of work had been done, but my conceptions bore no comparison to the reality. It is not so much that the ground about the famous centres of gold-digging as Ballarat, Bendigo, Castlemaine, and Maryborough has been turned over until the whole country round is bare. The marvel is that from Ballarat to Creswick, from Creswick to Maryborough, from Maryborough to Castlemaine, from Castlemaine to Sandhurst, and for twenty miles beyond towards the Murray, there is not a slight depression in the lay of the country, not a flat, nor hollow, nor gully, nor watercourse, that does not bear evidence of laborious prospecting and digging. To one who has not seen it the labour expended is simply incredible. What a sight it must have been when all this great extent of country was dotted with tents and alive with sturdy diggers! And where are they all now? Save a few Chinamen fossicking some old pile of soil that had been cradled a quarter of a century before, or a decrepit old fellow to whom panning-out had become a second nature, not a soul of them is left. They bore down

upon the land in swarms, inaugurated a spasmodic
activity over the face of the country, and then
disappeared, leaving no trace but hundreds of square
miles of bare, red gravel, countless mounds, endless
holes, and millions of tree-trunks; while others,
slower and less laborious than themselves, fattened
on the riches they had drawn from the earth.

But is it possible that all this immense alluvial
goldfield is worked out? I cannot believe it. When
I think of the rough appliances of the time, of the
inexperience of a great majority of the diggers, and
of the carelessness of the methods of men to whom
dissipation was the only recreation, I feel certain
that although most of the nugget gold may have
been extracted, there yet remains a very large percentage of the dust and small gold. Any one who
has watched an inexperienced sorter scraping at his
pile of gravel in the early days of the South African
diamond fields, knows well what an enormous
number were scraped away. The monotony of the
work was so extreme that it was most difficult to
keep the attention fixed, and if the thoughts wandered for an instant the chances were that a diamond
went at the same time.

Of course gold washing is different to diamond
sorting, for to a great extent it is mechanical, and
does its own work; still the operator is largely
responsible for the percentage of gold he obtains.
In 1874 I was on my way to Mashunaland *viâ*
the eastern Transvaal, and stopped one day at

Eersterling, where the previous year there had
been a miniature gold-rush. Taking a shovel and
a pan, I went down to the spruit and tried a little
panning on a spot where a good deal of work had
been done. A trader who was with me said at
once, " It's no use your trying there ; that is the
very claim where the Australian party were working."
Nevertheless the very first pan produced two pieces
of gold, one the size of a small sunflower seed, and
the second two pieces also. I believe I could have
made ten pounds a week out of that claim. Now it
is inconceivable that all these millions of tons of
gravel have all been properly and carefully washed,
even if we grant that all the gold-bearing soil has
been turned over. If a great washing machine,
something on the principle of the diamond washers
of South Africa, were set up in the centre of one of
these old alluvial fields, and the whole of the soil put
through it, I feel sure it would be a profitable under-
taking. Of course there would be no more romance
in the matter. Indeed, if ever gold-bearing alluvial
fields are discovered even richer than those of
Victoria, there will be little romance in them. The
bank-note sandwich and champagne ninepin digger
is a production of the past, dead and buried, and
never to be resuscitated. Railways, and the com-
monness of getting rich nowadays, have killed
him. In countries like Matabili and Mashunaland,
far from civilised centres, and where there are
strange animals and peoples, there may be a little

left, but it will be of a different kind. Bushranging and robbery under arms may survive, but the burly digger, bearded like the pard, and clad in blue flannel shirt, with his trousers tucked into his boots, racking his brains how to get rid of his wealth, is no more. He may drink himself to death, but he will not light his pipe with bank-notes. He will wear a coat, and have a bank account.

THREE VISITS TO THE DIAMOND FIELDS

IT was in 1867 that the first diamond was found in South Africa. It was seen by a trader in the possession of a Koranna child in a kraal on the Orange River, and was purchased by him for a trifle from the child's father, and resold to the Governor of Cape Colony for £500. Soon afterwards, another, much larger and weighing over eighty carats, was found on the banks of the Orange River, and was bought by a firm of merchants at Hope Town for £11,200. This diamond is now the Countess of Dudley's well-known "Star of the South."

It is strange that these two isolated diamonds should have been found in this way, for, so far as I know, no others have been found in this locality; but in consequence of their discovery the whole country round was prospected, and as a result the existence of diamonds on the Vaal River, about 100 miles above its confluence with the Orange River, became known early in 1870. On my return from hunting in the Gaza country at the end of November of that year, I at once took the post-cart at Harrismith and proceeded to Pniel, which was reported to be the chief of the diggings at that time. Pniel was a mission station that had been occupied for many years, and was over 700 miles from Cape Town, and about 500 from Durban. The country round about was in dispute as to ownership, being claimed both by the Orange Free State authorities and by the Griqua chief Waterboer. Arbitration by the then Governor of Natal resulted in its being awarded to Waterboer, and by him it was made over to the British Government, and eventually was incorporated with the Cape Colony. Apart from its wealth in diamonds it is a poor country, only saved from being a desert by the fertilising waters of the Vaal River, along whose banks are many pleasing oases of mimosa trees, which shelter large numbers of guinea-fowl and small bucks, many of the larger species of game being also plentiful.. The river itself was very beautiful, being lined on both sides with great drooping willows, whose trunks were gnarled and rugged with age.

When I arrived on the spot there were already several thousand diggers at work, and I was much surprised at the work that had been done. Although most of the country is deep sand, yet many rocky ridges, kopjes, and hillocks appear above it, and it was in the gravel among these rocks that the diamonds were found. The kopje at Pniel, which was the most prolific of all the river diggings, was in itself remarkable, as it was composed, not of stratified masses of rock, but of isolated boulders, rounded and waterworn, from the size of a cricket-ball to that of a haystack. The river as it exists now could never have brought these great rocks from the Drakensberg, whence no doubt they came. The accepted theory is that this part of the country, including the whole of the western half of South Africa up to nearly the 15th parallel, was once a part of the Atlantic Ocean, and was drained by a mighty upheaval. But though this was undoubtedly the case, it is quite insufficient to account for these great rounded boulders, inasmuch as an upheaval would cause a very rapid drainage, whereas the rounding of these boulders must have been a work of ages. There must have been a great torrent for very many centuries subsequent to the upheaval.

The *modus operandi* of extracting the diamonds is somewhat peculiar. The boulders have first to be removed, and the gravel found among them is taken down to the river to be washed. This gravel, when wet, is very beautiful, and glistens as though it were in itself a mass of precious stones; it consists of water-worn pebbles of quartz, jasper, cornelian, heliotrope, and other similar stones, together with corundum, tourmaline, and many garnets. It is taken down to the river and placed in the top tray of a "cradle," water being then

THE VAAL RIVER AT PNIEL, WHERE DIAMONDS WERE FIRST DISCOVERED.

12

poured over it, and the cradle rocked to and fro.
This top tray has holes in it about the size of a
shilling, and beneath it is another tray with smaller
holes, and below that again another with yet smaller.
When the water has washed all the smaller stuff
from the top tray the contents is searched for any
brobdingnagian diamonds that might be there.
This is done with the hand ; but the pebbles in the
other trays are placed upon a table of wood,
covered, if possible, with sheet iron, and are then
carefully scraped away, little by little, with a piece
of zinc, cut dagger-shaped on its upper edge and
straight on its lower edge. The " sorter " sits
down to the table with a pile of wet glistening
gravel in front of him, and with his sorting tool
spreads out a little heap and examines it with his
eye, and if there are no diamonds in it scrapes it off
the table, and spreads out another heap, and so on.
An expert sorter can work almost as fast as his arm
will scrape ; but, as a matter of fact, it is believed
that in those early days nearly as many diamonds
were scraped away as were found. The Boers
were especially bad sorters, and many a loafer made
a living by standing carelessly by watching them,
and noting when a diamond was scraped away, and
then, when the Boer had gone to dinner or knocked
off work for the day, returning to hunt for it in the
refuse heap. The work of sorting was very monotonous, and unless finds were tolerably frequent the
thoughts were apt to wander, when, of course, all

the diamonds were carefully scraped away with the
rest of the gravel. It was found that women made
the best sorters, as they probably have more patience.
It must, however, be said that diamonds could only
be scraped away through sheer carelessness or in-
attention, for it is next to impossible, when once
their appearance has become familiar, to mistake
them for anything else. There is a peculiar oiliness
in the rough diamond which is unmistakable, and
which is shared by no other mineral, or at all
events no other white stone. This smooth soapi-
ness is also immediately perceptible to the touch,
and the only substance that can be mistaken for a
diamond in this way is alum ; but alum does not in
the least resemble a rough diamond to the eye, and
is also very much lighter. Many queer stories were
told of the tests which used to be tried, before
diamonds were familiar to the diggers, in order to
ascertain if a suspected stone were really a diamond
or not. Perhaps the best was that of the Boer,
who, having heard that the diamond is the hardest
material in nature, placed a good-sized one on the
tire of his wagon-wheel, and gave it a mighty crack
with a sledge-hammer ! This, of course, splintered
it to atoms, for, strange as it may appear, a diamond
is not in reality a homogeneous substance, but is
laminated, or in layers. In some diamonds these
layers can be easily separated, especially in the
so-called "plate-glass" ones ; and the cutters always
take advantage of them in their operations. These

" plate-glass " diamonds are very white and peculiarly clear ones, having in reality more the appearance of crystals of glass than of diamonds. They are so brittle that they often splinter of themselves on being disembowelled from the earth and introduced to the light ; and I believe it is the practice now to wrap them in cotton wool, and let them receive light and air very gradually.

The diamond in its native state is always either a perfect or an aborted octahedral crystal, that is to say, a double pyramid, whose bases are jointed together. If not broken, this formation can always be traced, for even in those which have been crushed out of shape or rounded by pressure when in a semi-molten state, the faces can still, by careful examination, be distinctly traced. The origin, or supposed origin, of the gem will be dealt with when I come to describe the "dry diggings " ; suffice it here to say that the gravel in which they are found on the banks of the Vaal River is not their original matrix. What may be the theory of the scientists to account for their presence there I know not ; but I think it is unquestionable that they found their way there through the bursting up by seismic agency, or volcanic explosion, of some " mine," such as Kimberley, and the subsequent distribution of its contents by the torrent aforesaid. That this is certainly the case is as good as proved by the fact that the diamonds of every known " mine " have a distinctive character of their own, which is readily recognised by the experienced diamond-buyer. Some of these distinctive characters could hardly be put into words ; but there is the broad distinction of colour, which almost any one could see. Thus, Kimberley diamonds are very yellow, De Beers and Du Toit's Pan ones less so, Bultfontein still less, Jagersfontein almost white, and the "river" diamonds practically pure white. The value of the stones from the different mines follows, of course, the same classification, and I believe it to be a fact that diamonds found on the Vaal River are worth twice as much as the Kimberley gems.

At the time of this, my first visit to Pniel, the regulation of the fields was, I believe, in the hands of the diggers themselves. In fact, it was a small republic, with a president, a magistrate or two, and a few police, with a mining board, which issued licences for digging. The claims were thirty feet by thirty feet, and ten shillings per month was paid for the licence, this, together with liquor and auctioneer's licences, being, I think, the sole source of revenue by which the executive and police were supported.

The police had very little to do, for this community of diamond diggers was perhaps the most remarkable community ever collected together on the earth—that is to say, for purposes of manual labour. Large as it was, it consisted almost entirely of persons, male and female, of some education and position. The majority of them were men of in-

dependent means—university men, officers on leave
and retired, civil servants, professional men, farmers,
commercial men, tradesmen, and the better class of
artisans. Of unskilled labourers there were few, if
any at all, and the navvy and typical " digger " of
Australia or California was non-existent. There
were a few loafers, but they were of that kind that
had sunk to their position through drink. The
reasons for this state of things were probably, first,
that there was very little unskilled labour in South
Africa at this time, all rough work being done by
natives ; second, the distance of the fields from the
ports, and the consequent expense of reaching them.
Of course it did not last very long, and in a year
or two all the riff-raff in South Africa, and a good
instalment from other countries, were collected on
the diamond fields.

But perhaps the most remarkable feature of the
community was the number of ladies it contained.
Everybody who had one appeared to have brought
his wife, and many their daughters as well. It is
safe to say that no mining camp in the history of
the world ever contained such a large proportion
of respectable females as that of Pniel in 1870. It
gave a very remarkable aspect to the picture as one
surveyed the scene from some coign of vantage, for
it is hardly necessary to say that all these ladies
sorting at the tables, this being their special occupation, did not adapt themselves to the circumstances, and clothe themselves in convenient, if

unbecoming, mining togs; but, on the contrary, arrayed themselves in the very latest fashions their wardrobes would furnish, thus giving to the scene a brilliancy which, pleasing as it was, seemed almost incongruous. Nor was this the only display of colour that livened up the picture, for each fair sorter had erected on four uprights over her sorting table a sunshade, which was sometimes a red or blue or striped blanket, sometimes a piece of coloured print or other material, and sometimes plain white canvas or calico.

Let us cross the river to Klip Drift, now known as Barkly West, and survey the scene. As I have said, the river itself was most beautiful, with its long lines of great drooping willows and its lovely tree-girt islets, and even were there no diggings one could sit long and drink in the beauty of the scene. But it is its human interest that now engages our attention. The first thing that strikes the eye is the large number of English and colonial built boats (dozens of them) plying to and fro across the river. How they got there is perhaps the greatest mystery of all, for we are 500 miles from the nearest seaboard. One man who had five boats told me he earned three pounds a day to each boat, for there were diggings on each side of the river, and the executive offices, and the best hotel, were on the north, or Klip Drift, side, the charge for crossing the two hundred yards being half-a-crown. The river is running with great force, it being now full with the summer rains, and the water is brown and turbid. Immediately opposite, on the water's edge, is a double and treble line of cradles, some hundreds of yards in length, worked by swarthy niggers, hundreds of whom are also walking backwards and forwards into the water with buckets, and dashing their contents on to the gravel in the cradles. Behind the cradles, and higher up on the bank, for most of the willows had here been felled, is another double and treble line of sorting tables, with their gaudy sunshades, at each of which sits one or two sorters, male and female, the latter in the latest Paris fashions, and the former in moleskin or cord trousers, jackboots, brown leather bandoliers, brilliantly coloured flannel shirts, and slouch hats with puggarees. Behind these again are great masses of boulders, piled into fortifications, built into walls, or thrown promiscuously into heaps, and interspersed here and there with huge mounds of reddish sand, over all of which are sprinkled thousands of moving beings, picking, shovelling, wheeling, and carrying. In the rear of all rises gradually a low stony range of hills, reddish brown in colour, and sparsely decked with scattered thorn trees, every level spot of which is occupied by a glistening white tent or wagon. At the extreme left of the mounds of stone and sand these stand thick and huddled, the white surface they present being broken by a few galvanised iron roofs, where the little mining township of Pniel had established itself. Over all is the blue African sky, and the perspiration-inducing sun beating down in tropic strength. A stranger and more unique scene was never witnessed. It was no more like an Australian alluvial goldfield than it was like a Paris boulevard, and probably resembled nothing else in the world but a gold-digging set up on the stage by Sir Augustus Druriolanus.

Not less interesting was the one wide street which formed the little township. Here perspiring humanity trudged through the heavy sand with a fixed and determined mien of preoccupation. One was hastily coming up from his claim to wash the sand out of his throat with a long drink of pontac and ginger-beer ; another to buy a spade or pick ; another to sell a diamond he had just found, at the bank or store, or at one of the Jew buyers' canvas offices. Auctioneers were selling the mining imple-ments of departing diggers, wagons with goods from Durban or Port Elizabeth were off-loading at the stores, and business people were running hither and thither, all intent on some serious matter. The only idle people were the newcomers just arrived in the passenger wagon from Cape Town, who were standing curiously about, and a few loafers looking out for some one to stand them a drink. At mid-day hundreds of begrimed diggers trooped up and struggled for places in the dining - rooms and restaurants, and for a while there was peace.

Pniel and Klip Drift were not the only diggings

on the Vaal River. In fact, they extended from Hebron, twenty-five miles above, to Sifonel, seventy miles below that point. Among the best known and the richest were Gong-Gong, Cawood's Hope, Forlorn Hope, Delport's Hope, Blue Jacket, Moonlight Rush, and Waldeck's Plant. It was at the last-named place that the largest river diamond was found. It weighed 288 carats, and was found by an Italian who had once been in my employ as a gold prospector. He was offered on the spot £15,000 for this stone, but declined it. It was exhibited in many places in Europe, but I never heard what became of it.

I did not on this occasion personally engage in digging, but, after looking at the rushes up and down the river, left for Natal in a friend's wagon, and being dissatisfied with the pace made, made a bet that I could walk faster, and so left it and proceeded on foot, and did 450 miles to Maritzburg in fourteen days, beating the wagon by eight days. The R.M.S. *Cambrian* then took me to England, a voyage that was diversified by a collision with another steamer in the Bay of Biscay.

In the following May I was back in Cape Town, and proceeded by the newly constructed Overland Transport Company's service once more to Pniel. The start was from Wellington, sixty miles from Cape Town, this being the terminus of the only railway in the Colony. (There are probably 5,000 miles of railway there now!) The Company's wagon, drawn by eight or ten horses or mules according to the nature of the country, was a nondescript vehicle holding nine passengers inside and two out. The insides sat in cramped positions, each in a little iron pen, and looked ahead ; the outsides on a back seat with the conductor, looking the other way. It fell to my lot to be one of the fortunate occupants of this back seat, and I sat there for eleven days and nine and a-half nights, and, as it was exactly over the hind axle, and consequently received the benefit of every jolt and every stone the wheels passed over, I had a pretty lively time of it, but reached Pniel in safety with only three pitches out, which the conductor said was much below the average. He himself was thrown off five times.

At Pniel I found everything changed. The "dry diggings" had been discovered, and all the river diggings were almost deserted for the new treasure fields, where the diamonds were said to be as the sands of the seashore, and of a size marvellous to behold. Only a few who were in possession of undeniably good claims, or who preferred the quiet, healthy life on the river, with moderate finds, to the dust, dirt, and misery of the "dry diggings," though accompanied with fabulous prizes, remained ; and as I wandered among the chaotic piles of stones and sand, tenanted now by only a dozen or two of quiet deliberate diggers, I could not but marvel at the contrast it displayed to the scene I had beheld but

five short months before, when thousands of excited
diggers rusher hither and thither in busy haste, and
jostled one at every step. If Pniel awoke one day
to find itself famous, the reverse was equally true,
for it seemed already forgotten.

The "dry diggings" are thirty miles to the south-
east of Pniel. They are so called because the gems
are not found in river-wash, but in dry tufa,
which has apparently never been in contact with
water, although water once undoubtedly lay for
many ages above the mines. These so-called
"mines" are the craters of long-extinct volcanoes.
Of this there appears to be no doubt whatever, for
in the case of the Kimberley mine the walls of the
crater have been laid bare ; and its formation was
at one period of its existence clearly visible, while
the pipe or funnel has been traced to the depth of
more than a thousand feet. The volcanoes do not
appear to have been of the character of those from
which actual fire issues, but rather of the nature of
enormous "fumaroles," ejecting mud and steam.
Some investigators of scientific attainments have
professed to be unable to decide whether the
diamonds were forced up from beneath, or whether
the funnels were filled up with soil containing
diamonds from above ; but to my mind there
cannot be an instant's doubt on the point. If the
diamonds came from above, they would be found
all over the surface, as well as by digging anywhere ; but this is not the case. They are strictly

confined to these rock-cased cavities, the few stray ones that have been picked up on the surface having been evidently washed away from the top stratum of some mine by the sea that once covered them all.

As to the origin of the diamonds themselves, there have been many theories : but that which has met with the most general acceptance is, I believe, that they were formed by the liquefaction by great pressure, and the subsequent or coeval crystallisation by cooling, of carbonic acid gas, formed in cavities of the volcanic *ejecta* by the action of heat. This theory would appear to cover all the facts known concerning these mines, and it is a consequence of it that the original ejection must have taken place under water, the downward pressure of which was greater than the upward pressure from below ; otherwise the semi-liquid matter would have flowed over, which it appears not to have done. The colouring of the stones is a matter which, to my mind, has never been satisfactorily cleared up. It is, I believe, usually attributed to the presence of iron in some form ; but it is not easy to see how iron got into these crystals, and into nothing else.

On my arrival there were three "mines" at work— Old De Beers, Du Toit's Pan, and Bult-fontein ; but in a few days another was discovered, first known as the New Rush, then as Colesberg Kopje, and eventually as Kimberley. The last named was the richest of them all, and is un-doubtedly the most characteristic. In extent it is about thirteen acres, the outside reef consisting of friable shale. In the mine itself the surface stratum was sand, in which an occasional small diamond was found; then came a layer of sedimentary lime, as white as chalk, but harder. Below this was a rough, harsh, yellowish green tufa, or scoria, composed of a variety of substances with portentous names, and it was in this formation that diamonds began to be numerous. Indeed, this tufa was at first considered to be the matrix of the gems, and, when below it was struck a hard blue saponaceous clay, it was believed that the bed had been reached, and many left off digging. It was, however, afterwards found that this blue ground was the richest of all, and a mine is not now considered of any value unless this "blue," as it is called, is found in it. In the Kimberley mine it was, I believe, first struck at a depth of about 80 feet, and it is now known to continue for 1,500 feet down. This "blue" is, I think, identical with the saponaceous grey-blue mud that is ejected by the mud volcanoes of New Zealand, only in the latter case it is rendered semi-liquid by the presence of steam. The bubbles which are continually bursting in this mud are, perhaps, when not carburetted hydrogen, diamonds *in posse*, wanting only pressure to liquefy and crystallise them.

The method of extracting the diamonds from the soil was at this time quite different to that adopted on the Vaal River. Water was scarce, and it was

consequently impossible to wash the gravel ; it was
dry-sieved in sieves of different sized meshes, and
the residue was then sorted out as on the river.
The sieves used were long rectangular ones, such
as are worked by two men among builders, &c.,
only they had handles at but one end ; the other
end was swung between a couple of uprights, by
which means much labour was saved. The great
difficulty in working these mines lay in the apparent
impossibility of sifting out the whole of the ground.
The claims were, as on the river, 30 feet by 30 feet,
and on Old De Beers, Du Toit's Pan, and Bultfontein they were worked without any system, every
claimholder piling his refuse on the portion of his
claim he was not digging. The consequence of this
was that at least half of each mine was practically
valueless, being occupied by mounds of dust and
scoria. The mines were thus a confused mass of
mounds and yawning pits, and claims not near the
outside margin were very difficult to get at, and it
was a practical impossibility to remove the refuse
from them. When the New Rush, two miles from
Du Toit's Pan (all these four mines were within a
nine-mile circuit), was discovered, this drawback
was remedied by a very ingenious device. Thirteen
parallel roads were marked out right across the
kopje, in such a way that the longitudinal line
dividing one row of claims from the next fell exactly
in the centre of each road. As the roads were 15
feet wide, each claimholder gave up one quarter of

DRY-SIEVING AND SORTING: THE DIAMONDIFEROUS SOIL, DU TOIT'S PAN, MIDDLE OF 1871.

his claim to the common good. By means of these roads the soil was removed in Scotch carts outside the limits of the mine, and the sifting and sorting done there.

During the earlier period of digging, this system was almost perfect; but as the mine got more worked, and all available surface was removed, and the sinkings got deeper and deeper, the roads became isolated walls having yawning abysses from 30 to 100 feet on each side. In consequence then of the friable nature of the soil, the tremulousness produced by the carts constantly passing and re-passing, and the strain on the posts which were driven into each margin of the roads for hauling up the stuff in buckets, and for descending into the workings, constant slips occurred, and the roads became gradually narrower and narrower, until it was quite dangerous for carts to pass each other. At this time, therefore, accidents were shockingly frequent. For instance, two carts in trying to pass each other would get locked, and if drawn by horses the drivers would get frightened and jump off, and the carts, horses, and contents be precipitated, one on each side, into the chasms, and on to the heads of the unfortunates working below ; or if drawn by bullocks they would be difficult to manage to a nicety, and the result would be the same. Or an empty cart would be driven towards a claim, and in turning round to return the same way the wheels would approach too near the edge, and over it would all go. These scenes were of constant occurrence, and yet the carelessness displayed in the management of carts was wonderful. Slips, too, were frequent, and many a poor Kafir was buried in the debris. Ropes would also break when they were hoisting stuff, or were clambering up and down. Often men would be pushed over by carts, and sometimes when a horse was standing unattended while the stuff was being shovelled into the cart it would take it into its head to bolt, and then it was *sauve qui peut*, and every one on the road in front precipitately sought some place of safety, or perhaps fell over in doing so, until the cart came into contact with another, and both disappeared into the depths. From October, 1871, throughout the ensuing summer months, such accidents were of daily occurrence, and the number of people killed and injured must have been appalling.

To understand the very remarkable aspect of the mine at this time it is first necessary to realise its physical features. It was 250 yards by 300, or about 13 acres in all. The outside reef was laid bare in nearly all the claims on the margin, plainly showing its crater-like formation, and the lower the digging proceeded the clearer this became apparent. The dust and refuse that had been sorted were deposited on the reef all round the mine, until there gradually grew up a range of miniature mountains, the highest point of which was known as Mount Ararat, and the view from

"NEW RUSH" (KIMBERLY MINE) AS IT APPEARED AT THE END OF 1871.

this range was a very extraordinary one. Of course
every claimholder did not work with the same
amount of industry, so that the owner of one
quarter or half claim (for few worked a full claim)
might be down 100 feet, and his neighbour on the
left 50 feet, and that on the right only 20 feet,
while the one in front was 40 feet, and thus it was
all over the kopje. Standing on one of these
mountains of dust 40 or 50 feet in height, one
could take in the whole mine at a glance—the
outside range of mounds, scattered all over with
innumerable sieves and sorting tables ; the wall-
like roads, lined with posts and traversed by a
constant succession of carts and busy miners ; the
curious chasms and pits of all depths, and all
worked down with a plumb line, and the thousands
of Kafirs picking and hauling below, all enveloped
in a dull haze of dust. If the observer turned his
back to the mine he would find himself confronted
with an ocean of canvas tents, extending for miles
in every direction, in the midst of which the large
open market square and a few galvanised iron roofs
indicated the locality of the township.

This township was a study in itself. The great
galvanised iron stores, the innumerable canteens
and restaurants in all orders of iron and canvas
architecture, and the auctioneers' marts, where on
most days busy sales were always in progress, were
only such as could be seen in any mining town ;
but what gave this its distinctive character was the

amazing number of Jew diamond buyers' establishments. Almost every other stand was occupied by a canvas frame or iron house, on which was displayed a legend such as, Otto Goldsmidt, Diamond Buyer; Moses Aaron, Diamond Merchant; or Benjamin Abrahams, Diamond Broker. Although the fields had only been in existence a few months, it seemed as if the Jewish quarters of every city in Europe had emptied themselves on this dust-heap in the heart of Africa. If a walk were taken down the street during working hours hardly a face was to be seen that was not unmistakably of Hebrew type. No Jew was ever known to wield pick, shovel, sieve, or scraper. They toiled not, neither did they spin, but nevertheless it was into their pockets that most of the treasure surely flowed. The more respectable of them remained in their offices and waited for sellers to come to them; but the sharkier ones wandered about the kopje with their satchels over their shoulders, and spotted with unerring eye the greenhorn who had made a good morning's find, and eased him of them at half their market value. There is always a great outcry at any uprising against Jews, but, as a rule, it was not as Jews, but as avaricious and grasping sharks that they were objected to. No one who was behind the scenes during the early days of these fields could wonder much at this.

As the dinner hour approached, the Hebrew

"NEW RUSH," NOW CALLED COLESBERG KOPJE (KIMBERLEY MINE), AS IT APPEARED IN 1873. THERE HAD BEEN A FALL OF SNOW.

element was swamped, and the street swarmed
with thousands of dusty diggers in moleskins,
flannel shirts, bandoliers, and billycocks. The
canteens and restaurants were crowded, and the
rattle of plates and knives sounded like a dull
roar. Very little hard drinking took place, for
though the dust necessitated a good deal of
moistening, a great part of it was in such light
forms as pontac and ginger-beer, or shandy-gaff.
Never was such a wealthy community of bachelors
so abstemious. Every man one met had in his
bandolier one or two match or snuff boxes full of
costly gems, while many rattled in their trouser
pockets, like so many halfpence, a handful of
brobdingnagian diamonds, each worth a duke's
ransom. But they did not, like the Australian of
old, eat bank-note sandwiches, and drink champagne
out of buckets. There may be said to have been
absolutely nothing of that kind of folly. Nor did
they hoard their wealth ; on the contrary, they were
careless to a miracle. On one occasion I was in
the bar of Benning and Martin's hotel, when a
stranger handed round for inspection a fine diamond
of 103 carats (larger than the Koh-i-noor) which he
had just found. While it was in my hands he was
called out, and as he did not return for some hours
I was obliged to keep it, and it remained in my
pocket for several days, when I accidentally met
the owner in the street. He protested that he had
forgotten all about it.

Huge diamonds like this, and up to 150 carats, were quite common in those days, and it is a great mystery what has become of them all. It is the more remarkable because £20 a carat was more like the value of them than the 30s. of to-day, and the price was calculated something in this way : If a five-carat stone is worth £10 a carat, then a ten-carat is worth £20, and a twenty-carat £40 a carat. Whether these progressive prices were actually given for the larger stones I cannot say for certain ; but the sellers always declared they were. Smaller diamonds were literally in bucketfuls, and almost any buyer could show a good-sized basinful. It is extraordinary that there was little or no crime. Most of these buyers lived in canvas-framed houses, and few had safes ; yet during my nine months' residence there was no case of burglary, though one day a man put his arm through the post-office window and walked off with a mail-bag. Most of the diamonds, too, were sent away by post, and the cart travelled without escort, in charge of a single Hottentot, for 700 miles, through a country where there was sometimes not a house for 50 miles. But no case of bushranging occurred, though the driver once returned and reported that he had been stuck up ; but it was afterwards proved to be a plant of his own in conjunction with the keeper of a roadside accommodation house. Lady Florence Dixie relates some blood-curdling cases of sticking up as having occurred; but they were mythical, and born of that reprehensible practice of the colonists elegantly termed "filling up the jimmies." Mr. J. A. Froude was filled up in the same way, as the present writer knows only too well.

Instead of by drink and riotous living, after the Australian fashion, these diggers got rid of their easily acquired wealth by various methods of gambling. Light come, light go, was the order of the day. Although there was nominally a law forbidding them, gambling saloons were numerous, and some of them were fitted up with a degree of luxury which seemed anomalous in the midst of such surroundings. In these faro, rouge-et-noir, and roulette were the favourite games, and the stakes were very large. As soon as the evening meal was over, and a pipe leisurely smoked, these saloons began to fill, and remained so far into the small hours. The billiard tables were mobbed with black-poolists (neither devil's pool nor snooker were known then), and every table in the canteens and restaurants crowded with votaries of blind hooky, chicken hazard, nap, loo with the arbitraries, Davis's arrangement, euchre, fly-loo, and every other bedevilment for getting rid of spare cash that could be improvised. Fly-loo was, perhaps, the most extraordinary invention in the way of gambling ever conceived of. Half a dozen stalwart, bearded men might be seen sitting round a table, each with a spoonful of sugar on a piece of paper in front of him, and by the side of the sugar some coins or notes, or even diamonds. They sat perfectly still watching the flies, and the owner of the sugar on which the first one settled swept in all the stakes! There were variations to this game, but this was the usual form. In the private tents, too, heavy gambling was the rule, loo being the favourite game.

All this gambling is not, however, much to be wondered at, for there were no theatres or music-halls, or lectures, or libraries, or reading-rooms; and unless one went to bed it was difficult to avoid taking part in some game of chance. On Saturday afternoons the stock amusement was mob-meetings, to air political and technical grievances; and at these meetings republics were established, and overthrown with an ease and rapidity that put South America completely into the shade. The diggers had no real grievances, and they were looked at more in the light of amusements than anything else. Several who afterwards became prominent politicians had their first training at these meetings, including Mr. Rhodes and Colonel Schermbrucker. Usually, however, they ended in a fight between two of the audience, when the orators were at once left to waste their sweetness on the desert air, and a huge ring was formed and seconds appointed. A stand-up fight was also a favourite Sunday's amusement. I cannot remember if there were any churches at this time; but if there were, I do not think many attended them, one reason, perhaps, being that though there were between ten and twenty thousand whites, there did not appear to be a Sunday go-to-meeting suit of clothes in the whole place. They do things different nowadays, and a man in his shirt-sleeves and mole-skins would shock the delicate sensibilities of a Johannesburger or a Barbertonian. I prefer the unconventionality of the old diamond fields days.

It was not until late in the summer that the diggers had any real grievance. It was then found that the Kafirs had for some time been stealing diamonds largely, while working down in the claims, and selling them to low Jews and canteen-keepers. A public meeting was at once held, and as the result several hundred diggers went the round of the camp and searched a large number of canteens and other places against which infor-mation had been laid. At each one a regular inquiry was held, and witnesses examined, and if the offence of buying from the Kafirs was held to be proved, the whole place was burnt down, liquor and all, and in more than one case the cash-box was thrown into the flames. What became of the diamonds recovered no one ever knew, though they were supposed to have been sold for the benefit of the hospital. This was the beginning of the I.D.B. movement—those mysterious letters that are such a terror to society.

——Life on the diamond fields at this time was no

feather-bed existence. The heat was intense, 110° in the shade being no uncommon temperature. The deep sand under foot was often so hot that the leather of one's boots was almost frizzled. The air was full of impalpable dust, and now and again a great dust storm came along, when the atmosphere resembled a London fog in colour and density, and tents and houses were levelled with the ground. Sometimes the winds came as whirlwinds, forming columns of dust twenty feet thick and two or three hundred feet high, the lower stratum of which was composed of tents, clothing, bedding, tables, chairs, sieves, &c. Once I saw a lady's crinoline and parasol gyrating round thirty feet over my head, but on hailing it to ask if the owner was inside I received no answer. Many will remember two enormous pillars of dust, nearly 500 feet high, that stood stationary over Du Toit's Pan for some hours one Sunday afternoon in December, 1871.

During the day flies made life a misery, and during the night fleas murdered sleep. At meal-times it was hardly possible to tell a leg of mutton from a loaf of bread, they were so equally smothered with flies; and the nights were spent in discomfort—at least mine were, and I rarely got to sleep before dawn; but my partner, a military doctor with a hide like a hippopotamus, snored peacefully the night through, and roused my murderous instincts as they have never been roused before or

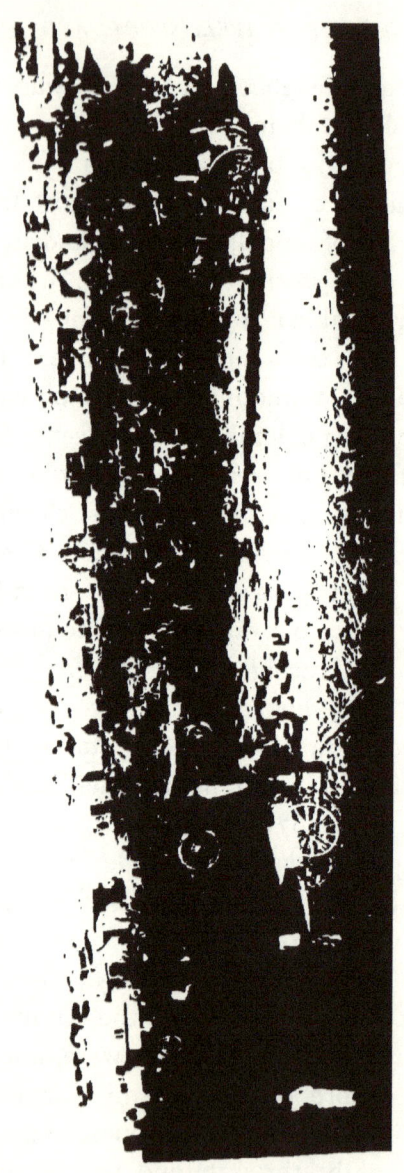

since. I rarely had two hours' sleep in a night that summer.

There were no sanitary arrangements whatever at this time, and the natural consequence was that fever decimated the camp. Hardly a tent escaped having at least one of its inmates stricken down, and the number of deaths was startling. The scarcity, badness, and dearness of water added to the evil, and led to dysentery following on the fevers. A couple of dams on neighbouring farms were the first sources of supply; but they were soon exhausted, and two or three wells were all the camp had to depend on. At this time water was half-a-crown a bucket, and often of the colour of coal-tar. Later on four shillings a hogshead was the regulation price. It used to be a common joke to go to an hotel before breakfast and order a soda and brandy, drink the latter, and wash in the soda-water.

Living was very expensive—for though meat was cheap, everything else was exorbitant, and vegetables were at famine prices. I once bought a cabbage in the morning market (where everything was sold by auction), after a spirited competition, for twenty-five shillings. This market, which was held every day, was a most interesting feature of the fields, and on Saturdays vast quantities of produce were sold by the market-master, farmers flocking in from hundreds of miles round. Fire-wood was one of the chief commodities offered, and was extremely dear; and maize, sorghum, wheatmeal, green and dry oats, pumpkins, four-footed game, peaches, and garden produce were also brought in by the farmers; and an occasional consignment of grapes was a cause of fierce competition. Later on, pineapples and bananas arrived from Natal. The unsophisticated Boers must often have stared with astonishment when they saw their poor parcels of vegetables going up to prices that a European millionaire would shudder at giving.

With all these drawbacks to existence it is really marvellous what a happy community it seemed to be, and how contented with their lots most of the diggers were. There were very few ladies—nothing like so many as on the river diggings—and the usual amenities of social existence were almost entirely absent. Indeed, the female element hardly existed at all, and Stafford Parker's five barmaids created a great sensation. Nevertheless it is safe to say that an equally large body of men so law-abiding, so mannerly, and so free from positive vice and crime never existed as during this summer at the New Rush. They sweltered in the sun, were smothered with dust, worried by flies, and tormented with fleas; they were often choked with stench, and thrown down by fever or dysentery; they were poisoned by bad water, and robbed by Kafirs; they chewed tough meat and ill-baked bread, and lay upon a rough pallet or on the ground at night; they had no society but of men like themselves,

OLD DE BEERS MINE, 1872-3.

no intellectual recreation, and no amusement but
gambling ; but they came up smiling through it all,
and rarely grumbled, except in a good-humoured
way. Perhaps the invigorating atmosphere had
something to do with it.

But this happy state of things did not last long.
Other times, other manners. All the riff-raff of the
colonial towns, with a large consignment from
Europe, found its way there, and when I revisited
the fields eighteen months afterwards, I could easily
see signs of deterioration. The mine itself, too, was
entirely altered. All ·the roads had disappeared,
and the stuff was hauled up on ropes fastened to
a two-storied circle of platforms, erected right round
the mine on the range of sand heaps, so that the
mine was covered with a gigantic ·spider's web,
each claimholder having his own standing rope.
The running tackle was worked with horse whims,
the wheels of which were in the lower story of the
platforms. The mine itself looked like an enormous
quarry, about the centre of which was a huge mass
of floating rock, which had apparently fallen in from
above. How deep the workings were at this time
I cannot accurately say, but in some cases I think
200 feet had been reached, and there was a good
deal of trouble from water. All the green scoria
was gone, and the entire mine was on the hard,
blue, saponaceous clay.

The appearance of the town had also altered, and
a good many elegant houses in wood, and even

brick, were to be seen; but it was long before Kimberley, as it was then called, became the elegant villadom it now is.

My personal experiences on these fields were unfortunate. It is an undoubted fact that in 1871–72 the large majority of the diggers made money, and many made immense fortunes; but this was not the case with myself. In partnership with a friend I first worked a claim at Old De Beers for a month, during which time the New Rush was discovered. We pegged off claims there, and did occasional work on them to prevent them being jumped, but gave most of our time to De Beers. The result of this month's work was one microscopical diamond, but the claim was in reality almost outside the diamondiferous formation. But if we found no diamonds, we made on two occasions rather remarkable finds in our shaft. On returning to work from our midday meal we found one day a Dutch child at the bottom, with its leg broken. Its parents would not permit the doctor to attend it, but set the limb themselves, by binding the leg between the straw coverings of a couple of brandy bottles. On another occasion we found a bullock stuck half-way down the shaft, which we had not made quite plumb. The animal had been shot at by a butcher, but being only wounded had run amuck and fallen in. As there was a Kafir working at the bottom, energetic means had to be adopted to get the bullock out before it slipped

KIMBERLEY MINE IN 1887.

down and crushed him. However, we need have
been in no hurry, for the Kafir, with an energy he
had never displayed in our service, had worked a
niche for himself in the side of the shaft, into which
he could retire out of harm's way.

We decided to abandon this claim, and as those
pegged out at the New Rush eventually proved,
with one exception, to be on the reef, we looked
out for a suitable one to purchase, as it so happened
that we had let this particular one for a percentage
on the finds. Attending an auction sale on the
spot for what appeared to be a good claim, I added
ten shillings to a bid of £17, but the bid being
unheard, it was sold for that sum. A month
afterwards half of this claim was sold for £1,700.
I was then offered a claim for £45, but as this was
then a long price I sought the advice of a more
experienced digger, and was advised to leave it
alone. The individual who purchased it cleared
out in a few months with £50,000, besides selling
the claim in portions for £60,000 more.

We eventually bought one for £16, and after
working it for a month, at an expense of something
like ten pounds a week, ·for one diamond worth
seven shillings and sixpence, we gave it up in
disgust. The buyer commenced working at once,
and in a few minutes turned out a diamond which
he sold on the spot for £800. On hearing of this
we sat down on a couple of buckets opposite each
other, and swore with vigour and ingenuity for fully

half an hour. We shifted operations to a quarter claim bought for £100, and after four months' work succeeded in paying expenses, discovering at the end of this period that while we had been sorting and sifting above, our Kafirs had been all along stealing the diamonds below. We were then both seized with fever, and I with dysentery as well, and while my partner went back to his regiment at Cape Town, I retired to Pniel, and sat every day on the bank of the beautiful river until I got well again. On my third visit I did not engage in digging at all.

These diamond mines are now, as probably every one knows, nothing like the above descriptions. The soil is extracted by mining, instead of by open quarrying, and is washed in huge washing machines, instead of being sifted, water being now brought from the Vaal River. Public digging has long ceased to exist, and the whole of the four mines is in the hands of two or three companies. De Beers, with a capital of something like ten millions, is probably the most gigantic and iniquitous monopoly the world has ever seen. It uses its wealth and power to prevent others benefiting by the existence of diamonds. If another mine is discovered it buys it up, and refuses to work it, and it will not permit poor people to wash out the debris cast aside by the old diggers, which still contains many diamonds. At its instigation the Cape Parliament passed the most iniquitous Act ever

enacted by a civilised legislature—the notorious
I.D.B (illicit diamond buying) Act. Under this
Act the police have the right to search at any time,
and without warrant, the persons and houses of any
one they choose ; and if a diamond is found, the
person or the occupier has to prove that he had
a permit to purchase that particular stone, in default
of which he is liable to a long tèrm of penal servitude. To this end they employ plants to sell
stones. To show the absurdity of the law, the
very governor of the colony once only escaped
penal servitude by favour, having inadvertently
bought a diamond for a keepsake without obtaining
a permit to do so! Private animus is easily wreaked
by enticing the other party to purchase stones at a
fraction of their value, and hundreds of innocent
people are now working in chains under the operations of this abominable Act. The mines produce
diamonds to the value of £4,000,000 a year.

CAMPAIGNING IN THE BASUTO COUNTRY

IN the early sixties the Dutch Boers were con·
stantly on bad terms with their neighbours the
Basutos, and these quarrels several times cul-
minated in open warfare. In one of these wars,
having nothing better to do, and being always on
the look-out for adventures, I served as a volunteer.
It is not necessary to enter into the question of the
merits of the war, but it is pretty safe to assume
that in any difference between Boers and natives
the former were the aggressors. Of this, of course,
being very young at the time, I was not aware ; and
had I been, should certainly not have volunteered
my assistance. As a matter of fact, I never gave it
a thought, and had no other object than a search
for adventure.

I went up from Natal with two or three others,
our objective point being the village of Harrismith,
a few miles beyond the Natal border, on the top of
the Drakensberg range. This village, nestled at
the foot of the great flat-topped mountain Platberg,
contained then not more thirty houses ; but it was

crowded with Boers, the people from the whole
country-side for twenty miles round having gone
into " laager." Consequently, there were hundreds
of wagons about, most of which were formed into
three great squares a few hundred yards from each
other, the vehicles being three or four thick round
each inner square. This was always the Boer
method of defence—and a very excellent one it is.
It is not, however, always effectual, and a laager of
Boers has frequently been annihilated ; the worst
case having been the destruction of the great Boer
camp at Weenen, in Natal, by Dingaan, the Zulu
potentate, some sixty years ago.

A Boer laager is perhaps the most uninviting
place of residence to be found in the world. Boers
are filthy in their habits and dress, foul in their
feeding, and, as companions, without one redeeming
feature. Consequently, I was glad after three days'
residence to be able to accompany a party of 150
bent on attacking an impi of Basutos reported to be
raiding deserted farms near the head waters of
Liebenbergs Vley, about thirty miles away. We
started in the afternoon, intending to camp about
twenty miles out, so as not to have far to go in the
morning. No fires were allowed in camp, and,
worse still, no smoking, and we just lay down on
the ground rolled up in a blanket, with the horses
tied together by their heads in dozens, taking it in
turns to do a sentry-go of two hours. We were off
again before daylight, but were unsuccessful in

surprising the Basutos, as we had hoped. Indeed, we did not find them at all till nearly midday, when we descried a mounted party numbering about a couple of hundred. As the Basutos are among the finest horsemen in the world, and possess a capital breed of wiry pony ; and as the country was quite open, without shelter of any kind, is was not thought that much would be gained by giving chase ; but no other course of action presenting itself, the word was given to canter gently after them in open order, in the hope that they might somewhere stand their ground and show fight. This was precisely what they did ; for on arriving on the crest of a long, low ridge they turned and faced us, spread out in a long, open line. From these tactics we were of opinion that they had a white man with them ; but if there was one, none of us saw him. The position was well chosen ; and had we advanced in close order they could have turned their flanks and surrounded us. However, we did not, and soon we were under a brisk fire, which we returned with interest, advancing at our best pace all the time. The Basutos did not shoot well, and had they done so we should have lost a good many men ; as it was, their elevation was all wrong, and I could hear bullet after bullet whistling over my head. A very few minutes sufficed for us to reach the top of the ridge ; but the Basutos did not wait for a hand-to-hand encounter, but turned and fled, scattering themselves all over the country. A chase under these conditions did not appear to be very hopeful ; but we kept it up for about ten miles, picking off two or three men, and capturing a couple of prisoners, when we gave it up. Our loss was only one man killed and two or three wounded, while the Basutos lost about twenty.

A few days after this, I was sent on an expedition which made a strong impression on my mind that will endure as long as I live. It was to try and recover a mob of stolen cattle that was supposed to be hidden among the fastnesses of the Witte Bergen. Only twelve were sent, the expedition being really of the nature of a reconnaissance. The Boer commandant assured us that it was exceedingly improbable that we should meet with any natives ; but from the fact that only English volunteers were chosen for the service, we formed the opinion that he considered it an extremely hazardous one. We had no commissariat, but were each supplied with biscuit considered sufficient to last us for four days, as we were told that even if we found no cattle we would be sure to fall in with game ; for my own part, I stowed away a bottle of brandy in one of my holsters.

The mountain range was a day's ride away, over some very rough country, and though it is, and was then, I believe, within the boundaries of the Orange Free State, it was to all intents and purposes in the enemy's country. On the second day we got into, I think, the wildest country I ever saw. Pen fails,

15

and words wax feeble in the attempt, to describe it. It was a confused jumble of mighty hills, of every conceivable shape and size, and deep sunken valleys, now of considerable extent, and, again, more like wells than anything else, all covered with luscious green grass, and scattered all over with enormous weather-beaten boulders of metamorphic rocks. Up and down, never resting, now plunging headlong down a well-nigh perpendicular grassy slope into a little valley buried almost out of sight among a forest of grass-green pinnacles ; now clambering up the face of a verdant cone, and then stumbling promiscuously down the other side ; now struggling through a rock-strewn pass between two rugged hills, and anon leading our horses along the edge of a rocky precipice. Riding was impossible, except along the summit of some rounded hill, and there seemed to be facilities among the hidden valleys, of whose existence one had not the remotest expectation until plunged into one, fit for hiding away untold thousands of stock. Under some of the rocky krantzes which fringe the edge of a square table-topped mountain we saw huge natural caves in the solid rock, where the dwarf and treacherous Bushmen are supposed to have at one time resided ; but we found no trace of recent residence, nor did we see any of those rock drawings said by some to exist in caves in these and other districts. Indeed, I am rather sceptical about them, never having in all my very extensive African wanderings come across anything that was not conspicuously the clumsy fraud of some white man. No sign of any path was seen, and we had nothing whatever to guide our search after the stolen cattle. Consequently, our day's wandering was unsuccessful, and we spent the night under a krantz at the summit of a high tableland. We met with no better success the next day, and were also unfortunate in coming acros no game except large numbers of partridges and some khorhaans, which were useless to us, as we had no shot-gun among us. Towards the afternoon huge volumes of heavy, black, forbidding-looking clouds came rolling up from the south-east, and piled themselves in dense solid-looking palpable masses all around, like large columns of troops taking up position preparatory to action. All nature seemed to herald the approach of a storm : the grass shivered in the shifting air ; the small birds flew aimlessly hither and thither, crying shrilly to each other ; the hawks sought shelter among the rocky krantzes, and the eagles wheeled majestically to their haunts in the crevices of the precipices. A general whispering seemed to pervade the atmosphere ; and even the horses became restive and impatient, and some of them were almost trembling ; it was. evident that we must find some shelter. So the word was given to make for a huge castellated krantz flanking a tableland, in the hope of finding a cave. But we were too late. Without any warning a fearful-looking

cloud, rolling and surging round immediately overhead, tore itself asunder and belched forth a broad
and fiery streak of liquid flame, and simultaneously
our ears were assailed with a frightful crack that
seemed to beat us into the earth, followed by a
rolling and rumbling and roaring and bellowing, as
though the world had split itself apart and were
groaning in its agony. Then the celestial sluices
were opened, and the pent-up waters fell over the
face of the land in drops the size of marbles, and so
close together as to seem almost a solid sheet, and
we were drenched to the skin in a few seconds. It
was now *sauve qui peut;* but the climb up to the
krantz was so steep that we could only manage a
snail's pace, and the lightning flashed around so
fearfully that one or two got alarmed and threw
away their rifles. At last we reached the foot of
the krantz in a half-drowned and sodden state, as
though we had been passed through a washing-
machine, and fortunately found a large cave capable
of holding ourselves and our horses comfortably.
Then we were at liberty to observe the storm; and
never in all my travels before or since did I see
anything so fearfully appalling. We seemed to be
in the very heart of it. Lightning was everywhere,
flashing and spitting and hissing in all directions,
above us, below us, and all around us; sometimes
so close and blinding as if an electric light had
suddenly been switched on at the ends of our noses,
and as suddenly extinguished, leaving all creation

for some seconds in Cimmerian darkness, although it was almost broad daylight. It danced and shimmered on the ground below, and, as night advanced, twisted and twirled and glittered among the boulders in the most fearsome fashion. Some flashes darted obliquely through the clouds, fine and straight as a line; more parted the heavens horizontally in broad zigzag coils; some flashed straight down and buried themselves in the quivering earth; and others again seemed to cleave the atmosphere from below; while yet more merely lighted up the universe in a blaze of dazzling glory. Not for a moment was there a cessation of the continuous flashing, and the thunder pealed, crack upon crack, roar upon roar, boom upon boom, crash upon crash, rolling and tumbling about as though it were trying to crush and crumble the earth into powder. A dozen different peals could be distinguished at once, now blending together, now all distinct; some receding, others approaching, and raising such a horrid din that the human nerves could scarce sustain the pressure. Huge masses of rock detached themselves from the face of the krantz, and went crashing and bounding with heavy thuds into the valley below; and over all was the dull level roar of the deluging rain.

Inside the cave matters were not particularly lively. Every one was drenched to the skin. A fire was unattainable, as all the scrub that grew among the boulders below was too sodden to burn;

it had turned bitterly cold, and some of the horses were rearing and plunging in mortal terror, and required all their owners' efforts to prevent them dashing out into the mad war of the elements, and careering wildly over the hills through the hissing fury of the storm. My own, fortunately, was perfectly quiet, being apparently a steady old stager with nerves of steel, so that I was able to turn my attention to the desirable object of endeavouring to persuade my rain-diluted blood to reassume its normal condition of free circulation. To this end I endeavoured to emulate the performances of the "Perfect Cure," but was surprised to find that my efforts were looked upon by some of my companions as little short of blasphemous! Such are the effects of superstition and terror. There was no thought of sleep, for even had we been dry and comfortable a pint of opium would have failed to produce somnolency in such a terrific commotion, and for the same reason conversation was impossible, so that each had to seek companionship and occupation in the recesses of his own mind. Those who were not engaged in attending to their horses were mostly huddled together in a corner, sucking at their pipes and shivering with cold. For myself, I spent the night pacing up and down under the rocky krantz, which faced the north, and, therefore, had the wind behind it; and the effect of the storm, as seen from here, was the most extraordinary spectacle I have ever seen.

Towards midnight the peals of thunder became gradually less numerous, and then were only heard at intervals, which became by degrees of longer duration, until at length, about three o'clock, they ceased entirely, although the rain showed no sign of leaving off, but had settled down to a straight, steady fall of heavy drops that seemed likely to last till the crack of doom. We now managed to get a little sleep, rolled up in our sodden blankets, and when morning broke we gazed out at a dreary scene of dripping country and monotonous falling waters. One and all declined to continue the search in such a downpour, so the horses were knee-haltered and turned out to graze on the side of the mountain, and we sat nibbling the last of our soaked and pasty biscuits, and gazing blankly at the dismal scene around. All that livelong day the rain poured down in one continuous, never-resting heavy drip, and it was perfectly useless making any attempt at shifting our quarters ; and at night the fall, if anything, increased in intensity, so we brought up the horses, fastened them to-gether by the heads, and made the best of another night, hoping that we should wake to bask in the warm rays of the summer sun. But, alas! for our hopes, the morning showed no change. There still, spread out below and around us, was the swamped-looking broken country ; there still the suicide-suggesting downpour ; and there the dull, heavy-laden clouds, seemingly as close and as solid as ever. A consultation was held, and the majority decided that it was impossible to do anything in such weather, and though we had nothing to eat, it would be better to remain where we were, as African rains generally break up on the third day. This decision arrived at, we once more turned out the horses, and prepared to make the best of another day. The weary hours dragged their slow length along, relieved by desultory conversation. Some huddled themselves together in a corner and went to sleep; others scratched out chequer-boards on the ground and played draughts with pieces of rock, and one produced a dilapidated and begrimed pack of cards and started a game of cut-throat euchre. Myself and a friend, utterly wearied out, could stand it no longer, so took our rifles and turned out into the deluge to reconnoitre, and in hopes that we might find a wandering eland, rietbuck, or rheebuck. But we saw nothing but water; wherever we looked there were only dense phalanxes of falling drops, sodden grassy hills, and inundated valleys. All life seemed to have become extinct, and the only living thing we saw was a manis, rolled up into a ball and apparently reposed to sleep for the rest of the season. We did not stay out long; the rain was altogether too much for us, and when we returned some of our companions wished to practice upon us the mechanical treatment recommended for the resuscitation of the apparently drowned.

So the day passed, and towards evening the rain began to fall lighter, and before dark it ceased, and the clouds settled bodily upon us in a soft drizzle, and then we knew that the morrow would be fine. About midnight a tiny star shot its rays through a rift, as though it were acting the part of a celestial wedge and attempting to burst asunder the gloomy mass and reveal again to our longing eyes the sparkling glories of the jewelled empyrean. Then, as the hours passed, the mist broke into rounded rolling volumes, silver-tipped and fringed with shimmering light; stars shone forth in all directions, and then the beaming moon appeared on her downward course, and threw her cold soft light over the drenched and weird-looking land, and slowly paled as the crimson gleam of dawn stole gently over the vaulted expanse of a bright and cloudless sky.

These African thunderstorms are among the most appalling things in nature, and woe to those of weak nerves who are caught in one among the mountains. No words could do them justice, and the most graphic word-painter that ever wielded pen would fail to bring the reality before those who had never actually witnessed one. The freaks of the lightning, too, are most extraordinary, and altogether inexplicable. Four strange instances have come under my own observation. I was once lying reading in my wagon, which was out-spanned about twenty yards from a Boer's house in the Free State, a fearful storm being in progress at the time. A blinding flash, with a simultaneous terrible crash, made me jump up, when I heard screaming proceed from the house. I at once hastened to see what was the matter, and found that the lightning had struck the house. Eight people had been sitting in the eating-room, and of these five were dead, and the other three quite uninjured. The curious part of the matter was that those killed were not huddled together apart from those who escaped, but all had been mixed up, each of the uninjured having one killed on either side of them. On another occasion I was riding over Van Reenen's Pass, in company with two others, when a storm broke upon us. Soon after the sudden lighting up of the country by a flash, which apparently had had no other effect, one of my companions all at once gave a yell, and said he had a terrible burning pain on the outside of his left ribs. We at once examined him, and when we opened his waistcoat he was immediately relieved. We found that his watch was actually reduced to a molten mass, and the hot metal had been burning him! Another somewhat similar case was in the Transvaal, when riding in company with another near Leydenberg. A blinding flash killed his horse, but neither of ourselves were conscious of anything but the glare. The fourth was when sitting in the coffee-room of an hotel at Colenso, in Natal, a village which then consisted of two hotels and a private house. The flash came down the chimney, rattled the fireirons, and knocked the things off the mantel ; but though three of us were sitting within a yard, we felt nothing, and on examination the only damage we could find was that the gilt frame of the overmantel was quite blackened.

To return to our cave. The next morning all was animation ; we did not wait for the rise of the sun, but as its aurora-like rays of coloured light shot up from the glowing east we rolled up our blankets, saddled our horses, and bade farewell to our rocky den. It soon rose, and as we led our horses through the dripping grass we basked in the welcome of its drying warmth. Up and down we wandered among those rugged hills and splashy valleys, without any sign of the stock. We had nothing to eat, but at ten o'clock we off-saddled for an hour to let the horses feed, and took advantage of the opportunity to spread our blankets and over-coats out in the heat of the sun, which was now as great as the cold had been severe on the previous days. All that day we climbed and clambered and scrambled and slid among the slopes and hillsides, all to no purpose, and at night it was agreed that, as it could not be ex-pected that we were to roam among the mountains for ever with nothing to eat, we should on the morrow turn our heads back to Harrismith. The next morning we moved before daylight, and after

riding some hours, found indications of the proximity of inhabitants in paths and patches of ground
that had a year or two before evidently been under
cultivation, and at last came across a field of
standing maize from which most of the cobs had
been plucked. Here we dismounted to search for
cobs to ease the gnawing of our hunger, when one
of our number called out that there were natives
hidden away among the stalks. We therefore at
once retired a short distance off, and one of us who
could speak Sesutu was told to call out in that
language if any one was there. No answer was
returned, and the interpreter was then ordered to
let it be known that if no reply was given to three
hails a volley would be fired, as the man who had
first called out was positive that he had seen a
black form sneaking among the stalks. No answer
was received to any of three inquiries, so the word
was given for half the squad to fire, and the sharp
ring of the rifles startled the mountain echoes.
Almost simultaneously with the reports a shrill,
piercing scream was heard to rise from among the
stalks. We waited on the defensive for a minute
or two, when, there being no further demonstration,
we rode round three sides of the mealie garden,
the other side extending down the slope of a hill
too steep to ride on. As nothing further could be
seen, and no answer was given to repeated hails,
half of the squad dismounted and cautiously advanced among the stalks. Recent footprints were

soon perceived, and presently, to our intense mortification, we came upon the body of a poor old Basuto woman, shot through the back and quite dead, and with a basket half full of maize-cobs at her side. It was now evident that there had been a party of women engaged in gathering the corn, and that this poor old wretch had been unable to keep up with the rest, who, the spoor informed us, had scrambled down the hill. There was no help for it; so we carried the body to the edge of the garden, scratched a hole in the loose soil, and buried it decently, piling a heap of stones on the spot. We easily absolved ourselves of any blame in the matter, as the hail was given three times, loudly and distinctly enough to be heard all over the garden, while the latter was large enough to have hidden away hundreds of men.

We felt so small after this exploit that some of our party urged the commandant to raid the village, which we found was about three miles off on the side of a square mountain. But on examination through a glass, it appeared to be tenanted only by women and children, the men being doubtless away with the impis. However, we rode down to find if we could get any news of the cattle. For a long time no one would come out, but eventually two or three old women crept out of huts, and, in reply to our inquiries, said that their men had been away for three months, and that they knew nothing of the cattle. As it was clear that only a few cows were about the village, we believed them, and, after roasting and eating some corn-cobs, departed. We made a bee-line as well as we could in the rough country for Harrismith, and when pretty well clear of the mountains, and in more practicable country, to our great joy came across the very mob of cattle we were in search of, on the trek home by themselves. We very soon sent a bullet crashing into the skull of a fat little ox, and with a lot of scrub from the banks of a spruit made a row of fires, and were soon luxuriating in frizzled beef, having been seven days without meat, and three days without anything at all but a few mealie-cobs. We rested till sundown, and then travelling all night without off-saddling, arrived in Harrismith the next morning, and delivered up the cattle to the authorities.

The war appeared now to be dwindling out; and as I had had enough of the Dutchmen, without asking leave I rode over the border one night with a couple of friends, and returned to Natal.

TRADE AND SPORT IN THE ORANGE FREE STATE AND THE TRANS VAAL

NOWADAYS every one knows all about "The Ship of the Desert." That wonderful product of the despised Boer mind, to which the most ingenious mechanics and engineers have been unable to suggest the most trifling improvement, has been so much written about by the vast army of African scribes, that it must be almost as familiar to the average Briton as the homely cycle of our roads. Its day has now (alas! that it has to be written) well-nigh passed. The iron road is driving it fast into back yards, from whence it will only emerge to be broken up into firewood. The romance of South African travel is becoming a tale of old fogies, and we now rush through the country with set and serious faces, intent on gold and diamonds, Companies and Syndicates, annexations and exploitations, and on other phases of greed and aggrandisement. The old South Africa has receded into the *ewigkeit*, and we who knew it in its glory, with its sport and romance, its good-fellowship and "don't-care-a-damnness," know it no more. A new race has arisen, whose divinity is lucre, and which has elbowed us out, and covered the face of our playground with the trails of its greed.

And so it has come about that the "Smouse," the travelling trader who went all over the country, from farm to farm, in his lumbering ship, bartering his soft and hard goods, his groceries and clothing, for cattle, horses, and sheep, ostrich feathers, hides, ivory, and wool, would be now regarded as as great a curiosity as a knight in armour. But he was an important man in his day, and that day is not more than a quarter of a century gone by.

It was in 1867 that I went into the "Smouse" line for eight months, and wandered about in my ship throughout the whole of the northern half of the Free State, and the southern end of the Transvaal. There were four besides myself in it—C., chief proprietor; R., business manager; H., manager of oxen and wagons; and N., a guest. We were all, except H., in the early twenties; and the combined business capacity of the lot of us might be represented as o—x. Four wagons were loaded up with prints, calicoes, moleskins, tweeds, plushes, cords, merinos, alpacas, winceys, silks, satins, ribbons, laces, shawls, fancy goods, clothing, hats, boots, canvas, flannel, saddles and bridles, tea, coffee, sugar, and all kinds of groceries, spirits, hardware, crockery and glass, tools, ammunition, and everything we could think of, the amount of capital invested having been about £3,000. The cavalcade of four wagons, sixty oxen, five horses, five white and eleven coloured people, and a number of dogs, was an imposing one as it left Grey Town, and many a *Deorch an Doruis* was drunk in honour of the occasion.

We leisurely climbed the great hill above Grey Town, and as leisurely dropped down into the wonderful bush valley known as The Thorns, and elsewhere described ; and on the third evening reached the Tugela. A regular heart-breaker followed in ascending the Biggarsberg by the well-known Helpmakaar. Our oxen were not yet in fair working order, and did not pull together, and this very steep bit of road proved too much for them, especially as it had lately been "repaired," that is to say, picked up, and the ruts filled with loose soil. The first wagon, driven by H., one of the finest wagon-drivers in South Africa, stuck fast, and no amount of shouting and lashing on H.'s part could stir it. Then the other three drivers, who were Hottentots or some sort of mongrel or other, were called up, and a scene of confusion ensued that it would be impossible to describe. The whips cracked, and lashed, and flew around, cleaving the air with the sound of a whirlwind ; and our ears were assailed with an appalling torrent of blasphemy in the very lowest of low Dutch. H., who only stood five feet two, was ubiquitous, and

16

his tremendous whiplash descended with a force terrible to behold, making the unfortunate ox on which it fell shrink almost into the ground. But it was of no use, and we had to fasten on another span, and with the thirty oxen we got the wagon to the top. It may be asked why all this cruelty? Why not have got up the other span at first? To do so would have been to ruin the oxen at once. Oxen are very knowing creatures, and if they find that they can stick fast without being severely punished, they would always be doing so, and there would be endless bother and delay; whereas if they are well punished at their first stick, and only receive assistance when it is found that the work is really beyond their powers, they will ever afterwards do their best at the mere sound of the whip, and rarely require more than an occasional gentle reminder, so that it is in reality a merciful proceeding. Nevertheless, it is idle to deny that the majority of South African wagon-drivers, English, Dutch, and coloured, were extremely cruel, especially the transport-riders, or carriers, and I have often witnessed scenes that to this day make my blood run cold to think of.

On the fine flat plains at the top of the Biggarsberg there were then numerous hartebeeste, and I had some rare gallops after them. Although this fine buck is to the eye most awkwardly built, the pace at which it can go is truly astonishing, and one has to be mounted on a real good horse to

have the least chance of coming up with them.
Here also I bagged one of the rather rare buck,
the vaal-rheebuck, a mountain buck the size of a
springbuck, and covered with woolly hair almost
white. They are only found along the stony edges
of mountain ranges, or on rocky ridges rising out
of the plains. C. made a fine shot and killed a
quagga 1,500 yards off, although I chaffed him for
firing at such a range. He fired into a troop closely
clustered together, and I watched the shot with a
binocular and saw one in the centre drop to it.
The distance we paced off to it was over a mile,
but there were several irregularities in the ground.
The rifle was a long Henry. On the road we
passed a spruit, or small river, in whose bank was
a large vein of coal of very fine quality, and the bed
of the stream is partly composed of the same. I
believe this is the locality of the well-known
Dundee coal mine. A little further, we reached
a couple of houses, and called at one to inquire
if we were on the right road for Newcastle, as
we expected to have reached it by this time, but
could see no sign of a township anywhere in the
wide plain. We were rather surprised at the reply
that it was Newcastle. This now flourishing town
then contained only these two houses—a store and
the magistrate's private house.

This same magistrate played us a nasty trick.
We were a light-hearted lot, and musically disposed ; H. was first-rate on the concertina, N.

fancied himself very much on the flute, C. could do astonishing gymnastics with the bones, and I could wring the very soul out of a tin plate, and we gave the magistrate a complimentary serenade at two o'clock in the morning, the rest of the company being provided with pots, pans, kettles, buckets, &c. The magistrate did not appear to take the affair in the same spirit as ourselves, for the next morning, before we had got a couple of miles (we always started at daylight), a mounted policeman, who acted as clerk, interpreter, sheriff, gaoler, messenger, policeman, magazine-keeper, and office-boy, appeared with a missive ordering us to present ourselves with all our belongings before his Worship. We might very well have declined, for we could easily have put the whole of the executive into the wagons and carried it off; but as the affair appeared likely to afford some fun, we returned. We found his Worship sitting in state, and he informed us that he believed that we were bent on an expedition to sell guns and ammunition to the natives, and ordered us to produce all our weapons. We did so, to the number of seventeen, all properly stamped (there is a duty of 10s. a barrel in Natal), some of which were valuable weapons, and made an affidavit that they were the private property of different members of our party, and were intended entirely for sport. But this did not satisfy his sapiency, and he confiscated the whole of them, and refused to release them. C. and myself had therefore to ride to Maritzburg and back, 400 miles, to get an order from the Colonial Secretary, to whom we were known, for their release, which was obeyed with a very bad grace. This gentleman became a K.C.M.G., and Commissioner in Zululand. His death was quite a recent occurrence.

We now ascended the Drakensberg over Laing's Neck, and under the shadow of Majuba Hill—a truly beautiful country to be desecrated in a three-fold manner—first by unnecessary and cruel bloodshed, then by incapacity and cowardice, and, finally, by dishonour. In the many times that I have crossed this pass I have seen none of these; I have seen nothing but Nature in her brightest mood. Near Sekoe Vley, on the other side of the divide, a lake swarming with aquatic birds, and also then containing a few hippopotami, C. and myself had a narrow escape of extinction. We were riding to a farm when we became aware that a large grass fire was bearing down on us on both sides of the road, which was only a slight wagon-track; the grass was a heavy and luxuriant crop, and as dry as tinder, and there was a fresh breeze blowing. We had no matches or appliances for meeting it with another fire, so we turned and ran, as we knew that with grass of that character, and in such a breeze, the line of fire would be some thirty feet in width, and six or eight in height. The fire came roaring down at the rate of at least twenty miles an hour, and the dense volumes of smoke were already enveloping us, and we plied whip and spur with all our might. But it was useless, for the fire rapidly gained on us, and had it not been that we reached the main road, on the other side of which the grass had already been burnt off, it would have gone badly with us.

It was about here that we first commenced the ostensible business of our expedition—trading. Let me give a description of the *modus operandi* of this smousing. Outspanning near a Boer's house, we spread a large carpet on the ground, and while R. and C., who both spoke Dutch fairly well, went in to do the polite and drink weak coffee made of burnt corn, according to orthodox Boer etiquette, the rest of us spread out the contents of one wagon, which was kept full of samples, and awaited the arrival of the purchasers. In the meantime the Boers sent for horses and cattle, or whatever they had for disposal, and pointed out those they were willing to part with, and after considerable haggling, for your Boer is a terrible fellow for a bargain, a price was agreed upon. Then the whole family, men, women, and children, trooped down to the goods. First, the head Boer, tall, gawky, and loose-jointed, with tangled reddish hair, flabby, un-wholesome face, plentifully ornamented with dirt, and short, thin, scrubby beard stained with tobacco juice; his hands were large, long, and bony, and on their backs could still be seen some of the dried

blood of the last wildebeeste he had killed, probably two or three days before. On his head was an old soft felt, wide-brimmed, caballero hat, stained with blood, grease, and dirt ; his coat was a tailless jacket of the schoolboy order, and was made of dark purple plush, with metal buttons ; his waistcoat of brown moleskin, and his shirt of unbleached calico, innocent of front, and last washed about a month ago ; he had no necktie. Round his waist was an ancient belt with pouches for bullets, caps, and grease patches, and his understandings were encased in yellow moleskin trousers, begrimed with blood and grease, and terminating above the ankle, exposing an inch or two of bare leg, the colour of which could not be seen for the dirt on it ; his sockless splay feet were shod in home-made veldschoens, blucher-shaped and unblacked. His *vrouw* was fat and frowsy, and clad in a dirty print gown ; her features could hardly be seen, being buried in a deep sunbonnet of the same material as her gown ; but what could be discerned of her face was as dirty and flabby as her lord's ; her stockingless legs were visible to the calf, and were only a little less dirty than the Boer's, and she wore the twin pair of veldschoens to his. The eldest son was a copy of his father, but wore a jackal's tail and an ostrich feather in his hat, and smoked a pipe of green soapstone of the old German shape. His wife was not so fat but no less frowsy than the old *vrouw*, and she suckled a dirty child, both her breasts being fully exposed. The younger

sons varied from gawky hobbledehoys, foul as their
elders, and dull and stupid as owls, to objectionable
brats to whom the use of a handkerchief is unknown.
The *meisjes* were the only members of the family one
could approach without disgust, as they were less
dirty, and their features when not buried in the
poke were often pleasing, and their eyes decidedly
shy, and were always wandering towards one or the
other of us. Their costume appeared to consist of
nothing more than a chemise and a print dress, and
as they sat round the goods a shapely bare leg would
occasionally be protruded, to be suddenly withdrawn
with a blush and a giggle when the owner saw that
we were glancing at it with humorous admiration.

Before any business could be done, Boer etiquette
must be complied with. Each of us, therefore, in
turn solemnly shook hands with the whole family,
from the old Boer to the youngest child in arms.
The Boer method of shaking hands is not of that
hearty character that *used* to be practised by
Englishmen. The hand is slowly thrust out and
placed in yours for a second or two perfectly motionless, and without a suspicion of muscular con-
traction. It feels as if a dead flabby codfish's tail
were thrust into yours. While the right hand goes
into yours, the left is raised slowly to the brim of
the hat, the front of which is lifted half an inch off
the brow. We always revenged ourselves for the
dirty, flabby, lifeless hands of the Boers, *vrouws*,
and children, by giving those of the *meisjes* a good

squeeze, which always made them run away and giggle to each other.

This function over, business commenced in earnest. All the women and children seated themselves on the ground round the goods, and the males made an outer circle, walking round and round, making critical remarks and asking questions. R. and H., as being most proficient in the Dutch language, exhibited the goods to the best advantage, and enlarged in glowing and mendacious terms on their excellences, and C. and N. hovered about talking to the Boers, doing the amiable to the *vrouws*, and acting as detectives to see that nothing was purloined ; while I seated myself on a pile of soft goods in the centre, book and pencil in hand, entering the articles as they were purchased, making sketches of any character that took my fancy, and keeping an eye on the *vrouws* and *meisjes*, whose notions of *meum* and *tuum* were decidedly shaky. In fact, whatever they may be now, the whole race of Boers, men and women, were in those days a pack of thieves. This seems a hard thing to say, but I had exceptional opportunities of observing, and so far as the Boers of the north of the Orange Free State and the south of the Transvaal were concerned, it is absolutely true. There seemed to be no shame about it, and, if discovered in the act, they only laughed. Seated thus in the middle, I have, I might almost say hundreds of times, seen them gradually work any small article at hand

towards them, and secrete it under their aprons
or in the bosoms of their gowns. If it was only a
reel of cotton or a skein of silk, or any similar trifle,
I said nothing, but entered the article in the book,
and if the purloiner was young and pretty gave her
a slow, quiet wink. But when the article was of
any value I was obliged to interfere. On one
occasion I saw a girl of about twenty, the daughter
of a rich and influential Boer, trying to secrete a
small case of watches. She had just got it half
under her apron, when she raised her eyes towards
my face, and seeing the expression of comical,
quizzical observation on it, put it back with a blush
and a laugh, and busied herself among the merinos
and laces. The men were just as bad, and a box
of caps, a knife, or any such useful article was never
safe lying about. On one occasion C. left his belt,
to which was fastened a pouch containing more than
£20, in a Boer's house, and never saw it again ; the
inmates, denied all knowledge of it, although their
guilty looks made it perfectly plain that they knew
all about it.

When goods to the amount of the stock purchased
had been selected, the accounts were made up, the
goods packed away, the animals branded and left
till our return, and then, accompanied with a flask
of "square face," we adjourned to the house and
had a general conversation, and did the agreeable
to the young ladies, who were by no means coy.
Often, if it was too late to move on, we got up a

dance. One of our wagon-drivers had a dilapidated
fiddle, and could grind out the two popular Boer
reels, " My Father was a Dopper" and " John
Filgee " (this name is spelt De Villiers, but for
some unknown reason is pronounced as written ;
it is the Smith of South Africa). To these delect-
able strains we would show our agility with a lumpy
meisje for a *vis-à-vis*. The only dance known to the
Boers is a kind of reel, in which the figure is more
spontaneous than constant. Energy in execution
was looked upon with greater favour than grace of
movement. At these dances we always supplied
the refreshments, and the Boer men and elder
women would often imbibe so freely that they
would fall asleep, leaving the *meisjes* and ourselves
to continue the dance until, the lights went out, at
which point both dance and paragraph must be
concluded.

The interior of a Boer's house at this time was of
the most primitive character, and in the case of
some of the poorer or lazier ones often consisted of
but one room, in which the whole family lived and
slept, one end being shut off by a curtain of
voerschitz (handkerchief stuff with patterns on it,
lions being the favourite one) for the married
ones, the rest sleeping on the floor, the girls at
one end and the boys at the other. They never
took their clothes off at night. Among wealthier
Boers on the Valsh, Rhenoster, and Vet rivers, and
on the Suiker Bosch Rand, there was more comfort,

cleanliness, and decency, and often we came upon houses quite respectably furnished, and generally with a harmonium. The womenfolk in these houses were always better dressed, and only wore the hideous poke when outside, instead of all day (and I believe all night as well). They would often buy silks and satins, but I never saw any of them wear these materials—probably they were reserved for high private functions. Often we would dispose of a hundred pounds' worth of goods at a single house, for there were few stores in those days, except at the half-dozen townships, and as our things were of the best quality and cheap (we found afterwards that we ought to have charged fifty per cent. more than we did), they would buy enough to last them for months. In this way we wandered about from house to house, going in no particular direction, but always trying to find out the Boers who had the most stock to dispose of. At first we found the Boers very poor, so we made for the direction of Potchefstroom, and soon entered the wildebeeste flats. While among the peaks of the Drakensberg four-footed game had been scarce, only a few vaal-rheebucks having been seen; but partridges were very numerous, and one day I accomplished what I always considered my best bit of partridge shooting. My cross-bred pointer, Don, was ranging up the side of a slope, and I was leisurely following him with my gun over my shoulder, when I suddenly flushed a brace of birds, one of which made straight away in front of me, and the other in exactly the opposite direction, straight away behind me, but I bagged them both. In the flats game was plentiful, especially wildebeeste, but it is not easy to understand why they preferred the poor grass of these shelterless plains to the richer feed and the shelter round about the feet of the flat-topped mountains, that stretch in a long line for many hundreds of miles where the uplands suddenly sink down to the broken country of Nomansland, Natal, Zululand, and Swaziland. Want of fuel troubled us a good deal, as nothing was obtainable but the dry ox-dung of the outspan places and farms, of which there were very few in these grass flats. There was very little grass either, and what there was was as dry as tinder, and we had to hurry along to get some decent grass for the cattle. One day, as we were trekking along just after sunset, a great herd of wildebeeste was seen bearing down upon us, and, without swerving from their course, they attempted to pass, and were soon mixed up with the oxen and wagons, and a scene of indescribable confusion ensued. There was no attempt at charging, and all seemed panic-stricken, and knew not which way to turn. We lashed at them with wagon-whips and sjamboks, fired at them with rifles, shot-guns, and revolvers, while the niggers yelled and waved their arms, the oxen lowed and struggled in their yokes, alarmed at the unwonted commotion, and the dogs barked and

17

snarled and charged wildly in all directions. The scene partook of all the features of a battle royal, and in the rapidly failing light was extremely weird. The poor beasts meant no harm, and would have been only too glad to get away, but when at last we got clear of them we found that nine had been left dead on the field, killed in self-defence. Our own damage amounted to only a few broken yokes-keys. We surmised that they had been chased by lions, for there were certainly no human creatures within miles of us, and I never before or since saw wildebeestes in such a complete panic. The lion is popularly called the "King of the Forest," but, as a matter of fact, they used to be quite as numerous in these open, treeless flats as in the bush country. They harboured among the reeds that bordered all the vleys and water-holes. These water-holes in the flats are very curious, for though often but a few yards across they are of immense depth. The water in them is olive-green, and not very wholesome. The number of jackals and hyenas in the flats at this time was astonishing, and on frosty moonlight nights the air was filled with a shrill chorus of barks, howls, and whines; and on looking out of my wagon I frequently saw them within a dozen yards, but they never did more harm than gnawing loose hides that might be lying about. If the oxen should not be tied up to the trektouws they will, however, make short work of the rheims and strops.

One night when we were doing a moonlight trek, R. and myself were walking in front of the wagons, when our progress was opposed by a porcupine in the road, which repeatedly turned its stern towards us and charged us. R. protected our legs from the quills with his greatcoat, which he had been carrying on his arm ; and when we had sufficiently amused ourselves with it I killed it with my revolver. On examination, the coat was found to be thickly stuck with quills ; and this is the origin of the fable that the porcupine can throw its quills. It makes a short, sudden rush backwards with astonishing celerity, and then, almost the same second, resumes its right position with a quickness that defies the eye. Its flesh is not bad, but is by no means a dainty. For a long time I would not eat it, though by no means fastidious ; but one day when I had been away shooting the whole day, a dish was set before me on my return, which I declared, being very hungry, to be the most delicious I had ever tasted. I was then told that it was porcupine, and I often subsequently ate it. But the animal must be young ; the full-grown one is exceedingly rank. There is a peculiar sort of glutinous skin on a portion of the back, quite half an inch in thickness, which is much relished by some.

As we neared the Vaal River we found that in addition to the herbage being eaten off by the game, the country had also been fired by the Boers, and for some thirty miles we passed through an expanse of country as black as a boot, relieved here and there by isolated patches of purple-brown grass that had escaped the fire. But as we approached nearer, we found that the fire had been stopped by a cross-road, and that there was a belt of grass about half a mile in width, parallel to the river, and kept comparatively green by its proximity; a long patch some miles in length also extended a mile or two to the south, enclosed by roads. With these exceptions, and a few isolated patches, as we afterwards found by riding, the country was burnt off for nearly fifty miles in every direction, the result, the Boers said, of accidental fires. Therefore, after consultation, it was decided to make a camp on the river until the grass grew again, in the meantime making rapid expeditions with a single wagon for the purposes of trading, leaving the others in camp for the oxen to fatten on the green grass that grew on the river's bank. The spot at which we first sighted the river was marked by what appeared to be a stony ridge running at right angles to the course of the stream, and about a mile in length, and as it seemed a most excellent spot for a camp we outspanned at once. It was about sixty miles from Potchefstroom and forty-five from Heidelberg, and five from the confluence of the Wilge River. Here we stayed for three months, trading, shooting, fishing, coursing, exploring, practising cricket, having athletic sports, shooting matches, horse races, &c.,

and working at different fancies during the day, and playing cards and other games at night. We placed the wagons in a square, and pitched a large tent in the enclosure, and thus had a first-rate camp. The Dutchmen soon found us out, and used to come in with ostrich feathers and cash, or driving

THE VAAL RIVER, BOUNDARY BETWEEN THE ORANGE FREE
STATE AND TRANSVAAL.

oxen and horses, and a little trade was done every day, R. taking charge of this department, as he cared little for sport.

The stones topping the long low ridge by which we were camped proved to be the ruins of an enormous stone town, or kraal, a mile long and a quarter in width. Though it had been apparently deserted for half a century, many of the huts were still perfect, and were made of undressed stone without cement, the roofs being formed by lapping flat slabs of shale one over the other until they met in the centre, exactly as in the ancient British stone huts found in Cornwall and other places. In fact, the resemblance of this town to the ancient British village of Chysauster, not far from Penzance, was, except in point of size, quite remarkable. They might both have been built by the same people, for not only were the huts erected on the same principle, but in each were the same stone kraals for cattle, and the same querns for grinding corn. But in this old Vaal River town there was an erection which has never been seen in a British village, nor, so far as I know, in any other African one. Its base was of the same size as the ordinary huts—that is to say, from 6 to 8 feet in diameter; but instead of being only about 4 feet in height and flat-roofed, it was built up into a cone 15 feet in height. In my extensive experience of South Africa this hut was quite unique. It appeared to be of more recent date than the ordinary huts, and was certainly a wonderful production. Let any one attempt to erect a conical hut 15 feet in height of loose stones without cement, and I venture to think that failure would attend 99 per cent. of the attempts. This town was a perfect labyrinth of stone, every hut having a large kraal for cattle, and a smaller one for calves. The Boers told us that the town had been built by Umziligazi (Mozilikatze of the English,

Dutch, and Bechuanas), the rebellious general of Chaka, the Zulu potentate, who, when sent by his master to chastise certain tribes on the Oliphants River, deserted and set up for himself, and eventually, after some wanderings, formed the Matabili nation. But this was clearly a mistake. Mozilikatze's route is well known, and though he once camped on the Vaal River for some time, he made no residence intended to be permanent there. It was in the Magaliesberg that he first made what was meant for a permanent settlement. The town was clearly that of the chief of the Bechuana race which in the first decade of the century inhabited these parts, and which was driven out by the Mantatee hordes. The so - called Mantatees were undisciplined hordes whose homes had been destroyed by Chaka, when he raided the whole east coast of Southern Africa nearly down to the Fish River, and who then wandered westward, and in their turn fell upon the Bechuana and Griqua tribes there established. They met with varying success in these struggles, but were eventually defeated by the Griquas at Old Lattaku in 1823. They then divided, some going north under Sibituani, and others east to the Basuto country under Ma'Ntatisi.

This ruined town was not the only indication of a former large population in the district. Facing the river was a great amphitheatre, three miles across and enclosed on three sides by a ridge

rising from one to two hundred feet above the
general level, and this semicircular ridge was
covered for its entire length with the ruins of huts
and kraals. At least 20,000 people must have
dwelt in the neighbourhood at one time. Similar
ruins are, or were, to be seen on all the ridges
throughout the Orange Free State, and therefore
these bleak open plains must have carried an
enormous population. From the fact of the ruins
being always on the high exposed ground, instead
of in the more sheltered hollows, it is certain that
they always lived in expectation of attack from some
quarter or other. The dispersal of this great population was undoubtedly due to four causes—inter-
tribal warfares, the raids of Mozilikatze and the
Mantatee hordes, and, lastly, the ravages of the
Boers. Whatever the Boers may be nowadays,
and whatever defence of them may be made by
apologists, it is within my positive knowledge that
in earlier times they were among the most ruthless
slaughterers and slave-hunters the world has ever
seen. In those days there was hardly a Boer house
in which there was not at least one absolute slave,
and often half a dozen, and each one of these
represented the slaughter of a family. This is no
guesswork statement ; it is the testimony of the
slaves themselves.

In spite of the bitter cold of the nights, our three
months' camp at this spot was a truly happy time.
Although there was no game larger than wilde-

beestes, there was sport, and plenty of it, of every conceivable description. Coursing on the flats beyond the amphitheatre was one of our favourite amusements. We had eight dogs — Spring, a magnificent dog belonging to H., which was a cross between a Scotch deerhound dog and a bull and pointer bitch ; Cæsar, a huge dog like a boarhound which I bought from some passing Kafirs, who had probably stolen it ; Carolus, a powerful Boer dog ; Caraval, a fast dog with deerhound blood in him ; Nell, a white mongrel, fast and staunch ; Tiger, a powerful, fast, and plucky mongrel, together with Don, the pointer, and Towzer, a foolish pup, which were generally left at home. With these dogs we could easily run down the wildebeestes, blesbucks, and quaggas, notwithstanding that the short stalks of the burnt-off grass made it very rough on the dogs' feet. But the springbucks told us a different tale, and it was rarely that we succeeded in fairly running one down. It is perfectly amazing how, with a few stiff springs into the air, for all the world like those the " Perfect Cure " used to make, these animals can put a distance between themselves and the fastest dogs. Nevertheless, I think these springs tire them very much, as it was only after making several that we ever succeeded in running one down. A more beautiful sight than one of these bucks making its spring, with a line of long snow-white hair erect along his back, it would be difficult to conceive. It

is a marvel that, on coming down from the heights
to which they spring, with all their limbs stiffened,
they do not break their delicate pipe-stem legs.
Indeed, I have heard that they sometimes do, but
I never witnessed a case.   Jackal hunting was also
occasionally indulged in ; but it was not often that
we could get them out of their holes, and when we
did there were so many aardvaark (antbear) holes
that they were soon to earth again.   Spring was
far the best at this kind of work—indeed, he was
a wonderful dog ; nothing came amiss to him, and
he was the only dog I ever knew that would go
into a porcupine's hole and bring the animal out
dead.

One day one of our Kafirs in charge of a squad
of the oxen managed, in that laborious way peculiar
to the noble savage, to lose them, but returned
with the information that he had seen a couple of
vlakvaarks, or wild-boars, in a vley two or three
miles away.   The next day was Sunday, and as
the horses had been well worked during the week
we determined to give them a rest, and do a bit of
pig-sticking *à la* South Africa on foot.   So after
breakfast we threw off our coats and waistcoats,
tightened   our   belts,   and   sounded   the   horn.
Curiously enough, none of us had thought to
carry an assegai, and the only weapons we had
among us were rifles H. and C. carried, and the
revolver I always had in my belt.   We soon
reached the ground, a reed-marsh or vley of no

great size, and piggies were evidently at home, and soon Spring, who was always foremost, was seen going at his best in the rear of two fine pigs, one of which was a boar. We gave a view-holloa and a tug at our belts, and started after them. It was awful going—the ground was boggy, and of that black, tenacious mud the African traveller knows so well, and my feet as I drew them up made sounds like the popping of corks, and the slush squirted up to my eyes. Soon we got on firmer ground, and the dogs gained rapidly, and before we had gone more than a mile Spring gave a bound forward and seized the sow by the ear, and then all the rest were on her. A battle royal at once ensued, and pig and dogs were so mixed up together that it was impossible to get shot or knife in. At last I managed to get a bullet into her broad forehead, but it was without effect, and it was not until the third shot, with the revolver almost touching her, that I succeeded in killing her. One or two of the dogs had slight gashes, but they were of no importance, and after a short rest we went after the boar. It had a good start, but Spring was again successful in finding it, and we all settled down in a steady run. The boar was a faster goer than the sow, and soon we were nearly a couple miles behind. When we came up a big fight was going on. Tiger had the boar by the hind leg, and Spring by the ear, and the rest were snapping round taking hold whenever they saw a chance, only to be driven off by a vicious snap from the boar's tusks. The boar was large, powerful, savage, and determined, and had immensely long tusks, and every now and again a howl would indicate that a dog had received a gash. Sometimes one would retire from the combat for a moment to lick its wounds, only to " at him again " with renewed energy, while Towzer prudently kept a yard or two away, and added to the din a continuous bark and howl in a shrill alto. I began to get anxious for the dogs, so I joined in and fired two shots at the boar without apparent effect; and as I had foolishly omitted to re-load the three compartments fired at the sow, I had only one shot left. However, I rushed in and seized the boar by the hind leg, and the moment I did so the dogs, which were all by this time pretty well cut about, left him, and lay down, and I was left to settle conclusions with the pig. This was not in my programme, and I danced round the pig, while he made vicious snaps at my legs, like a harlequin, and performed antics that would infallibly have brought down the house in any music-hall. " K-i-i-l-l him ! " I roared to the others ; " s-h-o-o-t him ! " Not they ; they *couldn't*. Some of them were stooping down with their hands on their stomachs, and the rest sprawling on the ground with their legs in the air, all in an agony of laughter. In reply a half-smothered " Why don't

you k-i-i-ll him yourself? ha! ha! ha!" arose. But
I did not know how; I had but one bullet, and
while the pig continued his frantic motions it
was impossible to take any aim, while the hunting-
knife I was carrying was a clasp bowie hanging to
my belt, which I could not open with one hand.
I dare not let go, and felt that I could not hold
on much longer, so I nerved myself up, and
clapping the muzzle of the revolver to the back
of the pig's head, by sheer good luck "blew its
brains out." Then I sat down exhausted, and
those wretches came up and patted me on the
back, and praised my display of agility, which
they said had been truly marvellous. "Well, my
boys," I said very slowly, as I arranged the rents
in my pants, "the next time you want any pigs
killed you can do it yourselves; the trade don't suit
this child." And so we returned to the wagons
carrying the two pigs among us.

We used to have good sport at the Wilge River.
It ran for a considerable distance between cliffs
about 100 feet in height, in the rifts and clefts of
which innumerable birds and animals made their
abodes. Eagles, hawks of all sizes, owls, wild
turkeys, addidores, great swarms of locust-birds,
dense flights of swallows and martins, and dozens
of species of smaller birds, flew out amid a great
whirring of wings whenever a shot was fired; while
rock rabbits darted about from hole to hole, and
made capital rifle practice from the opposite side.

On our first visit round black heads appeared every now and again on the surface of the water, and usually received a bullet before they could sink again. They were otters, and on searching the next day—for otters will not rise for some hours after death—we found that we had killed five fine animals. A sort of amphibious beast like a polecat, but of a brown colour, and which we called a skunk, was also killed, but as we had had previous experience of them through one which one of the dogs had killed in a small stream, by which he had acquired a horrible stench that remained on him for many days, forcing us to drive him away whenever he approached, we left it alone. Just at the confluence with the Vaal River the water was shallow, with banks and shoals of beautiful pebbles of agates, cornelians, jasper, flints, rock crystals, and other stones very similar to the gravel at the Pniel diamond diggings. Here shoals of silvery " scale fish" were often seen, and we amused ourselves with shooting them with bullets. Of course they were seldom hit, unless they were right on the surface, because a bullet cannot penetrate water very far, and in the little distance it can, its course is deflected ; but even if not struck they would turn belly up, and a Kafir was able to rush in and seize them. I cannot account for this, but often we would half fill a sack with fine fish of from one to three pounds, not more than two or three of which had been actually struck. In the Vaal River we

caught fine barbel (*siluris*) running up to forty
pounds. The fishing was not very scientific, a
huge sixteen-feet wagon whip serving for a rod,
and the bait was a quarter of a pound of meat on a
huge hook. The landing of them was a sheer
matter of " pull devil, pull baker," and often the
butt of the "rod" was placed on the shoulder and
the fish was dragged out by main force, as one
would drag a weight up a hill with a rope. Many
of these barbel were smoked in one of the stone
huts, and they afterwards afforded an agreeable
change of diet.

A flight of locusts visited us one day, and we
trembled for our grass, but luckily it was not a
large one, and as there was a fresh breeze blowing
it passed away very quickly. We fried some in the
orthodox manner, but I cannot recommend them
as an article of diet, and think a bundle of dried
nettles fried would be quite as satisfactory. Schools
of locust-birds, as usual, accompanied them, and
destroyed a great many, but the number they
destroyed could bear but a very infinitesimal proportion to the whole. These birds can often be
seen in large swarms at great heights, and it is
most interesting to watch their wheeling evolutions.
There is much talk of legislation to destroy locusts,
but to my mind it is an impossibility by any human
means. When a flight of locusts is a couple of
miles square, two hundred yards or so thick in the
air, and six inches deep all over the ground, it seems

idle to talk of destroying them. Such a flight would contain at a very moderate computation five hundred million locusts. Even the voetgangers and rooi-baatjes (young ones that cannot yet fly) could not easily be destroyed. They march through the country in the most stolid manner, taking no note of any obstacle. Even a river will not stop them, for they march in and get drowned until the dead ones become so thick as to form a bridge right across for the rest. I have even heard of the course of a river being turned by a swarm of walking locusts.

I nearly killed C. here. Several of us had been foot-hunting all day, and were returning in the evening dog-tired. C. and myself were walking in front side by side, and I was carrying a Sharpe's carbine—a weapon I did not much like, and seldom used—behind my neck, with a portion of the barrel in the one hand, and the narrow part of the stock in the other. It was a favourite way of carrying a rifle when by myself, but is a most objectionable method when in company. In this case the rifle was at full-cock, and by some unexplained means it went off, and the bullet just grazed the back of C.'s neck—as narrow an escape of death as could well be. This accident made me more averse than ever to shooting in company, and in after years I seldom did so. Another accident took place about the same time, and again C. had a narrow escape. We were having some pistol practice, and it became his turn to fire ; he had a bad right hand, having tried to knock down an ox which objected to being fastened up for the night—case of pot and kettle—and he therefore fired with his left. He was using one of those dangerous weapons, a Colt's revolver, and directly he pulled the trigger there was a terrific noise, as all the five compartments went off together, and he sat astride of the disselboom, from whence he had fired, looking foolishly at the weapon, evidently not satisfied with its performance. On examination it was found that the loading-rod and lever had been carried away, and they were found, of all places in the world, embedded in the wood of the wagon-box immediately behind him. How they got there I cannot pretend to say, but there they were, and the line they took showed that they would have struck him in the face had he fired with his right hand. Another revolver belonging to R. had a knack of going off itself at most inopportune moments, and C. had a revolving rifle which several times discharged two barrels at once, and was altogether an expensive, unreliable, dangerous, and useless toy. My experience on this trip led me to discard revolvers altogether, and always afterwards I used double-barrelled pistols, a splendid pair of which I had, made by Manton. These weapons were wonderfully accurate, and possessed astonishing driving powers. I could nearly always hit a sardine tin at fifty yards with them, and I once killed a buffalo with one by a shot in the head, right through the boss of the horn.

There are amazing numbers of animals which either burrow holes for themselves in the ground, or else live in holes burrowed by others, in these plains. Meercats of different varieties were, of course, the most numerous, and these charming little animals were to be seen in all directions sitting outside their holes and performing their toilets. It is a pity that their colonies are so dangerous to the horseman. Jackals and hyenas were everywhere, though not often seen, and there were at least two species of the cat tribe. The aardvaark (the South African antbear) appeared to be ubiquitous, judging from the evidence of his handiwork; but, as a matter of fact, they are not so numerous as would seem, as they are very industrious animals. Porcupines were plentiful, and there were occasional polecats and badger-like animals.

Temminck's manis, falsely called an armadillo, was occasionally seen. This is a scaly animal, which, when disturbed, rolls itself into a ball like a woodlouse, being then the size of a large football. I was one day carrying one to the camp when it made some movement, and cut my hands badly with the sharp edges of its large scales. An occasional spring-hare, an animal that jumps like a kangaroo, but is not a marsupial, was seen; and common hares often. We got specimens of all these animals by night-hunting, and porcupine hunting with assegais was a favourite amusement. They are plucky little things, and will charge back-

wards at one with the greatest ferocity. N. once
got one between his legs, and danced about like a
monkey on hot iron before he could stick it with his
assegai. The dogs fared badly with them ; and I
once extracted seven large quills from Cæsar's
throat. The badger, too, showed desperate fight,
and bit one of the dogs severely. But the greatest
surprise to us was the fight made by the only
aardvaark we killed. As many people now know,
this is one of the most curious animals in creation.
It has the head and snout of a fine-bred young pig,
the ears of a buck, the body of a pig, with a few
scattered bristles, and the tail of a kangaroo. Its
legs are so short that the belly is almost on the
ground, but are of the most powerful description,
with bones like a young bull's, and terminating in
paws as big as a boy's hands, and armed with long
sharp horn claws like fingers. It was through some
Boers living a few miles up the river that we got
this animal. They wanted to burn a portion of
the stretch of old grass already mentioned, and
asked our assistance to prevent it spreading beyond
a certain point. We therefore gave each of the
Kafirs a piece of old sacking to beat the fire out,
and all went to join the Boers, H. taking his rifle,
and I my revolver and an assegai. When the grass
was fired many animals were turned out, and several
knocked on the head ; and presently this aardvaark
was seen making for a hole. But this hole proved
too small for it, and was in such hard earth that, in

spite of its great strength, it could not work itself any deeper ; probably there was a rock at the end of the hole. Be this as it may, the animal stuck fast, with the tip of its tail just out of the hole. But we could not kill it. H. fired five bullets—all he had—with the muzzle of the rifle almost touching its rump, and I gave it all six out of my revolver, but they seemed to have little effect, and we sent a Kafir to the camp in hot haste for a couple of buffalo rheims. When they arrived one of the Boers cut a slit in the root of its tail, where the skin is nearly half an inch thick, and slipped the rheims through it, and then fourteen strong men exerted themselves to draw that aardvaark out of the hole. But, wonderful as it may appear, for a long time they failed to stir it. The animal prised its back up against the top of the hole, and dug its claws into the ground, and resisted their united strength, although it had eleven bullets in its body. But at length the vital forces waned, and after a quarter of an hour's hauling it was dragged out just as life was leaving it.

On returning to camp N. and myself, while foraging about in search of adventures, had one of a kind we cared little about. We got caught between the fire and the river, and as the grass was here very luxuriant the line of flame was ten feet in width and six in height ; if there had been any wind, it would have been thirty feet wide. N., of the two devouring elements, preferred the water, and jumped

into the river ; but I could not swim, and had therefore to face the fire. I took off my coat and fastened
it over my head and face, and, thrusting my hands
deep into my trousers pockets, dashed through it.
I escaped with a slight scorching, but N. had a two-
mile walk in his wet clothes on a frosty night, and
after all fared the worse.

After a happy month in this camp C. and myself
took one of the wagons and went to Potchefstroom,
doing a good trade in ostrich feathers on the road.
Potchefstroom, or Mooi River Dorp, as it was often
called, was at this time a small, unpretending,
arborescent town, surrounding a large open square.
It was the second seat of Government of the Transvaal, the first having been Origstadt, which, being
in the low bush country, was first decimated by
fever, and then deserted ; from Potchefstroom the
seat of Government was removed to Pretoria. It
was an out-of-the-way place, and was seldom visited
by English, except by hunters and traders on their
way to the Zambesi, Lake N'gami, and the Matabili
and Bamangwato countries, and in the colonies it
was very rare to come across any one who had been
there. On our way back we purchased at a farm
four young ostriches, a few months old, and not
quite half grown. We had considerable difficulty
in getting them off the farm. A little further we
bought three more, a little older and three-parts
grown, and these gave us proper work to get them
away. For a whole day we were chasing them all

over the country on foot, for we had brought no horses, not anticipating this kind of work, but they always returned to the house, and towards evening we gave it up. In the morning, at daybreak, we spanned or hobbled them with silk handkerchiefs, and in this way managed to get them six or seven miles from the farm. The next day we removed the handkerchiefs, as they were injuring the birds' legs, and for a little while they went along quietly, until they sighted a troop of wildebeestes, when they stretched out their necks and were off at their best pace to join them. We then each seized one of the two wagon whips we had, and started after them. If the birds had been real wild ones and full-grown we might as well have started after an express train, for I never sat the horse that could run down a full-grown ostrich in a fair course ; but they were only three-parts grown, and had been domesticated on a farm since they came out of the egg, and they were really more indulging in gambols than making a serious attempt to join the wilde-beestes. Consequently, we succeeded in driving them back, but the performance was repeated fifty times during the day, and we had not a moment's rest the whole day. It was quite dark when we at length arrived at the river, and but for the assistance of the rest, who came to our aid, we should never have got them through. At camp we threw our-selves exhausted on the ground, and both declared that it was by far the hardest day's work we had ever done in our lives. The distance we had run after those wretched birds was certainly over fifty miles, and for the greater part of the distance we were cracking heavy wagon whips as well.

These ostriches were afterwards a source of end-

OSTRICHES ON A FARM.

less trouble to us. They grew rapidly, and developed great kicking powers, until they became sometimes positively dangerous, the dogs and the Kafirs coming in for most of their attentions. Their appetite was insatiable; we used to make large quantities of biltong, or sun-dried meat, and there were usually dozens of strips of it hanging on rheims slung from wagon to wagon, and these were always objects of attention on the part of the ostriches. It was most amusing to see one trying to swallow a strip a yard long and two inches thick, just as a chicken struggles with a worm that is a little too big for it. Once we had to drag a huge strip out of one of the birds' throats to save it from choking. But it was the culinary department that interested them most. They would always attack the Kafirs bringing the viands from the " kitchen " to the tent, and sometimes were so pertinacious that the boy would get frightened and throw the dish away and bolt, and we would lose the best part of our dinner. They would even come into the tent and snatch things off the table, and we would take it out of them by smothering a dainty morsel with salt and cayenne pepper ; but after a while they seemed to flourish on it. One day, however, we got the laugh on our side. Dinner was preparing, and one of the birds was investigating the pots round the fire ; a great pot of huge potatoes took his fancy, and he incontinently seized and swallowed a red-hot tuber as big as a large pomegranate. Then we roared ; the antics that bird performed would have galvanised a corpse into laughter. He danced, he jumped, he kicked, he twisted his neck about almost into knots, he flapped his wings and waggled his tail, he ran amuck, knocking things down and banging himself up against the wagons and stone walls, he hissed and swore—yes, swore—and at last tore away into the veld at twenty miles an hour, until he was out of sight, and did not appear again for a couple of hours.

Every morning, soon after sunrise, these birds would indulge in a dance. They would rush away into the veld for about a mile, and then suddenly stop and commence waltzing round and round in the most ridiculous fashion, often till they dropped. I never could understand the meaning of this performance ; it might be mere gambolling, but if so it must be nearly the only case of young birds playing, as so many young animals do. Their keen sense of sight has often been noticed, but it is not generally known that their sense of hearing is quite as acute, and if they were feeding two or three miles away, a few mealies (maize) rattled in a tin pannikin would suffice to bring them back.

Although not strictly belonging to this " picture," it may be as well here to relate the trouble and loss these birds afterwards cost. On my return to Grey Town from this trip, I had at once ridden back to Potchefstroom, news having been received that a friend was lying there ill with fever, contracted in the Marico country. I took him in his wagon to the healthy mountain country at Wakkerstroom, and then rode back to Grey Town. These ostriches had been left there, and as there was no enclosure to put them in, they wandered about the village at their will. They had developed a habit of knocking children down and sitting on them, and another habit of rushing right into a span of oxen as it drew a wagon through the village, and craning their necks over them, flapping their wings, and frightening them to death, and they also frightened ladies when out riding. Consequently the magistrate ordered me to remove them from the village, and I therefore determined to take them to one of C.'s farms on the Drakensberg, near Harrismith, where there was a large sod-wall enclosure. The distance was about 150 miles, and I was rather uncertain as to how they would travel by themselves. We had brought them down easily enough, as we had a large mob of cattle, horses, and sheep, with a few tame bucks, and they kept with these animals quite naturally and only once went off by themselves; but I felt that driving them alone would be quite a different thing. However, there was nothing else for it, so I inspanned a wagon and started off with them. I had travelled about fifteen miles, and was proceeding along a cutting having a deep slope about two hundred feet deep on the left hand, when I perceived a Boer wagon approaching from the opposite direction. Mindful of the habit of the ostriches of craning their necks over oxen in yoke, and thus frightening them, I rode forward and asked the Boer to draw his wagon up against the inside of the cutting. But this he refused to do, saying that he had known all about the habits of ostriches long before I was born; and as I could not make him, I had nothing

else to say but to disclaim all responsibility. I
therefore put the birds behind my wagon and proceeded, and there they marched in their solemn,
stately, stupid, insolent fashion, looking to the
right and to the left with their piercing, unintelli-
gent eyes. Presently we came up to the Boer's
wagon, and then commenced the usual game—the
oxen got frightened, and went off at a run ; the
women and children inside screamed, and scrambled
out behind ; the Boer swore abundantly, and
threatened me with the pains of damnation ; the
foreloper (leader) threw away his touw (leading
rope of hide), and the wagon tore along, rolling
from side to side like a boat in a chopping cross
sea. Presently it approached too near the edge and
lurched over ; the disselboom broke short off, and
down rolled the wagon over and over, until it
landed at the bottom a shapeless mass of splinters.
Damages in the county court afterwards £15, which
was about a quarter the actual damage done. Two
mornings later when I turned out of the wagon, the
ostriches were *non est*. I scoured the country round
about for two days in heavy rain, and then found
them in the custody of a farmer, whose garden they
had destroyed. Damages £10. A day or two
afterwards we came to the Mooi River, and on
approaching it I noticed that a wagon stood
inspanned on the hither side, as if waiting to cross.
I walked down to the drift to see if the river was
fordable, and found there the owner of the wagon

watching a Hottentot whom he had sent across on horseback to test its depth. I stood with him until the Hottentot was nearly back on our side, when we suddenly heard a shriek behind, and turning round there were those infernal ostriches at their old game of craning their necks and flapping their wings over the oxen in yoke, which were just starting off at a canter towards a bend in the river. To rush into the water, drag the Hottentot off his horse and spring into the saddle, was the work of an instant, and I was not a moment too soon. The oxen made straight for the bight of a sharp bend, and when I galloped in front of them and seized the foretouw and turned them they had not fifty yards to go to plunge right over the high perpendicular bank into the river. The sudden turn very nearly capsized the wagon, but fortunately it recovered itself, and the only actual material damage done was the breakage of one or two yokes-keys. But to one of the ladies inside the result was premature delivery. The owner of the wagon was a former President of the Orange Free State, and the lady was his wife. He threatened me with dire consequences, and I believe consulted his solicitors, but these gentlemen must have advised him that premature delivery was not in the eye of the law a wrong that could be commuted by damages, for I heard no more about it. I made up my mind, however, to take those birds no further, for it was pretty clear we should all be clean ruined in damages before I got to Harrismith. I therefore sold them to a neighbouring well-known stock-breeder, who opportunely appeared upon the scene, and they formed the nucleus of the first ostrich farm in Natal. Three of them were males and four females, as I found by this time. When very young it is almost impossible to tell the sex, but as they grow old the scales on the front part of the legs assume an orange tint in the males, and a pink one in the females ; the differentiation in the plumage does not occur till later.

To return to our camp. While C. and myself had been away one of our Kafirs had found an ostrich egg some miles away, and on each succeeding day he brought another from the same spot, proving that there must be a troop of the birds somewhere in the neighbourhood, as it is well known that several birds invariably lay in the same nest. One day, therefore, we all turned out on horseback to find them, and hunt them in the Dutch manner. This is to make an extended circle round them, and gradually close in so that when the birds try to break out they would generally be within shot of at least one of the circle, and could, as a rule, be driven back before getting through the line. We had mounted four of our " boys " as well as ourselves, and when at length we sighted the ostriches, of which there were five, we spread out in a long line 500 yards apart, so as to drive them towards the river where it made a curved bend. When the line was completed, the signal was given from the centre to advance at a walk, the birds being about three miles in front of us. They apparently took no notice of us, but commenced moving slowly away from us, feeding all the time, which was exactly what we wanted. Occasionally the largest one raised his head and examined us, but always appeared reassured. Soon the signal was given to break into canter, and then the birds began to realise their danger, and to run hither and thither, one in one direction and another in another. The largest male tried to run the blockade between C. on the left flank and R., his right-hand man. It was a fine sight to see the great bird, with his glossy black coat and snow-white wings and tail, tearing away with a speed that seemed to defy stopping, his legs working like the spokes of a rapidly-revolving wheel, and every stride leaving his last footmark twenty or more feet behind. But . C. was equal to the occasion, and spurring hard, he pulled up with a jerk, and then I saw a puff of smoke and the noble bird fall in its stride, nor did it rise again. It was a fine shot, for the ostrich must have been travelling at nearly twenty miles an hour ; and large as they appear, there is not really much to hit in them. H. at the right flank then rolled over a female which tried to escape between himself and the river ; and only three were left. Of these one, a female, got over the river, which was shallow, and the two last, a male and female, tried to rush between the two Kafirs on my right.

I had seen their manœuvre, and spurred away to
where they would reach if they broke through.
This they did, for both Kafirs missed clean, and
I had an easy shot at fifty yards at the male; I
might have killed the female also, but I let her go.
The birds were in fine plumage, and the feathers of
each male were worth at this time from fifteen to
twenty-five pounds.

I made two more trips from this camp, one with
C. to Heidelberg and the Suiker Bosch Rand,
where we found many fine farms with magnificent
orchards, where the stones of the peaches that had
been allowed to drop off the trees lay two feet deep
on the ground, and this notwithstanding that every
Boer cut up and dried immense quantities every
year. We did a big trade in ostrich feathers and
cash here. It was not my first visit to Heidelberg,
which then consisted of not more than a score of
houses, and we made no stay. On our return the
only lion seen on the trip made his appearance one
night, but on C. putting his head out of the wagon
and yelling it turned tail, and disappeared before
we could get a shot. The other trip was in company with R. and N. up the Wilge River, where
we also found many well-to-do Boers, and traded a
number of fine oxen. There were many vleys and
small lakes in this part of the country, and the
number of aquatic birds was astonishing. Flamin-
goes were especially numerous, and there were
several varieties of the crane, including the lovely

mahem or crested crane, and the great bell crane ; there were also ibises, golden and Muscovy geese, and ducks of many varieties, as well as coots and other birds. But the most beautiful of all was a lovely white egret, with a few wing and hanging crest feathers of delicate fawn. It is not easy to make anything like a bag on these open vleys, as there is no cover under which to approach, and it is rare to get more than right and left shots ; but nevertheless I succeeded in getting specimens of most of these birds. One day we witnessed a curious scene in one of these vleys. It had got very low and shallow, and a party of Boers were marching through it in line armed with sticks, with which they were lashing vigorously about them. We found that their quarries were the yellow-fish, a fish averaging one to three pounds, which swarms in these pieces of water. As they killed them with their sticks their Kafir servants behind them gathered them up into sacks. In this way several sackfuls were obtained, which they smoke for after-use ; they said they do the same every year.

It was up the Wilge River that I witnessed a scene I have always regretted. A large party of Boers, with, I am sorry to say, some Englishmen, had gone into the plains and driven a great herd of game, chiefly wildebeestes, but with blesbuck, spring-buck, quaggas, and a few hartebeeste, towards the river. At first I did not divine their intention, and joined them ; but I stopped and remained an on-

looker when I realised what they were really doing.
There was a sharp bend in the river, with perpendicular banks ten or twelve feet in height, and it
was into this they were driving the herd. When in
the bend the herd had the river with its high bank
on three sides, and a line of mounted men, who
shot them down right and left if they attempted to
escape that way, on the other. In this way the
whole herd not otherwise killed was forced over the
bank, to the number of many hundreds, if not
thousands, and lay at the bottom (for there was
very little water in the river) maimed, wounded, and
groaning, in some places a dozen thick, while a
fusillade was kept up from the bank at those which
were unhurt and were trying to escape up or down
the river. It was the most ruthless slaughter I
ever saw, not excepting a *hopo* I witnessed in the
Bechuana country the year following. When I first
saw the elevated plains of central South Africa in
1863 they were positively black with game, and in
many parts were still so at the time of which I
write, but it got thinner every year. It was killed
off by every conceivable device, and the amount of
shooting that was done can be imagined when it is
stated that any one with ordinarily sharp eyes could
in galloping over the veld, after the grass had been
burnt off, easily fill his pouch with bullets in an
hour, these being only the bullets that had *missed*.
At an isolated store we passed on this trip up the
Wilge River we saw 40,000 wildebeeste skins piled

up ready for transport, the result of about four months' trade.

On our return to camp it was determined to break it up, as it was now September, and the grass was beginning to grow fast. As we had been on very friendly terms with all the Boers for twenty miles round about, we thought we ought to give some farewell entertainment, and, after consideration, decided on a shooting match. Messengers were therefore sent all round, and on the day appointed some sixty Boers assembled. The entrance fee was a sheep, and there were about thirty prizes, the first of which was a valuable double-barrelled breech-loading sporting rifle, the second a very fine new saddle and bridle, and so on. The display of ancient and obsolete weapons at this shooting match was wonderful and awe-inspiring. Old flint guns six feet long, with a bore that would almost have received a pigeon's egg, and which had probably been wielded by Marlborough's heroes at Malplaquet and Blenheim, were numerous, and so were flint guns of later date, which had dealt death and destruction to the serried ranks of Soult and Napoleon; Brown Besses, quaint old-fashioned percussion guns of a size and weight that made it difficult to understand how they could be used effectively, and queer weapons of Belgian, German, and Portuguese make were used by Boers as queer and odd as the guns. A few possessed good English double rifles, and some half a dozen were the proud possessors of breech-loaders. I tried one of the oldest of the flint guns, which had a crown and the letters " G.R." on the connecting iron-work between stock and barrel, and was probably contemporary with George the First, and my admiration for the men who could continually carry and fire such instruments, and win great victories with them, was great ; its weight was immense, and being mostly forward, was the more felt, while its concussion was terrific. It was at this match that my faith in Boer shooting was first shaken. I had heard so much about it that I expected to see something wonderful ; but, as a matter of fact, the shooting was decidedly poor, and much of it downright bad. The targets were of canvas, eighteen inches square, and the distance 150 yards, and though none of the Boers shot without a rest, most of them using a chair, few bullseyes were made. We did not ourselves enter, but on trying afterwards, three of us beat the best Boer score. My after experience, which was considerable, confirmed my want of faith. The truth about the matter is this : at target shooting Boers are poor ; at wildebeeste and other game shooting on the open flats they are first-rate, having somehow acquired what must be regarded as quite a knack at it ; at large game shooting in the bush, notwithstanding that they have produced several tip-top elephant hunters, they are much inferior to the average English hunter, being neither so accurate, nor anything like so venturous. They shoot better than Tommy Atkins, for the excellent reason that Tommy is, by some mysterious dispensation, probably the worst shot in the world.

While this match was in progress one of our rascally wagon-drivers distinguished himself in a rather peculiar way. The fellow was an incorrigible drunkard, and no terrors could keep him from stealing grog whenever he got the chance. We had brought a cask of peach brandy from the Suiker Bosch Rand, and it stood in a corner of the tent; I took two or three Boers in to give them a drink, and on entering found that degraded tippler lying on the flat of his back with the tap of the brandy cask in his mouth, and the aromatic spirit gently trickling into his throat. He had just reached the point of unconsciousness, and had we not discovered him would have been choked or smothered. We forced some tartar emetic down his throat, and then had him taken down to the river and ducked, and then soundly beaten with sticks to prevent him becoming unconscious again. He was very bad for some time afterwards. This same fellow distinguished himself again during our return to Natal. He managed once more somehow to get drunk, and when in that state always got out his fiddle, and ground out his two tunes until he was sober again. He established himself under my wagon after I had turned in for the night, and notwithstanding my yelling at him scraped away until

I was half mad, and turned out and drove him away. It was raining hard, and I neither knew nor cared where he went; but when I put my head out in the morning I saw him sitting on an ant-heap about a hundred yards away, still scraping away at his fiddle, out of which the rain had long taken the last vestige of sound. I was so exasperated at his folly that I seized his fiddle and smashed it to atoms over his head.

We now broke up camp, and went south to the Rhinoster and Valsch Rivers, where we found some wealthy Boers, with some degree of refinement in their homes. A fine barrel-organ we had bought from an eccentric Englishman highly delighted the *fräuleins*, and helped us greatly in our trade. We used to play it after outspanning at a house, and everybody within hearing would at once troop down. We afterwards sold it to Moshesh, the great Basuto chief, and it helped to solace his declining years. This part of the country is much superior to the bare flats we had been in so long, where, except at the Suiker Bosch Rand, the high rocky ridges of which were covered with sugar bush (a *protea*, I believe), and one or two other trees, with aloes and kindred plants, and on the banks of the Wilge River, where willows grow, no trees or shrubs whatever were to be found. Here patches of mimosa bush were plentiful, and were well stocked with guinea-fowl, francolins, hares, steinbuck, and duiker. Here, too, we found sand-grouse, quail, and korans (lesser bustard) of three different species. The harsh cackling of the black koran is one of the features of South African travel. Near Rhinoster Kop, a conical hill rising by itself out of the plain and covered with mimosa bushes, which was once famous for the number of rhinoceroses on it, we saw the extraordinary number of about one hundred and fifty pauws (great bustards), ordinary and crested, all at once. These huge birds, which sometimes attain a weight of more than sixty pounds, were at this time fairly common, but I never before or since saw anything like this number. They are wary birds, and not easily killed, except by long shots with the rifle, though it is sometimes possible, by circling round one and gradually contracting the diameter, to get within shot.

We got rid of all our goods among the Boers on these rivers, and proceeded up the Valsch River to Cronstadt to make final preparations for returning Natalwards. This river owes its name (False) to the fact that instead of widening out on its onward course, it narrows, so that while at Cronstadt it is over eighty yards wide, near its confluence with the Vaal River it is little more than a ditch, but very deep and rapid. At Cronstadt, a bright little town, we divided, H. and N. going back on our tracks to collect stock left on farms on the Wilge and Klip Rivers, and the rest of us proceeding by way of Winburg to Harrismith. We had with us more than a thousand sheep, two hundred head of

VAN REENAN'S PASS OVER DRAKENSBERG; INTO ORANGE FREE STATE.

cattle, and sixty horses, and some tame wildebeestes and bucks, besides the ostriches, and our cavalcade looked quite patriarchal. On our way to Winburg we lost thirty-eight sheep in a very mysterious manner. They were always counted, night and morning, and one morning this number was missing. We scoured the country round, but could find no trace of them, and what was stranger, could find no spoor. At first we thought that the thieves were wild dogs, those rare and curious animals which hunt in packs, and go straight through the country killing everything they come across, but as no carcases were to be found this theory was discarded. They might have been frightened by lions, hyenas, or jackals, but this was doubtful, as they would not have travelled so far away. My own opinion was that they had been driven off by some sneaking Boer, or wandering Kafir or Hottentot; anyhow, we never saw them again. We spent our Christmas by the side of a large water-pan swarming with aquatic birds, in a very desolate part of the plain. The whole country between Winburg and Harri- smith was deserted on account of one of the constantly recurring wars between the Boers and the Basutos; and the game had it all to themselves. We passed several deserted farms, and requisitioned large quantities of fruit and vegetables from the orchards and gardens. One day we nearly lost our ostriches. A troop of about a dozen wild ones appeared a few miles off, and ours immediately made off to join them. Then every one seized the horse nearest, slipped on a bridle, and, without waiting for saddles, sprang up and gave chase. It was a hard bit of riding, but we eventually succeeded in turning them, though more than once I thought we should have lost them. Had they been able to join the wild ones we should never have seen them again.

We reached Harrismith early in January, and the sheep were placed on a farm C. had near at hand. C. and myself then left for Grey Town in a dog-cart, leaving the others to follow with the rest of the stock. And so ended a most enjoyable eight months' trip.

THERE are probably men still living who can remember when Natal was the finest hunting country in the world. With the exception of giraffes, about which I am not certain, and of sable antelopes and gemsbucks, every species of South African game abounded in various parts of the country. The spot on which Durban now stands, and the surrounding hills now known as the Berea, where most of the well-to-do people of the city reside, was one of the most favourite resorts of elephants, and their paths could be seen in the Botanical Gardens as late as 1870. Indeed, I believe that wild elephants had been seen in the streets of Durban as late as 1855. In the interior they existed still longer, and had not entirely left the "Thorns" for nearly ten years afterwards. Lions were in the Colony certainly as far on as 1870, as well as buffalo, and though I have never myself come across either actually within the boundaries, I have more than once seen the spoor of both. Wildebeestes, blesbucks, springbucks, and quaggas abounded in the winter in the Newcastle flats, and I have several times seen ostriches there. Rhinoceroses, blue wildebeestes, waterbucks, and roan antelopes had disappeared, but when I finally gave up African sport in 1875 most other varieties were to be found in one district or another.

It was in the so-called " Thorns " that the greatest variety of sport was to be had. The " Thorns " is an extraordinary sunken valley, two or three thousand square miles in extent, through which the Mooi, the Tugela, and other smaller rivers run. The whole of this valley is covered with dense bush, the hills enclosing it being open grass. The depth of the valley is from one to two thousand feet, and in many places the surrounding hills show perpendicular faces a thousand feet in height, and in all places the descent is exceedingly abrupt. A stranger riding along, say, the road from Grey Town to the Biggarsberg would be cantering along the fairly level summit of a high grassy ridge, which seemed likely to continue for many miles, when he would be suddenly pulled up at the very edge of a precipice, and in a single second would be revealed to him this wonderful and unsuspected valley, and he would stand gazing over a vast tumbled sea of forest far down below him, and in the blue distance the enclosing hills on the northern side. How blue the distances are in Africa, none can conceive who has not seen them. In Australia the same phenomenon has caused the chief range of mountains to be called the Blue Mountains, but the blueness of these mountains, as seen from the Liverpool plains below, is not to be compared to the blueness of African distances.

Standing here, close under the wild, rugged, rock-strewn mountain known as Bothas Castle, the spectacle is a truly extraordinary one. The valley is not flat, like that in the Amaswazi Country, or like the Kalihari bush as seen from

HOW A FAMILY TAKES A HOLIDAY HUNT IN NATAL.

the Shoshong Mountains, but is broken up into a number of low ridges, with one central rib of considerable elevation. Bush, bush, bush, nothing but bush wherever the eye roams, all aglow in blue and purple haze, and rolling away in great billows like an angry sea in the roaring forties. Ten steps down, and we are in another climate. Farewell to the fresh, bracing breezes of the grassy hills, and the life-giving mountain air; nothing now but dry,

burning, dusty heat. Farewell to the eye-soothing
grassy slopes ; nothing now but thick tangled bush
—mimosas, flat-topped, round-topped, pyramidal,
all ablaze with a gorgeous clothing of golden pink,
white, or occasionally scarlet knobs, filling the air
with an all too powerful sweetness ; euphorbias,
lifting aloft their strange, ghostly-looking arms,
some rugged and spine-covered, others round and
smooth as a pipe stem ; prickly aloes, some tall and
upright, others bushy and straggling, but all vivid
with bouquets of scarlet blossoms ; rough-trunked
"olives"; glossy-leaved wild coffee, bedecked with
scarlet berries ; thick juicy-leaved succulent plants
throwing out sprays of yellow and red flowers; and a
thousand and one varieties of flower and fruit-bearing
trees whose names I know not, all intertwined with
clematis, jasmine, ivy-leaved geranium, convolvulus,
and a dozen other flowering creepers. Lower and
lower every step, hotter and hotter every mile ;
until at the bottom we fairly pant for breath, and
the perspiration rolls down us in streams. As we
ride down we are immediately beneath a forbidding-looking perpendicular precipice, more than
a thousand feet in height, from which pieces of rock
of all sizes are continually falling and crashing into
the valley below. This is the home of hundreds
of enormous baboons, as large as chimpanzees.
Perhaps we might see one walking deliberately
across the road, supporting himself on a stick.
Great eagles also have their eyries among its rocks

and may be seen floating about at vast heights, dark spots upon the vaulted blue.

On the right distance is Mount Allard, 6,000 feet in height, conical and bush-clothed to its summit; the little gleam of white close to the top being a house built by a well-known half-bred East Indian. The stifling heat seems to agree with insect life, for the air is full of winged creatures of various kinds, from great dragonflies and huge gaudy butterflies to the tiniest midges and sand flies, while on the ground crawl thousands of black round centipedes, sometimes eight inches long and as thick as a finger, and many scorpions, tarantulas, and lizards. But all the life is not noxious. Brilliant birds of scores of species flit about, conspicuous among which are gloriously jewelled humming-birds and honey-suckers; guinea-fowl scuttle across the road in hundreds; francolins whirr from tree to tree; startled duikers, impahlas, and steinbucks bound across to the shady depths of the tangled thickets, and perhaps a bushbuck, or even a kudu, may be discerned scurrying away into the densest brakes. The leopard will not be seen, though there are plenty of them. On the streams are many sleek ducks and geese, and gigantic kingfishers hover about in search of prey.

It was to the Tugela that I used to go in search of adventure. Here a well-known character called Yankee Dan, an old Canadian lumberman, used to keep an accommodation house and canteen, which

20

was in reality only an exaggerated Kafir hut with a
door to it. Here I used to spend weeks, and had
many curious experiences. The second time I
visited the place I was nearly drowned. It was
dark when I arrived at the river, and by some
mistake I entered the water at the wrong place.
A freshet had come down, and the river was rather
full, and the young horse I was riding got frightened
and plunged about a good deal. As the bottom
was of smooth round boulders, the inevitable slip
came, and the horse fell over on its side. The
saddle was loosely girthed, and my weight as we
went over dragged it right round, so that as the
horse came on to its side I was underneath, with
my feet entangled in the stirrups ; and so we floated
down the river. I managed to keep my head out
of water, but in spite of all my efforts I could
not free myself. We went down in this way for
about a hundred yards, when fortunately the horse
came right up against a tall upright stone, which
stood, among others, in the middle of the river,
here about eighty yards wide, and marked the
end of the shallow water. Here I managed to
clear myself from the stirrups and stand upright,
when I found the water breast deep, and running
with tremendous force. The horse also recovered
his feet, and holding him by the bit we endeavoured
to work up stream to where the road came down to
the river, as I knew that the bank opposite was
perpendicular. Although we were not much more

than a hundred yards from the drift, such was the force of the stream that it took more than two hours to reach it, and more than once I thought I would give it up altogether, and let the waters close over me for ever. I shouted myself hoarse, but neither Dan nor any of his Kafirs heard me, and when at length I reached the road I was utterly exhausted and chilled to the marrow. However, a dry suit of clothes, and a copious libation of brandy and water, soon set me right; but ever afterwards I disliked crossing rivers in flood. Of course, to those who swim such an adventure would be insignificant, but few can realise the sensations of a man who cannot in the middle of a breast-deep, fiercely-running river, in which alligators are common and hippopotami not unknown, on a pitch-black night.

The sudden way in which these Natal rivers rise is very extraordinary, and I have known this same Tugela rise 25 feet in two hours. At such times they are roaring floods that nothing whatever could withstand, and I believe it to be a fact that once every bridge in Natal was swept away on the same day.

Dan kept a large number of fowls for feeding passing travellers, and the leopards troubled him a good deal, and carried off a great many of them. It was indeed to help him kill some of these leopards that I had come on this occasion. Unfortunately, I had lost my rifle in the river, but Dan had a

Snider carbine, the regulation arm of the Grey Town Mounted Rifles (of which he was a member, and I then Quartermaster), and an old shot-gun, besides his own favourite shooting-iron, which was a double, one rifled and one smooth. After my work in the water I did not feel inclined to turn out that night, but the next night we took up a position under a tree, from which we commanded the whole roof of the fowl-house. We lay for a long time perfectly motionless, while occasional flashes of lightning illumined the distant horizon, and at last a few drops of rain began to fall. I was for resuming my bed, as a long day's buck and guinea-fowl shooting had made me sleepy, but Dan gave no indication of a desire that way, so I lay quiet, and soon it began to rain hard. About half an hour after the commencement of the heavy rain I felt Dan's hand placed on my arm, and gently squeeze it, and at the same time the fowls began to cackle and flap their wings. Still I could make out nothing, the darkness was so intense, but I could distinctly discern the straight line of the roof of the fowl-house against the clouds, unbroken by any foreign body on it. The dogs now began to bark, and I thought it was all up, but still Dan lay motionless, and kept so for a quarter of an hour, the dogs barking and the fowls cackling the whole of the time. The rain fell lighter, and presently left off, and we both sat up, it being probable that the leopards were working on the other side of the

roof, but presently I could distinctly see a rounded
form breaking the line of the ridge. I raised my
shot-gun, which was loaded with loopers, but Dan
again touched me, which I took to be a signal to
wait a little longer. Presently a break in the clouds
occurred behind the fowl-house, and by the light
thus given I could distinguish a long taper thing
hanging over the end of the further side of the
gable, which I concluded to be the tail of another
leopard. We now got impatient, as we were afraid
the leopards would soon finish their work and get
inside, so Dan whispered in my ear that he would
creep round to the other side, and I was to fire at
the one on my side when I had slowly counted
three hundred. He then left me, progressing on
his stomach, while I sat with my back to the tree
slowly counting. At two hundred and ninety I
covered my leopard, and just as I reached three
hundred I saw the flash of a discharge a little to the
left of the shed, and simultaneously I pulled my
trigger. I was on my legs in a twinkling, and
re-loaded as hastily as I could. The leopard had
disappeared from the roof, and I heard it fall to the
ground with a dull thud, and the two of them were
now snarling and caterwauling in fine style. It was
an exciting moment. It was so pitchy dark that I
did not care to approach, as I did not know how the
animals were wounded, so I shouted to Dan to keep
quiet, as I would run to the house and fetch a
lantern. This I did as quickly as I could, and on

my return I found my leopard half lying and half sitting up, and yelling away like a whole colony of cats with their tails cut off. When I approached he hissed and snarled at me, and attempted to paw me, but did not alter his position, and I at once perceived that what I had taken for his shoulder was his hind-quarter, and that I had broken the spine just in front of the quarter. This being so I knew he was safe, and went round cautiously to look for Dan, but could nowhere find him or the other leopard. Presently I heard a whistle a little way in the bush, and hastily made in the direction. Dan said he thought he had broken the leopard's shoulder, and had heard it creep in this direction, but thought it had now lain down. With the aid of the lantern we found a copious bloodspoor, indicating that the lungs had probably been touched. We followed it for about fifty yards into the bush, when Dan said he heard the leopard breathing, and holding the lantern high we saw the animal crouching in a bit of scrub not five yards from us, its eyes flashing, and its teeth showing. It appeared as though about to spring, but as I held the lantern up Dan gave it a settler in the head, when we returned and killed the other in the same way. After all, therefore, the adventure proved a very tame one, and no less tame was some more leopard shooting we had the next day. We went down the river in Dan's boat, our objective being a hill about two miles down on the other side, where he said

there was a regular colony of these animals. No
word can depict the beauty of the Tugela in this
deep reach. It is a veritable gem in the way of
river scenery ; everything that goes to make up
riverine beauty was there—tall, graceful reeds, hung
with the nests of weaver and tailor birds ; flower-
covered shrubs and bushes ; great overhanging
trees ; open patches of vividly green buffalo grass,
where guinea-fowl, impahlas, and duikers might be
seen feeding, and, occasionally, between the trees,
glimpses of the mountains in the distance. The
quantity and variety of the bird life was extraordinary, perhaps the most striking feature of which
was the great kingfishers, large as falcons, and
speckled like guinea-fowls. As we paddled down
stream we saw several small bucks, but took no
notice of them, until a fine bush-buck ram was seen
drinking under some tall reeds. This temptation
was too great to be resisted, for these bucks, large
as they are—and they have been killed weighing
four hundred pounds—are very difficult to find,
usually hiding away in the densest thickets. A
lucky shot brought it to the ground, and we got it
into the boat, which was a big clinker-built tub used
as a ferry boat. We landed opposite the hill we
intended beating for leopards, and made our way up
a dismal kloof where the tangled bush was almost
impenetrable, but soon came out on to more open
ground with great rocks scattered about among the
bush. Higher up the hillside absolutely stank of

leopards, but we beat about a long time before we could find one. At length one of the Kafirs with us said he saw something creeping through the long Tambouki grass to the left. Without waiting to think what would be the best course to pursue, I made a rush in the direction, and then saw not ten yards from me a beautiful leopard creeping rapidly away on its stomach. Just as I caught sight of it, it quickened its pace into a long, low canter, but a bullet from my carbine caught it at an angle behind the ribs, and came out at its chest. No feline creature could stand a shot like that, and it sprang into the air, fell on its back, clawing convulsively for a second or two, and stretched itself out dead without a sound. We found no more leopards, but killed a bush-buck doe, a duiker, and about forty guinea-fowl.

I did not, however, always find the Natal leopard such an easy, harmless prey as' on these two occasions. At a hunt on a farm in the Riet Vlei district, one of these animals was driven unwounded into a sort of cave in a rocky krantz, the entrance to which was low and narrow. Several bullets were fired into it without effect, and the rest abandoned the chase, but being young and foolish at the time, I thought I would creep in a yard or two and try if I could see anything of it. My body-Kafir followed me as I crept along with my rifle, but we had not gone more than five yards, when, from somewhere or other—I never could under-

stand where —the leopard sprang at me, and got
my right elbow in its jaws, its paws being curled
over my arm on both sides.   All I could do was to
dash my left fist in its face once or twice, when the
Kafir behind put his gun over my left shoulder into
the animal's ear and fairly blew its head to pieces.
As I had on a leather coat the scratches were
trifling, but erysipelas ensued on the bite, and my
arm swelled to a prodigious size, and discharged
astonishing quantities of matter.   Although this
took place nearly thirty years ago, I still bear the
teeth marks.

When I left the Tugela to go to the Transvaal,
a trip in which I rode more than 2,000 miles in
three months, Dan said he intended making a small
raft after the fashion of the Canadian lumber rafts,
and making a trip down the river before it assumed
its lower winter level, and asked me to join him.
This I promised, and duly put in an appearance.
The raft was made of logs joined together by
withes inserted in holes in the ends of the logs, and
kept in their places by pegs.   It was about 18 ft.
by 8 ft., and at the after end was a small raised
platform covered with a tent for sleeping in.   A
rough kind of rudder or broad-bladed sweep was
rigged up for steering round the sharp curves.
Provisions, arms, and ammunition were stowed away
in the tent, and we prepared for a start.   Several
hundred Kafirs had assembled to see us off, but our
start was not very dignified, for I pushed the after

end out too far, and the stream caught it and brought
the whole catamaran, as we called it, broadside to
the downflow, and then we whirled round in sweeping and jerking circles, to the intense delight of the
sable spectators, who testified their appreciation of
the humours of the situation by a deafening chorus
of guffaws and " Waws," accompanied by a torrent
of voluble exclamations and a marvel of excited
antics. However, with paddles, poles, and rudder,
we soon righted her, and went swimmingly down
the stream. Everything looked favourable for a
successful and enjoyable trip. The weather was
beautiful, the catamaran behaved admirably, the
water was clear, and there was little chance at this
season of a surging rush of flood. The only thing
that troubled us was the thought of the numerous
rapids we should have to shoot, as we stood a good
chance of being jerked off in case of a bump against
a boulder.

We did not go far the first day, as we had started
late, and before sundown we moored our craft to a
tree, and sent our Kafir ashore to make a fire and
cook the supper. The next morning we started
afresh, this time successfully. The scene was continually changing ; now we would be in a long, still
reach ; then under gloomy walls of blackened rock
intersected with white and gleaming quartz veins,
and slimy with dripping moisture and mossy
exudations. Anon we would pass out into more
open country, where here and there clusters of

Kafir huts nestled in a kloof at the end of a furrow, or stood alone in a large clearing on a rounded hillock. It was in these open places, where the river widened out in gently shelving banks of boulder and shingle, terminating in narrow level swards of velvety grass, that the rapids occurred. In shooting these, Dan and the Kafir, who were heavier and stronger men than myself, stood forward with poles, one on each side, to sheer off from any prominent boulder, while I managed the rudder. Our craft usually passed them admirably, sometimes bumping heavily on a large stone, which, however, had no other effect than to stagger us and wet our feet. But sometimes the river took a bend among these rapids, and then it became exciting. More than once it was touch and go, and only the frantic exertions of the polists saved us from catastrophe. However, there were not so many of these places as I had anticipated, long, smooth reaches being more common. We did not hurry ourselves, but landed repeatedly to do a little shooting or exploring, or to make acquaintance with the Kafirs and purchase amasi and other native delicacies.

On the evening of the second day we came to a slight fall, which, though only a few feet in height, was too much to shoot in safety, so that we had to do a little porterage. As to our ship, we fastened two long ropes to it, fore and aft, and then pushed it out into the river, following its course on the bank. It took the fall in fine style, without the least damage, and we determined to stick to it at the next one. The next day we passed the confluence of the Mooi River, where the scenery was very fine, and then, after passing between high walls of rock, we opened out into a wide valley, where the Buffalo comes down from the north, and mingles its waters with those of the Tugela. The river takes a great bend here, and widens out into a long course of rapids, and then flows in a long straight reach between high bush-clothed hills, until it is lost in the blue distance. We camped opposite the mouth of the Buffalo, just in front of the bend and the rapids, having the towering Mount Allard before mentioned behind, and a frowning wall of quartz-streaked black rock in the Zulu country in front. At night we took up a station on a rocky ledge overlooking the head of the long reach, to wait for sea-cows, or hippopotami, but none appeared during the three hours we remained, though in the morning the Kafirs said they had been heard blowing during the night. Consequently, the next morning we climbed the southern precipice to reconnoitre, and after much scrambling over rough rocks and through tangled bush, reached a point many hundreds of feet above the river, from whence we had one of the most glorious views I ever saw in any part of the world. Grand as it was, though, we saw something else which in those days made my blood course more fiercely than any scenery could. This was two or three tiny puffs of spray

RAPIDS ON THE TUGELA RIVER.

rising from the surface of the water, and, a little lower down, several black spots on the shining river. We knew these to be heads and blows of Behemoth, the mighty river horse. We could not descend the perpendicular face of the great cliff on which we stood, and therefore proceeded a couple of miles down, where we with difficulty managed to reach the water's edge. The sea-cows were now a good deal above us, and it became a question how we were to get up, as the cliff came sheer down to the water, which was of great depth. There was a small rocky promontory nearly opposite where we had last seen them, and by clinging to the face of the cliff, and working along little ledges, we managed to reach it, and took up our stations behind a rock to await events. Soon three or four heads appeared a good deal above us, and we were about to make our way up, when, not twenty-five yards from the end of the rocky point, a concentric ring of waving ripples appeared on the surface of the water; then, in the centre, a pair of huge pink open nostrils were seen, followed by a long black face and forehead, and a pair of small slanting eyes. Then the face rose higher and assumed a slanting angle, the ears became erect and the neck was lifted out, and there was Behemoth gazing upon the world around, the sparkling water dripping from his brown, rugged, and shiny skin, his small delicate ears moving gently to and fro, and his powerful yellow tusks gleaming in the midday sun. This was too good an opportunity to be lost, and before Dan could prevent me, I had sent a bullet right into the light pinkish mark behind the ear. Then we started back in amazement. It was as though there was an earthquake ; the waters opened before us in a huge cavernous hollow, and a mammoth mass of brown shot forth from it high into the air, lightly as a cricket ball, and fell back with a surging roar, causing rolling waves to chase each other far and wide, and covering us with spray. Then the waters were lashed into whiteness by a Titanic struggle, flashing visions of enormous extended jaws studded with great lumps of glistening ivory, and of gigantic writhing body and great sturdy legs, caught the eye, and then all was lost in a bubbling whirlpool, and the river flowed on in smooth and peaceful calm, telling nothing of the tragedy that had sullied its waters.

We left our Kafir to watch for the rise of the body, and then worked up stream again, and with much difficulty got clear of the cliff, and reached a little sandy spit, on which we saw the fresh spoor of a kudu. Dan went on to camp, but I determined to follow the spoor. It led me up the flat towards the foot of Mount Allard, but I soon lost it, and was making campwards when on the bank of a tiny trickling rivulet I suddenly saw one of the prettiest sights it was ever my fortune to behold. There was a sparkling stream, a fringe of graceful

reeds, a pink-flowered mimosa, and, in front, a
grand kudu bull, with magnificent horns, cooing to
a couple of large-eyed does. It seemed a pity to
spoil this idyllic scene ; but, alas ! the sportsman
has no soul, and the bull fell to rise no more. The
does were too startled to retreat, and stood for
several seconds gazing in distress at their dead lord,
and I am glad to say I respected it, and left them
alone.

The next day the sea-cow rose to the surface,
and was dragged up-stream to the spit of sand, and
hundreds of Kafirs came from all round to join in
the distribution of meat. While the dissection
proceeded I crossed into the Zulu country under
the guidance of a native, who said that there was a
small troop of buffaloes not more than five miles
away. We had a rough two hours' walk through
a lot of very dense bush before we found the spoor,
and then a long hunt before we at last came upon five
buffaloes in a thicket of trunkless thorns. These
were the first buffaloes I had ever seen, and my
ignorance of their habits very nearly cost my guide
his life. I had wounded the largest, and then
ordered the Zulu to take up the blood-spoor, I
following behind him. He evidently did not care
for the job ; but as I did not then know much of
the language, I could not quite understand why. I
soon found out. I was about six or eight yards
behind the Zulu when, without a sign of warning,
the buffalo rushed out of a dense clump of wattle-

like mimosas, and made a terrific charge at the
Kafir, which the latter only avoided literally by the
skin of his teeth. It was by sheer good luck that
I killed it by a snap-shot in the head, or it would
have fared badly with us. I afterwards knew that
it was madness to enter one of these thickets where
there are no trunks, and where the growth is so
dense that locomotion is difficult, after a wounded
buffalo. However, it was a good lesson which I
did not forget.

The next morning we prepared to renew our
voyage. I have already said that we were encamped a little above, but nearly opposite, the
mouth of the Buffalo, and that just below us the river
took a sharp turn, and ran for some distance over
a shallow stony bed. This shallow, or rapid, was
some three hundred yards in length, and the water
ran over the large stones, or boulders, with great
velocity ; it then widened out considerably, still
shallow and stony, and then passed on into the
long deep reach where we had shot the sea-cow.
Dan prophesied that it would be an awkward place,
and so it proved. Directly we were fairly caught
by the stream it urged us on with dizzy velocity
into the broken water, and carried us right across
into the surging eddies at the confluence of the two
rivers, where we paused for a second or two, as if
to gather strength for a fresh plunge. Dan and
the Kafir again stood forward, grasping, as it were,
the logs with their feet, and poising their poles in

readiness to sheer off in case of necessity, and I
took charge of the helm. Slowly she gathered
way again, and then, with a sudden bound, she was
lifted almost out of the water, and tore through the
rolling roaring shallows with a heave and a jerk
that threatened to dislocate the entire concern.
Then she swerved sharp round to the right, and,
" Hard over ! " roared Dan, and hard over it was.
But she did not answer, and Dan, who was franti-
cally trying to keep her head to the stream, got his
pole jammed between a couple of boulders, and in
an instant was thrown from his feet, and the craft
swept round to a broadside. Then she was lifted
over a line of boulders, and sweeping down the
rapid below, came against a half-submerged rock,
with a crash so tremendous that she was raised
partly out of water, and before we had time to
think we were all, with our possessions, in the river,
and the ship bearing away down-stream uncontrolled
and uncontrollable. The water was not a yard
deep, but before I could recover myself I was
carried some little distance down the stream, with
many a heavy bump against the rounded boulders.
Luckily my head escaped, and when I was able to
bear up I saw the others standing in midstream
looking half drowned, and lugubriously rubbing
their bodies and limbs. No bones were broken,
but we were badly bruised, and when we waded
ashore we sat down on a prostrate trunk and
looked at each other in comic dismay.

The catamaran had passed the shallows, and was calmly drifting down the smooth reach, and a number of Kafirs went after it. We paid little attention to them, as it was quite evident that our trip was over for the present, all our arms, ammunition, and supplies being at the bottom of the river. Presently we waded in to try and recover as much as we could, and got out all the guns, the portmanteaus, and some cooking utensils, and abandoned the rest. The craft we abandoned too, as it was impossible to haul it up-stream to Dan's place.

It was in this flat that, two or three years later, gold was discovered. A good many people set to work, but owing to want of knowledge on the part of those engaged it proved a failure, and a good deal of distress occurred among them, consequent partly on the poverty of those who flocked there, and partly from want of supplies, the place being almost inaccessible, and only to be reached by a very rough and steep bridle-path down the side of Mount Allard. On my return from the Zambesi early in 1869 I paid the spot another visit, and though nothing payable had been discovered, I am confident that the future will prove that payable gold does exist in the district. A rather curious sell took place in connection with this gold digging. A small parcel of quartz was taken to Grey Town, and, after being burnt, was crushed in an iron mortar in the presence of the leading residents. A little quicksilver was then introduced, and after the

CHARACTERISTIC VIEW NEAR GREY TOWN

quartz particles had been washed away the residue
was placed in an iron spoon and the quicksilver
evaporated. When it had all gone it was found
that the spoon was covered with a fretwork of
golden lines. The manner in which this metallic
matter was deposited was rather a surprise to some,
but in their ignorance they all accepted it as gold
from the quartz, and great, therefore, was the
rejoicing. A case of champagne was broached, and
success to the goldfields was drunk until the case
was empty. The next day the spoon was sent
round the village for inspection, and came into the
hands of a German lady, the wife of a storekeeper.
Immediately she saw it she exclaimed, " Oh, I can
do that," and she got an iron spoon, dipped it in
vinegar, and held it over the flame of a lamp, and
as soon as it became hot through, a golden fretwork, very similar to that upon the other spoon,
appeared. Then, from being unduly exalted, the
people went to the other extreme, and the enthu-
siastic shouter bemoaned the waste of his case of
champagne.

It was at the summit of the hill at the back of
Dan's place that I killed my only specimen of that
curious animal, the klipspringer. This is a very
small buck, with the habits of the chamois. It
inhabits the rocky summits of hills and mountains
throughout South Africa, making the most extraordinary leaps from rock to rock, and is an extremely difficult animal to kill. The curious thing

about this animal, however, is, that it is not covered with hair as other bucks—with the exception of the vaal rheebuck, which has a woolly coat—but with bristles, in every respect, even to the markings, like those of a young hedgehog. When I first saw the skin of one I would not believe it came off a buck at all, but insisted that it must be that of some rodent. The one I shot was pointed out to me by my Kafir, as I was skirting round the top of the hill, just under the summit krantzes, in search of rheebuck. It was standing at the extreme edge of the krantz immediately above me, surveying the surrounding scene. When I fired, the rifle could have been very little out of the perpendicular, and the bullet entered under the chest exactly between the forelegs, and came out through the spine, and the buck toppled over the krantz and came rolling to our feet with every bone of its body broken.

In these days there were many hartebeestes and some elands on the Noodsberg, and I had several fine gallops after them, and also got a few by stalking. I was always averse to killing elands after my early experience here. I have already, on page 22, given my reasons for this. It has always seemed to me to savour too much of murder, if merely viewed from the sporting aspect. The hartebeeste, however, tells quite another story, as it is a very game buck, and perhaps the fleetest in Africa. I believe it to be a moot point which is really the fastest; some say

JIM ROKKE'S HOUSE, AT ROKKE'S DRIFT. (THE CHURCH WAS BUILT AFTER HIS TIME).

the gemsbuck, others the oribi, others the springbuck, and others even the blesbuck. Of the smaller
bucks the springbuck certainly seems most built for
speed, and of the larger the gemsbuck ; but, in my
opinion, in spite of its awkward build, the hartebeeste can outstrip them all, if the ground is good
going. Its gait is most ungraceful, and to look at
it bobbing up and down, one would think that a
man mounted on a donkey could run it down ; but
the way in which, when it pleases, it can put a distance between itself and its pursuer, is astonishing.
On these high flats I was only once able to put
myself alongside a hartebeeste, and then only by
galloping hard down a long steep slope at the
imminent risk of my neck.

But I was not always the hunter in Natal. On
two occasions I was hunted, and once in a manner
such as I expect few have experienced. In both
cases the occurrence took place on the Biggarsberg.
In one I was returning from the Transvaal, and
about sundown had arrived near the end of the
Biggarsberg above Helpmakaar. At the edge of
the Berg, a few hundred yards away from the road,
is a long line of broken rocks, and as I rode along I
saw a number of moving objects on these rocks,
which I soon perceived to be great baboons. With
the high spirits of youth, I yelled and halloahed to
them, and challenged them to a race. As though
they understood me, they all set up a shriek,
bounded off the rocks, and actually came after me

in a body. This was more than I had bargained for, as I had never heard of baboons hunting men in this fashion. There must have been nearly two hundred of them, and I was for once totally unarmed, and they came after me at such a rate that I really thought they would catch me, as my horse was very tired, having done quite fifty miles on a very hot day. I dug the spurs into him, and forced him to his best pace, and it was not until we had galloped nearly two miles that I felt safe. I have never heard of a similar case to this. Had the creatures caught us they would undoubtedly have torn me, if not the horse as well, to pieces.

In the other case the pursuers were a herd of cattle, some three thousand in number. I was near the same place, but going in the opposite direction, and a dog had followed me from my overnight's resting-place. I had left the road, and was taking a short cut over the veld to a farm I wanted to call at, when I came upon this herd of cattle, and had to pass right through it. The cattle objected to the dog, and commenced chasing it, and then they tossed it, and had a regular game with it, tossing it from one to the other in the air as children would a ball. Then they began paying unwelcome attentions to myself and my horse, dancing all round us, and giving us playful prods with their horns. It seemed to me that I should never get clear of them, and when I at last succeeded, the whole herd gave chase in full cry, with their heads up and their tails

flourishing in the air. They kept this up for at
least five miles, the leading bulls never being more
than a few feet behind me. Had the horse stumbled
among any of the numerous meercat colonies, my

THE TUGELA RIVER FALLING OVER THE DRAKENSBERG ; THESE FALLS
ARE 2,500 FEET HIGH.

fate would have been sealed. Of course, I left the
dog for dead, as it seemed that he must have been
battered into pulp, but when I returned some weeks
afterwards, to my surprise I found him sitting sunning himself outside the door of his old home.

Natal possesses a great many very fine waterfalls,

that at Howick, 14 miles from Maritzburg, being probably one of the most perfect in the world. It is formed by the Umgeni River, which is here not more than 40 or 50 yards across in the winter, and 70 in the summer. The river plunges over a perpendicular precipice 320 feet in depth, into a fine bush-clothed ravine, or cañon. Except in the winter, when the river is very low, the water does not touch the face of the precipice, so that it presents a perfectly unbroken upright column. As the ravine is only two or three hundred yards across, a fine view is obtained from the opposite side. The descent to the bottom is easy, and one can stand within a foot or two of the column of water, and gaze through the mist up its shining surface. It is a fascinating sight, but the thud of the falling water makes the earth shake in an alarming manner, and the roaring is terrific. It is curious that while the flow of water is to the eye perfectly smooth and regular, the sound caused is a rapid succession of heavy thuds, like the working of the engines of a great steamer.

It is the Tugela Fall, however, which is the most remarkable in Natal. This is made by the river of that name plunging headlong down the Drakensberg Mountains. The height of this fall cannot be less than 2,500 feet, but it is not, like the Howick one, an unbroken one, but is a long succession of falls and cascades. Nevertheless, as seen from a distance of 50 or 60 miles, say from Colenso, it pre-

TUGELA FALLS.

22

sents the distinct appearance of being a regular, unbroken fall. I made an attempt early in my Natal days to reach the foot of this fall, and make my way up its side, starting from Dodds' well-known hostelry on the Van Reenans Pass road; but owing to the incessant rain, and the extra-ordinary number of roaring torrents that made a network of the amazingly broken, rockstrewn country at the foot of the great mountain precipice, I failed, and I believe it was some years before a successful ascent was achieved.

MY visit to these Falls, which have been well called the eighth wonder of the world, took place in 1868, and previous visitors have been Dr. Livingstone, W. C. Baldwin. Dr. Kirk, C, Livingstone, J. Chapman, T. Baines, H. Reader, Sir R. Glynn, Capt. Glynn, Capt. Osborn, J. Gifford, T. Leask, W. Horn, and one or two more. One or two Boers had also seen them.

My friend C., so often mentioned in these pictures, started early in the year for the Tati Gold-fields, and asked me to go with him, but as I did not care for that kind of work I declined. However, after he had gone I soon got tired of doing nothing, and therefore rode up to Potchefstroom, and thence to Rustenberg, where I heard that another friend was with his wagon on his way to the north. He was quite alone, except for his servants, and was glad of a companion, and we soon made the necessary arrangements. He did not exactly know where he was going, but was in search of sport wherever it was to be found. We therefore shaped our course for Shoshong, leaving it to chance to decide whether we should go from thence west to Ngami, north to the Zambesi, or east to Matabililand. We trekked through the beautiful Marico country, so charming after the uncompromising bleakness of the High Veldt that it seems to be another world. Indeed, I know of no other place where the 'change of climate and scenery is so abrupt and complete. I love the plains of the High Veldt, as they were in those days. The air was so pure and clear ; there was such a sense of elbow-room and freedom ; and the immense herds of game gave such delightful life to what would otherwise be but a desolate scene, that there was great fascination in them. Still, after a while one began to long for a tree, and to feel that there were other beautiful phases of nature not to be found within that vast and apparently limitless circle enclosed by the distant, and ever receding, horizon. And then suddenly to descend a mountain slope, and find oneself in a warm, soft, enervating climate, surrounded by a varied bush scattered with gorgeous flowers ; and to pass through orange plantations, brilliant with golden balls, and fields of coffee trees shining in the shimmering sunlight! The transformation is absolutely complete.

Across the beautiful Marico and Notuani rivers, still well stocked with game, although the elephants and rhinos, which were once so amazingly numerous on those rivers, had apparently disappeared, we passed through Kolsberg, and thence made for Butluami, a famous water-hole. We had with us a Hottentot driver who knew the country well, and besides other hunters had been with Baldwin and Hartley. We determined to avoid Shoshong, as it had a very evil reputation in those days, and an opprobrious name. There was also reported to to be a good deal of fighting between the respective adherents of Sikomo, Matjen, and Khama. We therefore kept to the west of the Mangwato capital, along a well-beaten road, past the water-holes of Lopipi, Mashue, and thence to Serotli. Although it was late in the season (August) these holes held enough water for our purposes. But at Serotli the bushmen reported all the holes ahead to be dry until Matuluani was reached. As this was quite 130 miles ahead, we turned off to the east and reached Kanne, and then struck north again. From this point the oxen were five days without water, until we reached a dry river-bed apparently running to the Maclutsi, where we got water by digging. We had but little ourselves, and on the third and fourth days our allowance was scarcely more than half a pint each ; on the fifth day we had not a drop until the evening, when we reached the spruit. As the heat was great the punishment was excessive, and only those who have undergone it can understand what it is. Perhaps the worst sensation is the swelling of the tongue, so that one can hardly shut the mouth.

To make matters worse we had continually to tramp alongside of the oxen to keep them up to their work. Some bushmen we met here said that there had been rain ahead, and that there was plenty of surface water in pans. This was most fortunate, as it enabled us to continue to the north, as we had made up our minds. Had we not received this news we should have had to make for the Shashi River and then to Matabililand.

The Bushmen guided us to a nice pan of rain-water, and we remained there three days to recruit, and bagged the first giraffe we had seen. We had no horses, as we could get no salted ones, and it was useless taking others, so that our hunting was very laborious work, this part of the country being very heavy and sandy. However, we had good sport, and before we got to the Nata River had killed giraffes, rhinos (black and white), gemsbok, and a roan antelope, besides buffalo and other commoner game. From the Nata we left the wagon spoor or "road" running due north, and turned off north-west to Metsi Botluko, where we camped for a week, and in one night shot three elephants that came to drink, one of which was a very good bull, with tusks of about 60 lbs. each. We also got a fine lioness here. At another water-hole, whose name I forget, about fifty miles north of Metsi Botluko, we remained another week, and got two more elephants, both of which we got by fair hunting in the daytime. One of them led me a fine chase of about seven miles. It was badly hurt and rested a good many times, enabling me to come up. At last it made a desperate charge, but a fortunate shot in front of the eye dropped it, and another fairly in the brain as it was trying to rise killed it. I was quite done up when I got back to the wagon.

From this pool we went east to the Gwai River, and had first-rate sport for three weeks, bagging almost every variety of African game, including my first sable antelope. The country here is very different to the desert to the west, being hilly and well watered, and game was very plentiful. Nobody seemed to have been there that year, as eastern Matabililand and Mashunaland were being opened up about this time, and all the hunters went in that direction. In November we inspanned again, and made across the desert to Daka. It was terrible hot now, and we made slow progress, but at the end of the month reached the stream, rather too low down as it turned out. We left the driver and one boy in charge, and with the other started on our tramp to the falls, which we judged to be about sixty miles off, but which proved to be at least eighty. The country began to get very rough, and the thick grass made it heavy going. On the fourth day we saw the tall white columns of spray, and on the evening of the fifth camped close to the goal of our journey. The atmosphere was very close and heavy, and everything very dank,

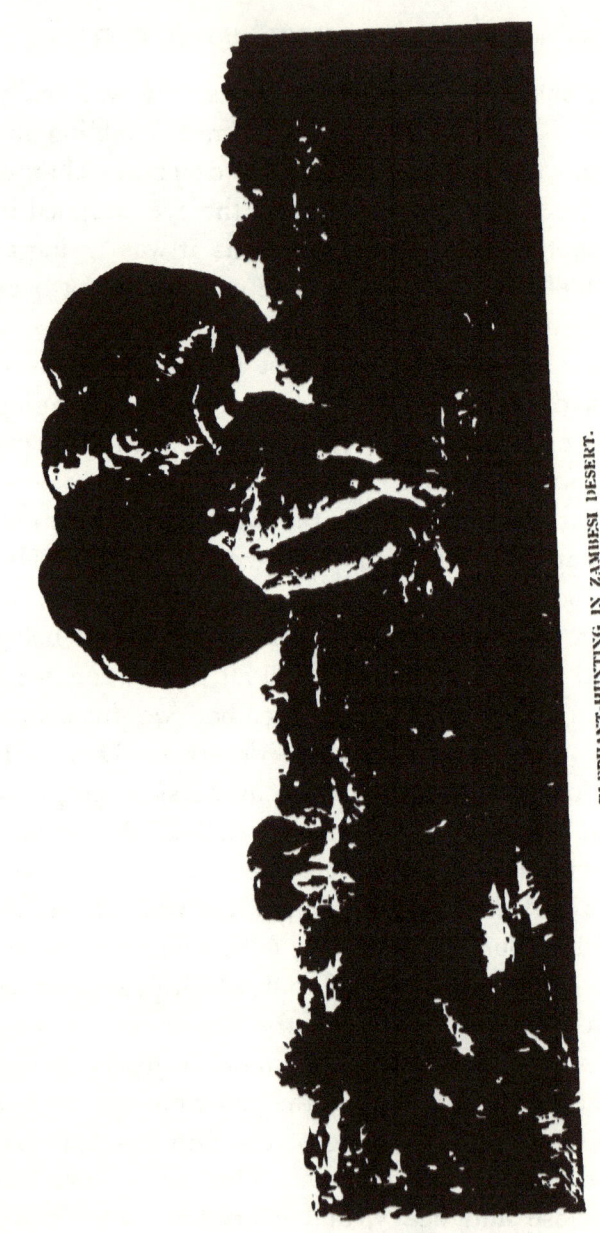

ELEPHANT-HUNTING IN ZAMBESI DESERT.

and we felt much exhausted, but were quite refreshed after a long night's sleep.

After a delicious breakfast of springbuck meat
shot the day before, and which was an animal we
never expected to see in these parts, we went to
take our first look at the eighth wonder of the
world. Our first view was from the westernmost
end, and from this point not a tithe of the whole
can be seen. What is there is, however, beautiful.
It is a series of lovely cascades rather than a fall,
with patches of dark rock standing out here and
there among the snow-white broken waters. When
the river is full after the summer rains no doubt
it presents an unbroken fall; but it cannot be
so beautiful then. At the risk of repeating what
every one knows, it must be said that the Victoria
Falls are unlike any other falls in the world. The
river does not fall over a mountain-side into a valley
below; it plunges into a marvellous slit in the
surface, right across the river's course, another slit
being continued through the country at right angles
to that into which the river falls, one slit opening
into the other at about two-thirds of the river's
width across. The depth of these slits is, as I
judged, about 250 feet, but I believe others give
different depths; its width varies from 100 to 400
feet. Thus the river simply seems to disappear
into the bowels of the earth; whereas it first plunges
into the narrow fissure across its course, and then
rushes through the other one, which I believe is

thirty or forty miles in length, and very serpentine in its course. These slits or fissures are cracks in the basaltic rock, how formed could not be said with certainty, except that water was not the power that operated. The cracks probably existed before the river assumed its present course, for, as far as I could see, there did not appear to be any continuation of the river's bed below the falls at the same level as that of the water above them. It would, however, require a much more careful explanation than mine to determine this matter. Indeed, the bush was so thick that no real examination was possible without following the slit a good way down. It ought to be said that the portion that crosses at right angles to the river does not lie north and south, but east and west, or nearly so, and that therefore the river has to take a turn to the south to fall into it.

Livingstone gave the width of the river above the falls as about 1,000 yards, but in this he was immensely out. Firing with a long Henry rifle, sighted to 1,100 yards, which was carried by our boy, the bullet was seen to strike the water a long way short of the opposite bank; and I judged it to be over a mile in width. Baldwin, I believe, reckoned it at 2,000 yards. This immense body of water, which, as it falls over the edge appears to be two or three feet deep, plunges into an abyss only 100 feet in width, and then the whole volume of it rushes into and through another of the same width. The turmoil may be imagined when a river a mile wide is suddenly contracted into one 100 feet in width. It has sometimes struck me that there must be a subterranean outlet for some of the water, because if a volume of water 5,000 feet in width, and three feet deep, is suddenly contracted to a width of 100 feet, it must be 150 feet deep. Certainly that is not such a tremendous depth of water, but when rushing along at a terrific rate its force would be so great that one doubts if even basaltic rock could stand it without being torn away by the mad impact; and yet, so far as I know, the outlet of this mass of furious water has not perceptibly widened since the falls were first discovered. Furthermore, by all accounts, the Zambesi is no wider in the Tete district than in that of Shesheke, although immense volumes of water are brought into it by the Gwai, the Sengwe, the Umé, the Sangati, the Uangwe, the Manyami, the Umsengesi, and other rivers on the south, and the Kafue, the Loangwa, and many more on the north.

I have implied above that there is no similar instance of a river being contracted in such an extraordinary manner. I was wrong, for I have seen two myself. In the Orange Free State the Valsch River at Cronstadt is a fine stream, as I have already mentioned well over 80 yards in width, but twenty miles lower down it is not 10 feet. A more remarkable case is at Waikato in New Zealand, which is like the Zambesi on a small scale, only reversed, the falls being at the end of the slit, instead of the beginning. When it leaves Lake Taupo it is a considerable stream crossed by a fine bridge, but it is soon forced into a gorge about 30 feet deep, across which I have jumped. In a mile or two the water rushes over the rock, forming the beautiful fan-shaped Te Huku Falls, into a lovely pool 150 yards across, and then continues its course at this same width.

The view from the western end is, as I have said, very much contracted, not only by the conformation of the abyss, but also by the great volumes of spray that arise from the bottom, and which in calm weather form columns ascending to a considerable height. There are in reality four or five of these, distinct from each other, but from this point only a confused mass is seen. It is, however, a charming scene. One stands looking down into a gloomy ravine, where at the bottom the surging waters are lashed into foam and spray, forming a turmoil whose leading feature is uncertainty of outline. On the left the snow-white slopes of water and dark patches of rock throw each other's characteristics into prominence ; and on the right rises a perpendicular wall of brown rock, crowned by a dense bush of varicoloured trees, whose leaves shine with the wet of the spray. All is wet and dank, as though there had just been heavy rain. Close by where we stand is a huge baobab, its swollen, bloated trunk steaming with moisture, and its ghostly arms spread out as though to warn one off.

To get the best view of the Victoria Falls as a whole, or, at all events, of so much of them as can be seen at once, it is necessary to get on to the wall of rock opposite the falling waters. This is really a tongue of rock, for the fissure which carries off the waters almost immediately after it opens out from the cross slit takes an abrupt turn to the west, and runs for some distance almost parallel to the line of the falls. Owing to the density of the bush and undergrowth, it is, or was then, impossible to walk along this tongue on the side of the falls, or in sight of them ; but nearer the further side there was a kind of path, made apparently by buffaloes. This was indeed a favourite resort for these animals, and they appeared to revel in the steaming atmosphere. It was certainly about the wettest place I ever got into. Every leaf and every blade of grass was edged as with pearls, and great drops formed at each apex, and at irregular intervals fell to the ground. The atmosphere was filled with tiny globules, so light that they floated about, and attached themselves to anything they came into contact with. Of course we were very soon wet to the skin, for although there was a path, still there was a great deal of forcing through the undergrowth, and the trees overhung it almost all the way. In about half a mile or more we suddenly came to the end of the bush, and found ourselves standing on the apex of the tongue. The sight here was truly marvellous. Facing the falls, which seemed almost within touch, to the right and to the left was a vast perpendicular mass of water, broken by one or two islands of rock on the edge, one of which, far to the left, was partly tree-covered. Columns of spray rose up white and steamlike, and a circular rainbow danced about to the left, half-way down the abyss. The falling water did not present a smooth, unbroken surface, but was corrugated in rounded columns and depressions, showing alternately dark and light effects that were very curious. In some places, where the rocky edge came nearer to the surface, it was beaten into snowy froth and spume. The thunder of a thousand guns pervaded the atmosphere, booming and thudding in irregular rhythm. The whole world seemed in a tremor. The water quivered and flickered as it fell. It throbbed and pulsated at the bottom, like the throbs of a mighty engine. The spray shimmered and whirled; rolling back and forth in great lambent masses; ascending and sinking; sometimes dense and heavy, and then fading away into diaphanous clouds, which as they spread themselves out were dissipated into invisibility. The gleaming rainbow to the left, although in reality stationary, seemed to oscillate in measured motions, as though softly dancing to the music of the pulsations below. The iron-bound rock on which we stood shivered as if its very foundations

were assailed by a furious convulsion. Even the
sun, as one looked up to it through the floating
vapours, seemed to have lost some of its immobility,
and to flicker in unison with the writhing of the
mist. Looking over the edge into the far depths of
the abyss the sight was appalling. The mighty
mass of water as it reached the bottom was beaten
up into a surging sea that would assuredly deal
destruction to any craft that ventured upon its
swashing surface. It was not a bit like the billows
of the ocean nor the surf of the shore ; nor did it
resemble the boiling of a volcanic pool. It was a
long strip of water lashed into frenzied fury ; dis-
traught and chaotic. There was no purpose in its
movements, no order in its fluctuations. Whirlpools
and eddies, vortices and billows, breakers and water-
spouts were mixed up into inextricable confusion.
As one looked down upon it the only thing one
could make sure of was the immensity of its unrest.
A surging billow, crested with snowy sud, was a
billow but for the fraction of a second ; before the
eye had fairly seized upon its being, it was trans-
formed into a vast vortex, whirling in eddying
circles, and lined with an unctuous facing of foamy
lacework. Then, almost before the vortex was a
vortex, it appeared as a hundred little pyramids of
greeny water, each throwing from its pinnacle a
cloud of frothy bubbles. And so changes revolved,
with a rapidity that defied the eye, and a diversity
that no words could convey. And with them all

23

went a sense of power and force that almost
made one's heart stand still with terror at its
stupendousness.

It was not so easy to look down into the outlet
and watch the waters escaping, because the rock
here sloped a little, and the edge was some distance
away. However, by careful scrambling the edge
was reached, and then was revealed below a rushing
stream whose velocity seemed incalculable. It
would almost appear that here, at last, the irresistible force had met with the immovable object ;
for surely nothing could resist the mad rush of that
torrent, and surely nothing could hurl that solid
basalt rock from its foundations.

It was all very beautiful, very wonderful, very
majestic, very awe-inspiring ; but also it was *very
wet.* Our enthusiasm began to get damper ; our
ardour had too much cold water thrown upon it.
We turned our backs to all its glories, and tramped
out of reach of the all-pervading spray. On the
way we shot a couple of buffaloes, and at camp we
stripped, wrapped ourselves in our blankets, built
a roaring fire to dry our clothes, and, impaling the
buffaloes' tongues on a couple of sticks, waited
patiently until they were nicely grilled.

The next day we went up the river to a village
or kraal, the name of which I have forgotten.
Here we obtained a canoe, and were paddled on
to the largest of the islet rocks on the edge. It was
ticklish work, and I did not much care about it ; but

the men who stood up, the one in the prow and the other in the stern, with long poles, seemed to know their work, and landed us safely through a good deal of broken water on the island. The view from this point is rather disappointing, and not to be compared to that from the opposite side; but we could see more of the eastern end, where the water falling over appeared to be deeper, and the fall consequently more solid. It was very fascinating to sit on a rock close to the edge and watch the waters falling over. Falling, indeed, is not the right word; the water slipped or slid over, as a man slides who slips on a snow-slope and slides leisurely before he attained any velocity. There was no hurry in it, and the sense of force was not so great as when watching the water fall perpendicularly.

We had heard of a tree on this island on which were carved the initials of Livingstone, Baldwin, and Glynn's party, but we could not find it. Probably it had been thrown down by the hippopotami, as the island appeared to be a common resort of these animals, which were numerous in the river, their heads being seen in considerable numbers near the northern bank.

Paddling back was hard work, and at one time the canoe seemed to make no progress at all. The thought of being carried over the fall down into that appalling abyss was far from pleasant. Nor did we desire to make near acquaintance with the sea-cows, who were quite equal to biting our canoe in two.

However, we got safely to shore, and the next day started back to the wagon. We encountered quite a large troop of elephants on the way ; but not having much ammunition with us we only fired a few shots at them, and failed to bag one. From the wagon we went on a regular hunt after the elephants, taking several bushmen with us as bearers. We travelled north-east to the Matietsi River, and were away nearly a fortnight, but only got four elephants, although we saw a good many. They were all, however, picked bulls, and had fine tusks. When not a great way from the Zambesi, near where the Matietsi joins it, we were much surprised to find, on the side of a low hill, and nearly overgrown with undergrowth, the skeleton of a boat with copper plates. Of course it was Chapman and Baines' boat, intended to take them to Tete or Quillimane ; but at the time we knew nothing of its history, not having seen Chapman's book, although we had heard of the expedition.

F. began to show symptoms of fever here, and we hurried back to the wagon. It proved to be a mild attack, and he was soon all right. It was now the end of the year, and rains began to fall, and as there promised to be plenty of surface water we shaped our way across the desert towards the Tamalukan. As it turned out, there was a good deal too much water, and as our driver, who knew the country, assured us that the Mababi Flats

would be inundated, we turned to the south, and
in due time reached Kama-Kama, and thence the
Maila ponds. I do not know why this desert is
so seldom traversed, for it presented no particular
difficulties, except in cutting away undergrowth.
True we met with nothing that could be fairly
called permanent water, although many of the
pools must hold water until quite late in the season.
But then, on the other hand, we did not particularly
look for any, for by noting the depressions in the
country we generally found surface water when we
wanted it. Game was fairly plentiful, but much
scattered, and our hunting was not very successful,
for we pushed on as hard as we could, sometimes
trekking nearly the whole of the night, as the
days were very hot. At Maila, both of us and
the driver as well were prostrated with fever, and
we had a bad time of it, as all our supplies were
pretty well exhausted. We did not want for meat,
for one of our boys was a capital hunter, and always
kept the pot full; but meat alone is poor food
for sick men. I ought to have said that we ate
our last loaf of bread and drank our last cup of
coffee before we left Daka, and we had not so
much as a pinch of salt. We found a tin of
desiccated potatoes, which somehow had been over-
looked, and there were two bottles of pickles, and
these constituted our variety from plain meat.

Maila is the place where, in 1860, Reader,
Lamont, and Burgess's three wagons were blown

up by an explosion of gunpowder, the last-named
and two Hottentots being killed. Only two wheels
were left, and many of the oxen and horses were
killed. Reader and Lamont, with Piet Jacobs, the
famous Boer hunter, were lying flat on the ground
by the fire at the time, and their recumbent positions
saved their lives. Reader made a cart with the two
wheels, and travelled back to Shoshong with it.

When we had shaken off the fever, we made for
the Botletli, and struck it near the great bend
which turns from north to west, or from east to
south, for this river runs both ways, the direction
of its course being determined by the height of
Lake Ngami. If the level of the lake is high
it flows east and south; if low, in the contrary
direction; that is to say, that if the lake gets
too full for the Teogi, which runs through very
level country and is therefore a sluggish river,
to carry off the water fast enough, it backs into
the Botletli from whence it came, and reverses the
course of that river, in which case the water fills
.up the Makarikari salt pans, and makes lakes of
them, until such time as the Teogi, or Okavango,
drains Ngami.

We trekked leisurely down the Botletli, having
good sport, although we only saw one troop of
elephants, out of which we secured three. A few
years before these animals swarmed all along its
course. The Botletli is a beautiful river, placid and
tree-lined, its immediate banks being festooned with

a variety of graceful rushes. There are a good many huge baobab trees on the banks, and one of them which had partly fallen down has been measured to be 162 feet in circumference six feet from the ground, and to be, therefore, the largest tree in the world. Although I am not sure that I have also seen the actual tallest tree in the world, for I do not think it is positively known (or, at all events, was not in my time) which claims that distinction, I have seen the bush which contains it in the Dandenong ranges in Victoria. Some of the eucalypti here are said to reach 600 feet in height.

Many of the baobabs on the Botletli and in other parts of Zambesia are carved with the initials of various hunters and traders. I wish I had copied them all, as they would have greatly assisted in compiling the early history of these regions, which can now never be exhaustively known. One at Ngabisani, on the western bank of the river, had quite a large number of names carved on it, dating back to 1851, two years after this river was first discovered. Many of the early martyrs of these parts have preserved their names in this way, as Rider, who died of fever at Lake Ngami in 1850; Maher, who was killed by some Baralongs in 1852; Wahlberg, who was killed by an elephant on the Teogi in 1857; Dolman, who died of thirst in the desert east of the Botletli in 1852; Robinson, who was killed by an alligator in that river in 1851;

Holden, who died of fever west of Ngami in 1862 ;
Pretorius, who died of fever near the Victoria Falls
in 1862 ; Bonfield, who was killed by an alligator
in Omaramba, Utoko, in 1861 ; and Burgess, who
was blown up as I have already described.

As I was again attacked with fever we left the
river and struck into the desert by way of Kubi
Wells, and made straight for Nchokotsa.   On this
part of the journey we came across a surprising
number of giraffes, and I shot a fine fat cow while
sitting on the wagon-box as the wagon was trekking.   Cow giraffe meat, be it said, is, after eland,
the best of all African game meats ; but at this
time of the year no meat would keep beyond
the second day, and we had therefore to kill
something every day or go without.   Fortunately
there was generally feathered game about the
water-holes—guinea-fowl and sandgrouse, and often
bustards, floricans, and francolins, otherwise pauws,
korans, pheasants, and partridges—yet, stay, were
all these there? alas, my memory fails me, but I
know some were.   At Nchokotsa we expected
our troubles to begin again, as between us and
Shoshong, more than 150 miles distant, lay perhaps
the worst portion of the great thirst land, with
less than six known permanent waters.   Our
driver had been over the road two or three times
before, and we left the route entirely to him,
and, in fact, put ourselves under his orders.
He entirely justified our confidence, and although

the oxen were two and a half days without
water south of Mathuluani, they did not suffer
much, as we trekked in the night. A couple of
lions followed us one night, but when we stopped
and outspanned for a rest of a couple of hours
we stood sentry over the oxen tied to the touw,
and were fortunate enough to shoot them both. On
the following day, however, we lost an ox, which
was killed by one of these animals, and although the
lion was wounded it got away. At Serotli we
turned off to the south-east to skirt the north-east
side of the Mangwato Mountains, and arrived at
Shoshong in February. We only stayed long
enough to purchase a few supplies from a trader
on his way to Tati, and then headed straight
for the Transvaal.

ALL Nature wrapped in a mantle of snow? Trees arrayed in glistening festoons of diamonds, and hedges like solid hummocks of alabaster? A great log-fire, rum punch, and ghost stories?

No; not one. A flat sandy desert, sparsely covered with prickly shrub, and specked with scattered clumps of acacias. A brazen sky, whose lower portions are dull ochreish reds, dirty lustreless yellows, and dingy slate-blues. A glaring sun, blazing down with a savage intensity that seemed to betoken that the end of the world was approaching, and that ere long it would suddenly flare up in one mighty conflagration, and then disappear from the universe of orbs as a drop of rain disappears upon the ocean. The atmosphere reeking with furnace-blasts; the sand under foot like a thin crust of *scoriæ* hiding volcanic fires; and everything dry, parched and crumbling, like a mummified land dragged out of the obscurity of a tomb and exposed to the light of day, and the breath of a living world. Not a drop of water in the whole region ; not a globule of moisture to be squeezed out of it ; but in the distance a flickering expanse of dry white haze, that distorted the stones into grotesque boulders, and the tall withered grass stalks into palm trees. Of native life there was none. The very chameleons and lizards were driven into the hollows of the tree trunks ; the great beetles saved themselves from being roasted by burying themselves under decaying leaves in the scrub ; and the ants retired deep into the cooler chambers of their dwelling-places.

And through this appalling Stygian shore crept a dilapidated wagon. Its canvas tent was hanging in ragged ribbons ; it wheels, wobbling from side to side on their axles, were held together with strips of green hide, which, bound all over them, held together the axle-boxes, the spokes, and the felloes, and bound the tires to the latter as well. It was drawn by twelve emaciated oxen, whose starred and scabby coats, hanging tongues, parched black and rough, and wild bloodshot eyes, told of prolonged deprivation of water. On the wagon-box sat a young man of three or four and twenty, clad in tattered shirt and moleskins, and raw-hide leggings still showing some of the coloured hairs of the gaudy zebra from which it came. His face, half covered with a short growth of scrubby beard, was thin and careworn, and his eyes betrayed the anxiety under which he laboured. From time to time he turned his head round to the interior of the wagon, and looked wistfully at the figure that lay upon the cartel covered heavily with blankets. Though the temperature was at least a hundred and ten inside, the teeth of the man thus swathed chattered in his head, as though he were deadly cold, and his whole body shivered violently enough to impart vibrations to the wagon. The oxen were led by a tall Maka-laka, whose bones looked as if they would be all the better for a thicker covering of flesh, and by his side walked a little pot-bellied Masarwa, from whose body hung a variety of mysterious things that to others than his own strange race were nameless and useless. The driver, a mongrel of Hottentot extraction, walked by his oxen and vainly tried with whip and with appalling expletives to en-courage them to a faster pace. It was barely more than a mile an hour, and when an ox fell in the yoke from sheer weakness, he turned to the man on the box and said : " Very hot now, Baas ; must outspan till night." " All right, Jacob," returned the other wearily, and got down to help. It was only ten o'clock in the morning, but the heat was terrific, and the oxen when released from the yokes, with the rheims left hanging to their horns, stood about moaning and bellowing in a manner pitiful to hear. They could not eat, but clustered round the wagon, licking the ironwork, and sniffing at the empty water-cask at the back. Four days had they been without water, and they would get none till the following day. Copious rains had fallen in the desert to the north, but in this peculiar part of it, as the wagon headed for the Botletli, it looked as though none had fallen for years.

And it was Christmas Day ; the time for feasting and rejoicing ! No feasting and rejoicing here ! I looked in the *vatje*, where I had put the last of the water for safety's sake to keep it for Fred, and there remained but about three pints. Of provisions there was absolutely nothing left in the wagon but a few sticks of biltong, as hard as wood, and as dry as tinder. Meal and coffee, and sugar, and tinned stuffs had all been finished before we left Daka, weeks ago, and no game of any kind had been seen for days past. As I examined the contents of the keg, the three coloured men regarded me with sullen expressions, and when I suddenly looked up and met their eyes I saw in them something very like menace. But I put my hand on my revolver in its case on my belt, as a hint that attempts on it would be dangerous. Then I took out of the wagon-box the little bottle of quinine, now nearly empty, and shook some of it into a spoon, stirred it into a little water, assimilating the two as best I could, and administered it to poor Fred, who, though still shivering violently, was now sitting up. Then I put the keg in the wagon-box, locked the padlock, and put the key in my pocket.

Fred lay down again and tried to sleep, and seemed to get a little better, for the shivering

ceased. For myself it was too hot to sleep, too
hot to do anything but sit and muse. Inside the
wagon, outside, or underneath seemed all alike.
The hot air grated one like a rasp as it went down
the windpipe into the lungs, and my tongue and
palate rattled against each other like pieces of dry
parchment when I spoke. I put a bullet in my
mouth and sucked it, to try and create a little
moisture, but with small success. As the day
advanced it seemed to get hotter and hotter, and
the atmosphere more and more like particles of
molten matter. And then my dinner hour approached—my Christmas dinner! I stood upon
the wagon-box and scanned the country round
with my glasses. Not a sign of life could I
discern, but a few loathsome *aasvogels* which had
descended mysteriously from the brazen skies and
settled on the branches of an adjacent camel-thorn.
They clearly seemed to have greater expectations of
a Christmas dinner than I had, for more than one
of the oxen was apparently at its last gasp. Should
I take my gun and try and get some fresh meat?
What was the use? If there was any living thing
in this parched-up desert it was as likely to be near
the wagon as far from it. Besides, the prospect was
grievous. To tramp through those burning sands,
after having had but half a pint of water a day for
three broiling days, on the offchance of dropping
across a wandering buck, and then having to carry
the meat back to the wagon, did not strike me as

KLIP DRIFT (BARKLY WEST) AND VAAL RIVER IN 1871.

the occupation for a joyous Christmas Day. Nor would the remaining water be safe from the boys if I went away. I could not send them, because they had been on their feet for many hours, and would have to tramp throughout the night.

There was nothing for it but the biltong. So I selected what appeared to be the juiciest strip, and sharpening my clasp knife on the disselboom, shaved it into the thinnest shreds I could. What a glorious Christmas dinner! One by one I put the dry shavings in my mouth, and slowly masticated them. My teeth and gums were sore from much eating of hard meat, and my tongue was dry and swollen. It was like eating sawdust, and the difficulty in getting the meat to travel down the gullet was extreme, and caused frequent violent coughing. I carefully measured out a quarter of a pint of water for each of the three boys and myself, leaving barely two pints for Fred. The Masarwa, who was our guide, declared confidently that with a long night's trek we should reach water early on the morrow, or I should not have encroached upon our little store even to this extent. How I longed for a tankard of foaming beer! Even a bottle of champagne—nay, a bucket of the foulest water ever issued by a London company would have been a gift from heaven; but it was towards beer that my thoughts particularly tended. Plum-pudding I hardly fancied, but for a big plate of tender sirloin, and a quart pot of

24

bitter ale, I would have given all my worldly goods.
As for poor Fred, he could barely eat half a dozen
of the thin shavings. He had had a little sleep, and
seemed decidedly better, but after a heavy sweating
was consumed with thirst. I gave him half a pint
of the water, but was obliged to refuse any more in
case of accidental delay.

And so the Christmas Day wore on. The pitiless
sun slowly moved down upon its course, and the air
got preceptibly cooler. The small creatures of the
desert came out from their hiding-places and foraged
about for *their* Christmas dinners ; and the *aasvogels*
swore audibly to each other at the churlishness of
the oxen in refusing to die. And as darkness suddenly fell, and shut out the ghastly horrors of the
desert, we inspanned the wretched oxen, and at
an hour when we should have been assembled
round the Yule-log telling our questionable stories,
and burning our fingers over the bowl of snap-
dragon, we were slowly labouring through the
sand and scrub, and disturbing the awful solitudes
and grim mysteries of the wilderness with sulphurous
invectives hurled at the patient and long-suffering
oxen.

         *　　　　*　　　　*　　　　*　　　　*

Another, and a brighter one.

In the Free State, this time ; the year before the
last. There were five of us : Self, C., R., H., and N.
Our four wagons were outspanned midway between
Cronstadt and Harrismith. Round about us, grazing

on the rich green herbage, was a varied assort-
ment of animals collected during our eight months'
trading trip. There were two or three hundred
head of fine cattle, more than half a hundred
wiry horses, and some fifteen hundred merino
sheep ; and among them wandered, quite at home,
seven ostriches, three-parts grown, and several
tame wildebeeste and springbuck, with two or
three young blesbuck and hartebeeste, and a pair
of half-grown elands. A number of dogs of all
sorts of breeds lay about. And there were other
animals which did not catch the eye, for in a big
Kafir basket under a wagon snoozed a couple of
lion cubs, a young jackal was tied up to a wagon
wheel, and some meercats peered through the bars
of a sort of rabbit-hutch set upon one of the fore
chests.

The camp itself was in a state of bustle, for all
hands were preparing for a royal Christmas dinner.
A merry-eyed Makateese boy was plucking the
feathers from a great pauw, and another was engaged at the same work on some handsome wild
ducks ; a Hottentot was skinning and cutting up a
delicate springbuck, and a wildebeeste lay upon the
ground beside him awaiting his intentions. The
coolie cook was busy making bread and cakes, and
we five men were deep in the mysteries of a plum-
pudding. One, sitting on a bucket, read the recipe,
copied for us from a cookery book by a young lady in
Cronstadt, another stoned the raisins, a third washed

the currants, and a fourth weighed out the flour, sugar, and spices, and the last man cut up the wildbeeste suet and candied peel, and powdered the bread-crumbs. Then, amid breathless interest, all the ingredients were put into a large enamel washing-basin and solemnly stirred. The brandy was mea-sured out and poured in, and the stirring proceeded again. From time to time pinches of the savoury mess were taken up and tasted, and voted so good that one declared that boiling it would be a work of supererogation, and that it would be much better to eat it there and then. But this was out-voted, and the prospective pudding was tied tightly up in a cloth, and put into a great cooking-pot already boiling over a cowdung fire.

What a charming scene it was! How the blood tingles in my veins when I recall it! The busy camp was close on the shore of a large water pan, almost to be dignified as a lake. To the right it was fringed with reeds and rushes, where the weaver-birds' nests hung like great fruits; but the rest of the shore was bare, so far as vegetation goes. But instead, there were birds in thousands upon thousands, in lines, in phalanxes, in regiments, and in armies. Glorious crimson and white flamin-goes stood upon their long legs in masses, looking like the flush of dawn as the sun approached the horizon; ibises, with their strange great beaks and yellow bags, as solemn as a conclave of judges; tall blue cranes, pert and alert; crested mahems, in black, brown, purple, and scarlet; snow-white egrets, with delicate fawn tufts at the back of their heads; huge black, green, and scarlet Muscovy geese; golden brown geese; ducks of all sizes and colours; black and white coots, and tiny, saucy wagtails. And beyond, on the other side of the water, feeding on the slopes and silhouetted against the skyline of the rising shore, were herds of wildebeeste, quagga, blesbuck, and springbuck, with a few ostriches and hartebeeste, all roaming about together in friendly amity.

And the weather was just glorious. We were neither snow-bound nor sun-baked. It was just comfortably warm enough to make shirt and trousers the most appropriate costume, and therefore we were all in shirt sleeves—clean ones, mind you, in honour of the day.

And how we did enjoy that day! It had been voted a public holiday, and we took it out at that. When the culinary arrangements were completed, and the famous dinner all ready for the cook, we lay upon karosses in the glowing warmth of the sun's rays, smoking our pipes and passing desultory remarks concerning the events of our long expedition. Sportsmen as we were, not a shot was fired that day. The birds performed their antics, preened their feathers, caught their fish, and took excursions into air and water undisturbed. The wildebeeste tore about like things possessed, stood upon their heads, and lashed out with their hind legs at things in general and nothing in particular ; the blesbuck wheeled awkwardly round in circles, bobbing up and down like Punch and Judy in a street show ; the springbuck leaped over imaginary obstacles, springing high into the air, and raising a snow-white line of hair along their backs ; and the ostriches waltzed clumsily round in spontaneous figures ; but no gunshot startled them from their gambols, and no bullet whizzed in among their ranks. It was indeed a day of peace.

And then the dinner was served ! The dining-room was the pea-green veld ; the ceiling was the blue vault of heaven, painted with scarlet flamingoes, white egrets, and long-tailed black sacaboolas ; and the walls were decorated with lacustrine scenery, herds of wild and domestic animals, camp pictures, distant flat-topped mountains, and long vistas of grassy plains. The table was the ground, and the seats, too, were the ground, except that the master of the ceremonies occupied an upturned bucket. We took Macbeth's advice, and minded not the order of the viands coming, but let all come at once. With an enamel plate on the ground before one, loaded up with half a duck, a slice from the breast of the pauw, a piece of larded springbuck leg, a large slice of pumpkin, and a fid of stamped mealies, who among us would have exchanged places with those sitting, faultlessly attired in evening dress, around the loaded mahogany, and daintily nibbling morsels of course after course in their prescribed order? Not one. True, the feminine element was missing, but then—let me whisper here—the feminine element is not always an unmixed blessing. But the pudding was—until the next morning. It was just scrumptious, boiled to a turn, rich, fragrant, and toothsome. Two pounds apiece, fizzling in flickering blue flame, was about the allowance, and belts were cast aside, and all, eager for the fray, attacked the savoury mess.

Then the Chairman on the bucket: "Gentlemen, charge your glasses!" The tin pannikins were filled with brandy and water, or gin and water, or rum and water, or a mixture of each, according to taste. "Hats off! The Queen!" "The Queen! God bless her!" Song: "God Save the Queen." Once more: "Charge your glasses! The Old Country!" Song: "Britannia Rules the Waves!" Again: "Charge your glasses! Absent friends!" Song: "The Stirrup Cup!" And then songs, stories, hunting yarns; concertina, flute, fiddle, and barrel organ; brandy, rum, and gin, until the boundless plain had long been shrouded in the solemn veil of night, and the twinkling of the stars upon its waters alone told of the existence of the lake.

*   *   *   *   *

A third, three years later.

Who remembers Klip Drift? Its very name is lost in the snobbish cognomen of Barkly West, as New Rush is lost in Kimberley. But Klip Drift was a place of note in its day, and on Christmas

Day, 1870, its day had not yet waned. It was in fact crowded with bustling humanity, athletic diggers all, muscular, good-humoured, and pleasure-seeking. They had come in in their hundreds from all the rushes up and down the river—from Pniel opposite, from Hebron, Cawood's Hope, Gong Gong, Waldeck's Plant, Blue Jacket, Moonlight Rush, and all the rest of them. A finer looking lot of men it would be hard to find, and outside of the Orient certainly not a more gaudy one. For there was scarcely a coat in the crowd, and every man wore a new coloured flannel shirt with embroidered front, collar, pocket, and cuffs—such shirts as are probably not made in the world now. Rich cobalt blue, magenta, and scarlet were the favourite colours, but there were green, violet, and yellow, and white and pink as well. And every man had a brilliant coloured puggaree wound round his grey cavalier hat, with fringed and tinselled tails hanging down behind. A broad leather belt having several pouches on it, moleskin or cord pants and long boots, completed his attire.

At first sight it would be difficult to say what had brought them all to the spot. The river, with its fringe of great weeping willows, was beautiful enough in all conscience, but it is equally certain that they had not come for that. Nor could there be any attraction in the vast expanse of chasms, pits, boulders, and hummock heaps behind them. But still farther back, where suitable ground could be found, there were horse races, foot races, and jumping matches. There was even what purported to be a cricket match, but, to my critical eye, brought up on the Brighton Brunswick ground, and matured on the Oval and Lord's, the cricket part of it was not quite apparent. And in a leafy kloof in the river's bank a little way up-stream there was a stand-up fight between two noted coloured bruisers, and afterwards (*proh pudor!*) one between two Hottentot women. Then there were boat races on the river—how did all those heavy English and Colonial-built boats get there, 600 miles from the nearest sea, and not fifty miles of railway in all Africa? What a contrast to to-day, when there are nearly 7,000 miles open south of the Zambesi! And there were billiard-tables, card-rooms, and bars. Yea, and there was dancing over at Pniel, where there were considerable numbers of ladies, and at night even a ball! And as for feasting! Oh, ye gods and little fishes, was such feasting ever seen? Restaurants by the score, all in canvas, and the rough tables made of loose boards on trestles bending under the weight of beef, mutton, pork, and ham; wildebeeste, blesbuck, and spring-buck; turkeys, fowls, and geese; pauws, guinea-fowls, khorhaan, and bush pheasants; pumpkins, potatoes, and mealies; big tureens of soup, and sometimes even barbers and "salmon" from the river. And then came the mighty puddings, not unseldom, it must be admitted, related to the variety known to nautical men as "spotted dog," but as often fit for the most fastidious taste in Christmas fare. As for the drinks, it would require the pen of a Kipling to do justice to them. How many gallons of beer, champagne, port, sherry, brandy, gin, rum, and whisky—whisky had not then the vogue it has to-day—were consumed I should not care to calculate ; but I venture to think there were few there that day that had not got outside of their gallon. And yet there was little or no drunkenness. The air of these dry African uplands is too thin and exhilarating; all the noxious fumes and dregs pass off through the skin, and leave only the good-humoured jollity that lies in the heart of good liquor.

I believe that there was also a big political meeting, called to discuss some obscure governmental question. I am not sure, for though I have some faint recollection of something of the sort I must have paid little heed to it. The question of the ownership of the diamond districts had not then arisen, and being only a visitor I cared nothing about the cost of licences, or the removal of boulders, or whether the President of the little self-constituted Republic should be an autocrat or only a figure-head. And so I passed from one sporting scene to another, peeped into this bar, and that restaurant, and t'other billiard-room ; sampled the liquors, ate my beef and pudding, potted myself off the black, took miss at loo, and when tired out as the small hours approached, and as full as I could conveniently hold, retired to my wagon, lay down upon the cartel, and, smoking my pipe, congratulated myself upon having done my duty and upheld the time-honoured institutions of my native land.

DURING my adventurous career it has been my fortune to travel more than 150,000 miles on the ocean, in about thirty mail steamers and sailing vessels. It is of course impossible for any one to engage in such a number of long voyages without meeting with adventures, and though I have never been actually wrecked, I think I must have been face to face with every other phase of phenomenon the ocean has to offer. But though I have never faced shipwreck, I have been a passenger in quite a number of vessels that have afterwards been totally lost. Among mail steamers I can call to mind the P. and O. *Bokkahra*, the N.Z.U.S.'s *Taupo, Tararua* and *Taranaki*; the U.S.'s *European, American, Natal, Basuto*, and *Kafir*, besides two full-rigged ships and a barque. I believe, too, that the R.M.S.'s *Syria, Saxon, Dane, Celt*, and *Cambrian* have also been lost, but of these I am not quite sure. And though never actually wrecked, I have been so many times on the very verge of such a catastrophe, that, combined with the subsequent loss of the vessels

I have named, I can hardly subscribe to the claim of modern maritime authorities that one is as safe on the ocean as on land. No doubt in the case of the huge steamers of our foremost lines, the care of them has been reduced to a very exact science indeed ; but it is at the cost of such fearful wear and tear to those in charge that the system is bound sooner or later to break down. Few human frames can stand for long the terrible strain, the command, or the control of the steam power, which a modern liner demands. One day a captain or a chief engineer will suddenly go mad, and a frightful catastrophe will ensue. (This was written many years before the loss of the *Mohegan* and the accident to the *Paris.*)

With regard to sailing vessels, and speaking entirely of the period between ten and forty years ago, my experience leads me to the conclusion that the prime cause of disaster has been intemperance on the part of the masters. I have been once to Cape Town, twice to Natal, once to New Zealand, and once home from New South Wales, in sailing vessels, and of these five voyages the masters of the vessels in three were in a chronic state of delirium tremens from start to finish, and in each case the vessel had at least three exceedingly narrow escapes of being totally lost. It must, however, be admitted that in one of the other cases, when the master was an abstemious, steady, and careful man, an error of judgment, only rectified with much difficulty, and by great good luck, almost led to the complete wreck of the vessel on a rocky shore.

My first voyage in a sailing vessel was to Cape Town, at the end of 1862. It was a most unfortunate voyage, and took 112 days, consequent entirely upon the cause I have mentioned. We beat backwards and forwards in the Channel for twenty-eight days before we cleared the Land's End, and then were blown northwards and nearly wrecked on the coast of County Cork. Then in some mysterious way we found ourselves off the Morocco coast, and anchored close to Mogador, where, after a good deal of difficulty, two or three of us, myself among them, were allowed to land. The coast of South America was the next surprise, and here again I had another run on shore at Pernambuco, over a bar as bad as any I have seen. But perhaps the greatest of all was when one dark night we nearly banged our flying jib-boom up against the frowning cliffs of Tristan D'Acunha, where we had no more call to be than at the North Pole. The final eccentricity of the befuddled skipper who took us this lively jaunt occurred in Table Bay. There were no docks in those days, and we anchored in the bay late on a Saturday evening. The Health Officer would not come off to pass us on the Sunday, so I amused myself with catching the great crayfish which used to swarm at the bottom then. I had a good pile of them on deck, when a boat full of ladies and gentlemen, officers from the garrison and their friends, rowed round us. The skipper roared rudely at them, and asked them why the blank blank they did not come on board, with the further information that we had neither small-pox nor cholera. As no notice was taken of this, he took up one of the crayfish and hurled it into the boat with a "Take that, you blank, blank, blanks!" Then another went, and then another, until the boat was out of range. This escapade cost him a visit to the police court, and a lightening of his *rem pecuniam.* This worthy afterwards carried off another man's wife from Algoa Bay in a small sailing boat, with the intention of reaching Mauritius, but was chased by a steam tug and brought back. It was to men of this sort that the charge of thousands of human lives and millions of pounds' worth of property was entrusted, and it is small wonder that so much loss took place.

Nevertheless, to myself personally, this voyage was a dream of delight. I found that I was a natural-born sailor, and acted as sort of third mate throughout the voyage, keeping watch and watch with the chief mate, and at the end of it I believe I could have passed the examination for a master's certificate. To this day I have a vivid recollection of the chief incidents of the voyage. The mate, bos'un, and carpenter were the only reliable seamen on board. The second mate was a sprig of the aristocracy who had been kicked out of the Navy; he was a regular daisy, a fine, handsome, manly-looking fellow, but a blackguard to the soles of his boots. The short-handed crew—it was a "cheap ship"—were as nice a looking lot of cut-throats as one would wish to see, and the inevitable mutiny occurred in its due time. It was after the usual broaching of cargo when near the line, and the ostensible ground of complaint was the excessive amount of pumping the vessel required. Certainly there seemed to be some reason for complaint, for, as a matter of fact, she required pumping for two hours every watch, that is, for two hours out of every four. It being my first voyage, I did not at the time appreciate the significance of this, but, knowing what I know now, it is a marvel to me that the ship kept afloat in some of the weather we had. The mutiny resulted in a fight in which handspikes were freely used, but the crew were such a miserable lot that the captain, mates, bos'un, carpenter, myself, and the second-class passenger (there was one other first-class passenger, a delicate, nerveless youth, who had a call to convert the heathen), had no difficulty in driving them into the fo'cas'le, where they were kept on bread and water for two days. The leader, a French Creole from the West Indies, was seized, put in irons, and kept in a sheep-pen on the poop deck for the rest of the voyage. We had terrible hard work pumping while the crew were confined.

It must be often well for passengers that they do not realise the risks they run at sea. With a leaky

ship, a mutinous, incapable crew, and a drunken
captain, we had a combination of circumstances
which might have made the bravest man nervous
if he had grasped the meaning of them, but it never
· for an instant occurred to me that there was
anything out of the ordinary run of the incidents
of sea life.

The idiosyncrasies of individual skippers when
they become whisky-sodden are very marked.
This particular one had a craze for "carrying on,"
and the more drunk he was the more he would clap
on sail. He had a great fancy for that almost obsolete sail the "stunsail," and as long as he had a
boom left nothing could prevent him running it out at
the most unseasonable times. How many stunsail-
booms he broke on this voyage I cannot charge
my memory, but I am quite certain that if he had
had three times as many he would have broken
them all. I believe that every sail on the ship was
at one time or the other torn to ribbons, including
two sets of fore and main topsails and to'gallantsails.
Besides this, his fore and main royalmasts were
carried away, and his main to'gallantmast sprung.
And yet we had no really heavy weather such as I
have seen in other vessels, but a great deal of what
might be called very bad weather; but the more
intoxicated he was the more he would carry on.
On the other hand, the skipper of a large barque
which took me to New Zealand, and who was quite
as whisky-sodden as the present one, developed an

25

undue amount of caution in precise proportion to the degree of his intoxication. One could always tell, by the way in which the sails came off, the depth of his potations for the time being, and when he was very drunk indeed he would heave-to altogether. Of the two, one would perhaps choose the last to confide our fortunes to, but they were both most undesirable custodians of our fates.

The captain of a barque in which I voyaged to Natal in the early sixties was, if possible, worse than either. He used to get not merely sodden, but mad-drunk, and in this condition was downright dangerous. More than once I consulted with the mate as to the advisability of putting him under restraint; but this mate was a timid, diffident person, without a bit of go in him, and he refused to undertake the responsibility. I personally saved this man's ship from total wreck for him, and small thanks I got for it. After we rounded the Cape we had no sight of the sun for nearly a fortnight, and did not know where we were, as the Mozambique current running down the coast made the laying down of our position by dead reckoning very difficult. One afternoon land was sighted, and soon a lighthouse was made out. The skipper at once assumed that this was the light on the Bluff above Durban Harbour, and made for it. I had been up this coast before, which was the case with no one else on board; and I knew that it was the East London light, at least 350 miles from Durban, and told him so. But he would not listen to my repeated remonstrances, and towards dusk we got close to the land. I then went to him and told him that I was not going to be wrecked to please him, and that if he did not put the ship about while there was time I would knock him down and do it myself. He swore at me, and tried to strike me, whereupon I gave him a push, and he fell on deck, and did not rise again, but went off to sleep; and we got the vessel round just in time. Another quarter of an hour and she would have been a total wreck, for at this time East London was a most dangerous place and had the worst bar I ever saw, no vessel being able to cross it unless the sea was quite smooth. The next day we had a sight of the sun, and were able to ascertain our true position, and finding that I was right, the captain, who did not wake up for fifteen hours, said nothing about the matter.

Doubtless owing to their having more society than masters of sailing vessels, the captains of steamers do not appear to develop these soaking habits. At all events, all the two dozen or more with whom I have sailed, with one possible exception, have been steady, reliable men. It is open to question, though, whether they do not sometimes get too much society, to the danger of their neglecting their duties to their vessels. The inconsiderate way in which passengers make demands upon the time and attentions of the master of a mail steamer is one of the most striking features of present-day sea life ; and if he does not comply with all these demands, but prefers close application to the care of his charge, he is at once voted a boor, and adjudged to be disrespectful, forsooth, to his passengers. This is especially the case in the Australian and South African lines, the *nouveaux riches* of which countries appear to think that the captains have no other duties than to find constant amusement for them. On a voyage to Natal in one of the largest of the Cape mail steamers, about four years ago, a few of those bumptious brokers and company promoters who now rule the roost on these lines, seriously proposed to prepare a written remonstrance because the captain, who was much troubled with rheumatism, owing to his habit of passing his nights on the bridge, preferred to take his meals in his own cabin, instead of at the head of the table, where they made the saloon hideous with their noisy vulgarities.

I have often been asked which is the pleasantest —a voyage in a sailing vessel, or one on board a mail steamer. The reply is that it depends entirely on the passengers. To a person who is not self-contained, and has no resources within him or herself, the being cooped up for four months with a lot of people with whom he has absolutely nothing in common must be a most intolerable infliction. But, on the other hand, to one not utterly frivolous the ceaseless racket of so-called amusement on board a mail steamer is unendurable. When I first voyaged in mail steamers we looked upon it as a yachting trip, and did not sit on the safety valve and urge the captain to shorten the passage at all hazards. We enjoyed it. There was no fever of excitement; we dawdled away the day basking in the sun and drinking in the glory of the mighty ocean and the blue sky. We were not elbowed to one side by a mob of sharebrokers and company riggers. We did not eat ten or twelve courses at dinner, and then quarrel with the cook because we had not had enough. We had—thank Heaven—no music-room, and were not squalled at day and night by squeaky sopranos and broken tenors, nor spanked at on the grand piano by husband-hunting spinsters. We did not listen at night to melancholy niggers, or to ranting histrionic geniuses. We were not danced off the deck every other night, or turned out of the saloon for a dismal concert. We took things easy, and were satisfied with a mild rubber or a hand at limited loo, or a game at backgammon; and only now and then indulged in an impromptu waltz, or a little music in the moonlight. We had no electric lights, and no luxurious sofas, and our panels were painted a pale sea-green. This is all altered now, and a voyage in a mail steamer is a restless, noisy round of human nothingness.

For those who wish to study the phenomena of the ocean, and a more interesting study there is not, a sailing vessel is undoubtedly the best. Mail steamers nowadays travel at such a furious rate that it is well-nigh impossible to make any observations, and the rapid shifting of latitude, and therefore of climate, precludes any attempt at forming a symmetrical conception of the phases experienced. Those whose experience of the ocean has been entirely confined to mail steamers know but little of what the ocean has to show them. They may have seen storms, but the modern steamer is such a powerful creature that the fight between him and the forces of Nature hardly, save in exceptional cases, gives one an adequate idea of what they really are. One only realises her terrible power when it is met by resistance which is practically passive. The reverse of a storm has its terrors too, and those of a tropic calm are unknown to the steamship voyager. He glides through it at racing pace, probably deep in the mysteries of nap all the time, and never dreams of the awfulness the man on the sailing vessel experiences when for weeks the sun glowers down with furnace heat from a brazen sky, and is reflected with increased intensity from the oily waste of waters, and his abode rolls from side to side until her yard-arms almost touch the water with an awful dip that sometimes makes the hardest heart quake, and a ceaseless monotony that is well-nigh maddening. Nor does he see much of the marvellous cloud and atmospheric effects of the ocean, and, except a few porpoises and flying fish, rarely any of its denizens.

It is generally supposed that the North Atlantic

passage is the stormiest in the world, and if by this
is meant that sudden and deep, but passing, depressions are more numerous there than elsewhere,
this may, perhaps, be true ; but those who wish to
witness the sustained fury of the elements must go
down into the Southern ocean.   The heavy westerly
winds which almost constantly prevail here apparently belong to enormous cyclonic systems, which
must have their centre at the Antarctic pole.   The
effect of this constant passage of violent winds in
one direction is to build up seas of the magnitude
of which those who have never seen them can have
no conception.   I have seen seas that could have
been little short of a mile from crest to crest.   The
height of these great seas is not easy to ascertain
without an aneroid, which, unfortunately, I never
had when in the Southern ocean, but judging from
the fact that when down in the bottom of a trough
they seem to tower far above the mast-head, they
must be considerably over a hundred feet, if not
two.   The sensations as one of these great mountains of water passes under the keel, and the ship
then slowly sinks into the trough behind, are very
extraordinary.   Though under close-reefed topsails
the vessel will travel before the wind at twelve knots
an hour, but so much faster do the seas race along
that she is in a constant condition of rising and
falling, of laboriously climbing up mountains, and
then rushing headlong down into awesome valleys.
As the ship sinks down into one of these troughs

one feels as though rising up to the mast-head in a balloon, and involuntarily catches hold of the first thing to hand to keep oneself down. With many a shiver, many a creak and groan, she goes down, down, down, apparently into the bottomless pit, and one's fingers dig themselves hard into one's palms, and one's teeth set firmly together. At the bottom she pauses for many seconds, her timbers and rigging tremble as though exhausted with an awful struggle, and her abbreviated sails hang loosely as the wind is shut out by the wall of water astern. One is, as it were, in the valley of the shadow of death. There is an awful loneliness that is never felt when there is a wide horizon around. The view is shut out fore and aft by grim and menacing mountains that seem to have volition and angry intent ; to port and starboard there is a dreary waste of waters, green and sickly, and streaked with white, and bounded at but little distance by the haze and glow of the driving spray ; overhead, and but little higher than the crests of the seas, are dense and glowering clouds, scudding along at furious rate, and plunging the scene into semi-darkness. Even if there should be a few albatrosses, molly hawks, and Cape hens shrieking defiance to the fury of the storm, they do not lessen the feeling of loneliness, but seem rather like attendant demons mocking at our fears. Then the topsails slowly fill again, the stern rises, the timbers give an answering groan, and we climb stern first up an angry steep of hissing water. Now we feel as if we were being doubled up into the deck, and we stiffen our backs and stand defiant to the surging mountain that advances to overwhelm us. Higher and higher we rise, deeper and deeper we seem to sink into the deck, and, towering far above us like a huge mountain of glacial ice slipping down upon us, is the crest of the sea. We stand breathless, every moment expecting to be pooped and swamped. The men at the wheel dare not look behind them lest they should turn and flee from their impending doom. Then with a shiver we are on the very summit, like Noah's Ark upon Mount Ararat, and gaze round, as from a mountain peak, upon a vast world of sage-green and rageful waters. The air, too, is full of rage. The tempest howls and shrieks and roars and whistles through the rigging as though it would tear the masts out by their very roots. Our clasp tightens round the shroud we are holding, fearful lest we should be carried bodily away. The spray flies over us in sheets, and buries the ship out of sight, and when we emerge from it we are once more sinking down a sickening slope into another death-like valley. And so it goes on, day after day, for weeks together. The only break in the monotonous climbing and sinking is when, as sometimes happens, the wind veers to the north-west and blows harder than ever. This causes a confused and dangerous sea, and most cautious shipmasters heave-to until it has backed again to the west.

But, terrible as these furious winds and mountainous seas are, there is a grandeur and beauty in
them that is fascinating in the extreme. Notwithstanding the awe they inspire, one almost feels
inclined, when poised, as it were, in mid-air on the
pinnacle of a dizzy ridge, to throw wide one's arms
to the fury of the elements and perform acts of
adoration and praise. Indeed, all sense of awe very
soon disappears, and the dominant sensations are
wonder and enchantment—wonder at the might of
the forces let loose, and enchantment at the marvellous, weird magnificence of their effects. Standing
on deck in this wild and lonesome world, and gazing
around at this chaos of fury, one becomes spellbound
with the glamour of the tumult, drunk with the
might of Universal Will. The splendour of the
spectacle takes possession of us, and we become
lost to ourselves, lost to the puny world of human
creatures and human civilisation, and know only
that we stand in the presence of the Infinite, and
are watching the evolution of a world.

But all is not enjoyment in these mighty turmoils.
When one tears oneself away from their fascination,
it is found to be cold and dismal. Everything is
saturated; the deck is inches deep in water; the
uproar of the storm is so deafening that conversation
is only possible by shouting; the ship tumbles about
so that the cook can only cook the plainest comes-
tibles, and those in the roughest and most inadequate
fashion; the stewards can serve them with the

greatest difficulty, and they can only be eaten by a series of gymnastics which accord neither with the dignity nor the digestion of the individual. At night one's bed is as lively as the balls in a washing machine, and the noise of the elements and the creaking of the timbers drives sleep from the drowsiest head. Voyagers in steamers never experience these seas. They keep to the north out of their range; it is only in circle sailing that they are attained.

In illustration of the force of the wind in these latitudes, I may relate that once on a voyage to New Zealand, when it became necessary to heave-to owing to a veering to the north-west, the chief mate and two men endeavoured to rig up a tarpaulin to the mizzen shrouds, as the wind was much too strong even for a storm staysail. With much difficulty they got into the shrouds, but when there it freshened temporarily in a squall, and for some minutes they were jammed hard and fast up against the rigging as though they were bound with ropes, and could move neither hand nor foot. I had a rather curious experience on the same voyage. The cuddy and sleeping cabins were so small and stuffy that almost from the commencement of the voyage I had given up sleeping in my bunk. On deck, and in stocks amidships, between the fore and mainmasts, was a large lifeboat, and over it, keel uppermost, was lashed a smaller boat. There was just room to creep in between the two, and in there

I had taken my bedding, and had a lovely large airy cabin all to myself. After we had rounded the Cape we bore away to the south-east for the circle. The following night as I lay asleep in my private abode I was suddenly awakened by a tremendous crash. Starting up, I found that the boat was full of water, and was tilted up at an angle of about forty degrees. With much difficulty I struggled out, and found myself waist-deep in water, although the vessel was a flush-deck one. The bow of the lifeboat was resting on the bulwark, the stern end of the keel being still in the afterstock, which was wrenched right round. It appeared that we had suddenly entered these westerly winds, and a great sea had struck the vessel almost broadside on. The boats being in the most open part of the deck received the full force of the blow, and were completely smashed, the fore-stock was torn out of the deck, and the boats themselves very nearly carried overboard to leeward. It was a narrow escape for me, and a complete marvel that the vessel was not utterly swamped, as she was a yard deep in water from stem to stern.

The actual force of the wind is, perhaps, often greater in some of the ordinary travelling cyclones than in this great stationary one of the Antarctic Ocean. (It may here be said that the much-talked-of cyclones of the Indian and China seas differ only in intensity from the depressions which reach our shores from the Atlantic.) I think the strongest wind I ever experienced was on a voyage between Natal and Ceylon (I cannot now call to mind in which direction) in the R.M.S. *Natal.* We were head on to it, the engines going dead slow, and it was absolutely impossible to stand and face it. If for an instant I turned round to it, my face felt as though I were being flayed alive ; and I am convinced that if I persisted my skin would have been peeled off. Among several strange exhibitions of the wind's force, perhaps the most remarkable was the heavy brass bell on which the hours were struck being lifted out of its sling on the fo'cas'le, and after being banged about against the rigging from side to side, landing on the poop right aft. During the same storm a sea struck the steamer, which, besides smashing a couple of boats, actually bent one of the iron davits on which they were slung nearly double, although it was as thick as a boy's leg. It is absolutely inconceivable how this could be done when one considers the smallness of the resistance, but I could not disbelieve the evidence of my own eyes.

The Bay of Biscay has got a very bad name in the matter of stormy weather, but, unless my experience has been exceptional, its reputation has suffered as undeservedly as many others. I have been through it sixteen times, and I think only in four has there been anything like bad weather, while in several I have run through it without seeing a fiddle on the table, and only a sailor can realise what that means. The worst weather I ever saw there, which was in the R.M.S. *Mexican*, was not bad enough to keep any but the elderly and delicate people off the deck.

"After the storm comes the calm," though, as a matter of fact, I think the sequence is more often reversed. Be that as it may, a calm is in its way as awful as a storm. Sixteen days was my first and longest experience of a tropical calm on the equator. Others have known forty days' calm, but I think sixteen will be found sufficient to satisfy the most insatiate craving for observing the phenomena of nature. Sixteen days of blistering heat, when the sun seems absolutely to throw itself bodily at one, and the air is so still and stagnant that a wisp of swansdown dropped from the mast-head would, if it were not for the rolling of the ship, fall in plumb-line on deck, and yet so heavy that it would take it half an hour to do so. I have never felt such absolute stagnation on land in any part of the world as in this particular tropic calm. In the stillest days upon land there are almost always slight moving airs, caused usually by the irregularities of surface, and in the mornings and evenings there is sure to be some soft waftings of the atmosphere ; but here at sea not the slightest movement could be traced. It seemed absolutely to press down upon one, and sometimes a long deep inspiration had to be taken in order to keep the lungs up to their work. The shade temperature does not exceed 100 degrees, and is perhaps more often nearer ninety, as the great body of water must have some lowering effect. Many foolish people talk about the Red Sea being the hottest place in the world, as though it were not a natural necessity that it must be still hotter on shore. But the sun heat is sometimes as much as 150 degrees to 160 degrees, and rarely falls below 130 degrees. Consequently, one has to avoid touching anything, for the pitch in the deck and rigging boils ; the paint blisters ; and the metal work is as though it were red-hot. The glare is fearful, for the sea is as oil, and glitters like a looking-glass, and the brazen skies are as one great sun. But the most trying feature of all is the monotonous rolling of the ship from side to side. It is difficult to say what causes this extraordinary rolling. One would imagine that in absolutely still water a vessel would remain absolutely still ; but such was not the case in any one of the sailing vessels in which I have voyaged. Even steamers, notwithstanding the way on them, sometimes roll in the same manner, but this is not always the case. In this first voyage of mine the rolling would have been quite terrifying to some constitutions, for I really thought on several occasions that she would roll right over, and never recover herself, and it was always a marvel to me that the masts were not jerked off her. Of course it made taking meals a matter of great difficulty, and the attempt to partake of soup was nearly always disastrous. Being very young at the time I used to think it great fun, but I am sure that now I should look at it as an intolerable infliction.

There is another curious thing about these calms. As a vessel does not remain stable in them, neither does she remain stationary. As a matter of fact, vessels drift about in the most extraordinary manner. The cause of it is as obscure as that of the rolling. That it is not caused by currents is evidenced by the fact that they do not drift in any particular direction, but quite capriciously. In fact, two vessels within a mile of each other will drift in exactly opposite directions, quite independently of the direction of their heads. They are said to attract each other when drifting in this way, and cases have been known in which serious collisions have occurred between sailing vessels in an absolute dead calm. I had rather a disagreeable experience of this drifting in this very calm of which I am writing. There was a large vessel about two miles from us, and after dinner one day (we dined in the middle of the day) I asked the skipper if we might take a boat and pull off to her. To this he assented, and the first mate, the three passengers, the carpenter, and four hands, pulled away for this vessel, whose name I now forget, but which was bound to Rangoon. We had a long jollification on board, and as the afternoon wore on became decidedly lively, and the captain politely suggested that it was time to return to our own vessel. But

when we came to look for her we could not make
her out. There were quite twenty vessels in sight,
but so far had our own drifted that we could not
pick her out. However, we made for the one which
the mate (he was rather "squiffy") believed to be
ours, but before the sudden darkness fell we were all
convinced that he had made a mistake. We therefore shaped our course in the dark for another, but
owing to the men evincing a preference for going
to sleep rather than rowing, we were some hours on
the water without reaching it, when all at once we
saw a port-fire flare up in quite another direction.
We altered our course for this, and after pulling in
a desultory way for the rest of the night, gained our
own vessel at break of day, all pretty well exhausted,
and fortunate in not having to take a passage to
China or some other undesirable place.

Notwithstanding their monotony, these calms are
interesting in enabling one to observe the life of the
ocean far more closely than is possible when the
vessel is moving. Unless a few migrants should
pass over, or unless the vessel should be tolerably
close to land, there is little or no bird life, but in
and on the water are many interesting organisms.
Pieces of the beautiful Gulf Weed, most elegant of
all sea plants, are often to be picked up, though the
greatest quantity is to be found outside the calms.
(It may be mentioned, by the way, that this weed
can be gathered even when the vessel is moving at
a good rate. The plan is to take the ribwork of an

26

umbrella, fasten to it a broom-handle to which is attached a line, and, closing the ribs, use it as an assegai, hurling it through the desired · clump of weed. On drawing it back, the ribs will open and catch the weed as in a net.) Another extraordinary plant I have seen is a long, smooth, round leafless stalk, such as we sometimes see on our shores, but as thick as a man's thigh, and a hundred yards long. I have no doubt that some of the supposed sea serpents have been pieces of this weed. Further south, I once passed through an immense bed of many thousands of acres of it, so thick that the vessel could hardly force its way through. Lovely Portuguese men of war float about in thousands, and the true nautilus may occasionally be observed. Turtles are sometimes seen, and sharks and their attendant pilot fish are almost always present. On this occasion we caught one no less than fourteen feet long, the biggest monster I ever saw. Among other fish I obtained were flying fish, which, of course, were ubiquitous, porpoises, bonitos, and an albacore. I also shot a black fish, a small species of cetacean.

This calm broke up, not with a storm, but with the heaviest fall of rain I ever experienced. The great bank of black, forbidding clouds came up apparently without any wind ; the sky became dark ; the lightning flashed continuously ; and the thunder was appalling. Then the rain came down in a plumb-line, and continued for full two hours.

So heavy was it that, notwithstanding that it was running out of the scupper-holes all the time, it was sometimes more than a foot deep on the main deck. It was truly a delicious bath after the fort-night's frizzling and steaming we had had.

On this voyage occurred one of those strange and unaccountable, yet not uncommon, appearances of a phantom ship. It was a fine moonlight night, there was a light breeze right aft, and we were moving at about five knots. We were all sitting on the grating abaft the wheel, smoking and keeping up a desultory conversation, when, casually turning round, I saw a full-rigged ship, all sail set, bearing down on us about a mile astern, but a point or two to port. She stood out bright and clear in the moonlight, and we all turned round and looked at her, and discussed her probable destination and cognate matters. We stood thus watching her for several minutes, and then sat down again, and resumed our lazy talk. About a quarter of an hour afterwards I turned to take another look, when, to my surprise, she had disappeared. We scanned the horizon long with night glasses, but clear as it was not a trace of her could be found, and she was never seen again. It has been attempted to explain these strange disappearances by supposing that the vessel becomes enveloped in a thin fog-bank. I offer no opinion on this explanation, I merely record the fact as it occurred.

After manifestations of natural force, perhaps the

most appalling things at sea are fires and collisions.
Of the former I have had small experience, the only
fire having any element of danger in it which I have
known having occurred on a sailing vessel, when
the crew, after broaching cargo and getting drunk,
managed to set fire to some bales of Manchester
goods. They smouldered for some time before the
smell attracted the attention of the officer on watch,
but though nearly all the hands were lying about
drunk, the officers, assisted by the passengers, soon
extinguished the fire. But in the matter of collisions
I was present in a rather dangerous one, though of
somewhat unusual character. I was on board the
R.M.S. *Cambrian*, homeward bound from Natal,
and we were in the Bay of Biscay. There had
evidently been some heavy weather, but it had
subsided, leaving, however, a nasty chopping sea.
When we came on deck after dinner a steamer was
seen in the distance making signals of distress, and
we altered our course to see what assistance we
could afford. When within hailing distance her
captain informed us that she had broken her shaft,
and he wished to be towed to Southampton, and,
after some parleying, our skipper agreed to do so.
In the nasty sea there was running I knew very well
that the proper course by which to get a line on
board was for one of us to lower a boat ; but both
skippers apparently thought otherwise. They therefore approached each other in order that the *Mary*,
which was the name of the disabled steamer, might

throw her line on board of us. The inevitable consequence ensued, and both vessels got broadside to each other in the trough of the same sea. Then they rushed down the two slopes of the trough like toboggans coming sideways down a hill, and crashed into each other with a terrific noise. Then they got locked together by the yards, rigging and boats, and jabbed into each other with every heave of the sea. Both masts of the *Mary* toppled over, and her port boats were smashed to splinters. A like fate awaited our starboard boats, and our mizzen topmast and to'gallant yard went by the board, and all the starboard bulwarks were smashed in. It was a difficult job to get clear of each other, as all the wreckage was inextricably mixed up together, and all the time we were continually banging into each other. When we at last succeeded, we both presented a very sorry appearance ; but we got the hawser on board, and proceeded on our voyage.

When our topmast came down, I was standing just behind a windlass which stood forrard of the wheel and binnacle. I saw the mast coming down, and saw by the line it was taking that it would come very near my head, so I quickly stooped down behind the windlass. The mast came right down across the middle of the top of the windlass, and broke across it, I being out of harm's way right under it. Fortunately it missed the binnacle and wheel. Of course, a good deal of confusion occurred. Some of the lady passengers were screaming, or in

hysterics, and others took to praying, and some of
the men were no better. While the captain was
busy giving orders about the wreckage, a missionary
rushed up to him, seized him by the coat-tails, and
in a terrified voice cried, " Oh, Captain, Captain,
there is a hole in the ship's side big enough to put
my head into." The answer he got was, " Then go
down and put your head into it, you blank, blank,
and don't bother me ! "

Eventually we got the *Mary* in tow, and steamed
successfully for some hours, when the line broke,
and then the very same crashing together occurred
again, though in a much less dangerous form.
There was really no excuse for it this time, and
both masters were equally to blame. However,
we took the disabled steamer to Southampton, and
heavy salvage had to be paid—indeed, I was afterwards told that the share of the captain of the
Cambrian amounted to no less than £1,500.

Breaking a shaft is one of the most dreaded
accidents on a steamer, and this too has happened
within my experience. . It was on the R.M.S. *Syria*,
returning from Natal in, I think, 1875. We had
just left St. Helena, and the island was still in sight,
when, as we sat at dinner, a great crash was heard,
and then the engines rushed round with tremendous
velocity, deprived of the resistance of the water on
the blades of the screw, making the vessel vibrate
to her very keel. We all jumped up and looked
at each other, but there was no need to make

any inquiries, for all knew by instinct what had happened. Captain Vyvyan held a consultation with the passengers on deck, as to whether we should endeavour to reach England under sail, or return to St. Helena and wait for the next monthly steamer. It was fortunate that the balance of opinion ran in favour of the latter course, for, unless my memory plays me false, it took us seven days to regain our anchorage at St. Helena, although the island was in sight the whole time, and the weather perfectly fine. At that rate it would have taken us many months to fetch the Channel, and if we met with bad weather we should probably have foundered. The result of this accident was that we had a not altogether unpleasant stay of three weeks at this beautiful island. Driving, riding, and boating parties, cricket matches, dances, fishing, and music filled up the time, and some were quite sorry when it was all over. One of our favourite amusements was getting up races against time among the native boys, up and down the well-known Jacob's Ladder. This was then a rickety wooden concern of 900 steps, not as it is now, a stone and brick flight. Nevertheless, the time in which these little boys left the hotel, ran up the ladder and down again, and regained the hotel, was simply astonishing. We were eventually trans-shipped on to the ill-fated *European*, which was consequently most inconveniently crowded.

A curious little accident occurred on board the

Syria. A Jew diamond-buyer was one day showing round a very handsome diamond ring, which he
valued at £300. The group was standing close to
the starboard rail, and at their feet was a scupper-
hole. As the ring was being handed by one of the
group to its owner, the latter fumbled it, and it
slipped from his grasp, and fell right into the
scupper-hole, and of course went down into the
sea.

Whether it was from the *Syria* or the *Dane* I
cannot now remember, but from one of them, or
from the *Celt*, a young fellow jumped overboard one
day. On reaching the water he at once struck out
for the ship, and cried out in piteous tones to be
taken on board again. When he was fished up he
disappeared into his cabin, and was never seen
again for the rest of the voyage. It was believed
that it was a love affair, but his courage failed him
when he got into the cold water. On an outward
passage in the *Mexican* there were two successful
suicides, one by a first-class passenger, who cut his
throat in delirium tremens, and the other by the
baker, who jumped overboard. Besides these, there
was a sudden death from heat apoplexy, and, of
course, all these cases threw a great gloom over the
voyage. Indeed, it is very strange what a solemn
feeling a death at sea causes. I have witnessed
more than a dozen burials at sea, and in every case
it had a much more solemn and lasting effect than a
similar occurrence on land.

Only once have I seen an iceberg. It was in the Southern Ocean in 1875. It was a beautiful sight, but there was no element of danger in it, as it was broad daylight, and the ship was well in hand. It is at night or in foggy weather that these lovely things are dangerous.

TRAPS AND HORSES

ONE of the very first things that strikes the
wanderer in the great expanses of the
southern hemisphere is the strength and
endurance of the horses. He notes that, though
to look at they are the sorriest scrags he ever set
eyes on, yet they appear to be possessed of a
power of getting over the ground that is little short
of miraculous, and so astonishing in its persistence
as to seem automatic. A very striking instance
came under my notice only a few days after first
landing in Cape Town in 1863. I was sitting one
Saturday afternoon in the stoep of Park's Hotel,
which occupied the corner of Adderley and Strand
streets, when a dust-covered horseman stopped and
dismounted. His horse was taken to the stables,
and in the course of conversation in the bar I learnt
that he was a member of the Legislative Assembly
for an up-country district. There was no railway
communication with the interior in those days, and
he had ridden in from his home at Colesberg in
less than six days, having started on the previous
Monday. Now Colesberg is more than 500 miles

from Cape Town, and the country is very rough
going, much of it being heavy sand, and other
parts very mountainous. No English-bred horse,
fed according to English methods, could have
accomplished such a ride as this, more especially
when we consider the temperature of the Cape
Colony. I went to look at the animal on which the
journey had been performed, and found it to be a
little roan schimmel barely fourteen hands, and
apparently as fresh as paint. Another very remarkable ride that came under my notice was
performed by a Boer who lived a few miles from
Grey Town, in Natal. His wife was taken ill, and
a particular medicine, not to be obtained in Grey
Town, was imperative. So in the early hours of
the night he started for Maritzburg, fifty-five miles
distant, through an extremely hilly country, and
was back on his farm in sixteen hours. The
remarkable thing in this ride was, that this Boer
weighed over seventeen stone.

In my own experience many instances of the
wonderful staying powers of African horses have
occurred. To mention one, in 1866 I had been
appointed Honorary Secretary for the first Athletic
Sports held in the Umvoti County of Natal. They
were to be held in Grey Town on Boxing Day,
which fell on a Monday. All preparations, entries,
&c., were concluded early in December, when I
received an urgent request to go to the Transvaal to
look after a friend who was lying very ill in his

wagon with no attendants but a couple of raw Kafirs. I rode up as hard as I could, and found him among the kopjes of the Drakensberg, between Lydenberg and Wakkerstroom, very bad with fever, which he had contracted somewhere in the low country to the north-west. I tended him for some days until he was clearly out of danger, and then suddenly remembered that I had to be in Grey Town on Monday morning. I was then sitting on the wagon-box drinking my morning coffee at 6 a.m. on Saturday morning. Grey Town was 220 miles away, but I was at my post there at 10 a.m., and in addition took a second prize both in running and jumping competitions.

Now, even if the country had been fairly level, this would have been a good ride for any horse, if we consider that it was performed in the height of an African summer ; but to any one who knows the country it becomes simply astonishing that any single horse could stand such a strain, though it is only fair to add that my weight in those days did not exceed nine stone. The wagon was out-spanned about 60 miles from Wakkerstroom, and the intervening country, though heavily undulated in places, was fairly easy riding. At an elevation of nearly 6,000 feet the air is most exhilarating, and the fine granite kopjes of a thousand, or even two thousand, feet in height, scattered about in all directions among the rich green of the luscious grasses, made a delightful picture. Nor was game wanting, and I and my horse frequently amused ourselves with scampering after ostriches, running down elands, or challenging hartebeestes, zebras, blesbuck, and springbok. True, vast expanses of black, tenacious mud often impeded our progress; but, on the whole, we got through to Wakkerstroom in remarkably good time. But it was after leaving this benighted vlllage—then inhabited by a few scamps and loafers, for whom hanging was too good—that our troubles began. It was not my first visit to this part of the country, and I was aware of the existence and route of a bridle-path to Utrecht, over the mountain ranges, which was considerably shorter than the wagon road. Therefore, after a brief rest, I again saddled up, and commenced the ascent of twelve or fifteen hundred feet to the top of the Drakensberg Mountains, on attaining which I was more than 7,000 feet above sea level. There was a good many miles of fairly level cantering ground up here; and when I approached the edge, and could see a hundred miles into Natal, the shades of night began to fall. I now had to descend more than 3,000 feet down a narrow bridle-path, in some places as steep as the roof of a house. Of course, I was obliged to dismount and lead the horse, for no horse could be ridden down such a place, even in daylight, and in a very short time it was so dark that, though the atmosphere was perfectly clear, I could not see five yards in front of me. The steepness of the path was not the worst ; it was the rocks in it, some lying loose, others protruding from the soil, that bothered us. We floundered about, barking our shins, stumbling among the loose stones, kicking up against the fast ones, and sending rocks crashing down the mountain - side at every step. I was in constant dread lest the horse looming above me should slip and pulverise me, or bring down an avalanche of rocks and sweep me off my feet. Nevertheless, we made the descent in safety, and reached the God-forsaken village of Utrecht just as the last lights were extinguished, having ridden 90 miles. There was nothing to eat there ; there never was in those days, and I think the inhabitants must have lived on peach-brandy. By daylight I was off again, and had a fine gallop over the flat and along the level plateau of the Biggarsberg, then enlivened by large troops of magnificent hartebeeste. At the bottom of the steep descent of Helpmakaar, I called at a Boer's house and asked for something to eat, explaining that I had eaten nothing since the previous afternoon ; the Boer placed a plate containing two peaches in front of me, and that was all I had until late in the evening. I had then to descend into that wonderful thorn valley so well known, and I am afraid anathematised, by all travellers to Utrecht or Wakkerstroom, and by dusk reached the welcome " hotel " (*i.e.*, Kafir hut) of Yankee Dan on the Tugela, having again ridden about 90 miles. Off again before day-

light, I had about thirty-five miles of the roughest
country conceivable to traverse before ten o'clock,
including the ascent and descent of a ridge quite
2,000 feet above the valley. This ride has always
seemed to me a remarkable instance of the endurance of grass-fed South African horses. It was
the very height of summer, and the heat tremendous ; three very considerable ranges of mountains
from 2,000 to 3,000 feet in height had to be crossed
over , and three large rivers and several smaller
ones to be forded, and except on the top of the
Biggarsberg there was scarcely a mile of level road
anywhere.

Although this particular ride was performed
without any accident, this luck did not always
accompany me on this same road. I have
in another paper described how I was nearly
drowned in the Tugela, and a few days afterwards
I barely escaped an even more terrible fate. It
was in the Buffalo River. The upper courses of
this river run through the sandy plains known as
the Newcastle Flats, and in some portions of its
course dangerous quicksands are formed. I was
crossing over and had got through the deepest
portions of the bed, the ripples on the water
showing that it was only a few inches deep in the
remaining part of its width. But directly I got into
this apparently shallow reach my horse began to
sink, and in a few seconds his belly was in the
water. As he seemed unable to move I slipped

out of the saddle to ease him by removing my
weight, when of course the same fate at once befel
myself. I saw that energetic measures were called
for, or I should be swallowed up in a very short
space of time. On starting on this journey I had
purchased a huge pair of riding boots, which came
right up to the tops of my thighs. They were very
hot and uncomfortable things, and I had been
cursing them all the way up, but they now saved
my life. I soon found that I was as hard and fast
as the horse, and ever second getting deeper. The
boots were large and loose, and it occurred to me
that if I could make the horse struggle out he could
pull me out of my boots. Therefore, catching hold
of the rheim twisted round his neck in my left hand,
with my right I commenced to belabour him with
my sjambok. The poor brute's struggles were
frightful, and I was almost inclined to give it up
rather than torture him more. But it was life or
death, and I hammered away. At last he succeeded in raising himself out, and I clung on to the
rheim with both hands. I thought he would have
dragged my legs out of their sockets, but soon I felt
them slipping out of the boots, and in a few seconds
we both of us floundered ashore exhausted. It
was about the toughest pull I ever had in my life.

On riding back to Grey Town from this journey
I had another rather curious adventure. Since I
had gone up an alteration had been made in the
road on the hilly ground just above the Thorns on

the Grey Town side. In order to avoid a very
steep bit a new road had been marked out, and a
cutting made which crossed the old one nearly at
right angles. When we arrived at this place it was
dark, and the clouds had settled down on the
mountain-tops, so that I could not see a yard in
front of me. Consequently, I let the horse choose
his own way, confident that he would keep to the
road. This he did right enough, but, naturally, he
kept to the old one, and when we came to the cross-
cut he walked right over. I was half asleep at the
time, and I never had such an awakener as when I
found myself still in the saddle, at the bottom of
the cutting, and the horse on his knees. For some
time I could not make out what had happened,
and to this day I cannot understand how I kept in
the saddle, or how the horse got down, for the
cutting was 15 feet in depth and nearly perpendicular. Nevertheless he was not in the least hurt,
and at once gathered himself together and continued on his way in the right direction.

On another occasion, perhaps a still more curious
accident happened to me on the same road. This
time it was with a trap. A friend and myself were
on our way to Pretoria, driving a pair in a kind
of dogcart. We had left a roadside shanty in
the very early morning, and were approaching a
Boer's house where we expected to get breakfast.
My friend was driving, and I was sitting with a
rifle between my legs, as we had been passing

27

a good many hartebeestes and other game. The house stood a little off the road, which did not appear to go up to it, so my friend guided the horses across the veld in a direct course for it. When close to the house a line of tall Tambuki grass ran at right angles across our course, and thinking there might be a ditch I stood up the better to see. My friend did not stop, and as I was standing the horses, which were a wild young pair, made a sudden jump in a manner I never knew horses in harness to do, and lifted the cart clean over the line of grass, which did in reality conceal a ditch. I was pitched out like a sky-rocket, and fell at full length on my face, and the rifle, which had been shot still higher than myself, came down muzzle first, the muzzle striking me exactly in the centre of the neck. It was a double sporting rifle, and one of the barrels were at full cock, as only a few minutes before a herd of spring-buck had passed close to us, and I was ready for a shot if a suitable one presented itself. That the shock of the rifle falling on my neck did not cause it to discharge was remarkable ; but as it fell to the ground something caught the trigger and off it went, the contents passing within an inch or two of my head.

When we were returning from Pretoria on this occasion we were witnesses to an accident which caused me almost more laughter than anything I can remember. After leaving Utrecht we found that the Buffalo River was too full to cross, and we had to go some miles down to where there was a punt. When we reached it, a number of Boers going to Nachtmal at Utrecht were crossing over. They were regular doppers, and all in their Sunday best—mulberry plush schoolboy jackets with metal buttons, new yellow moleskin pants, new veldschoens, and cavalier hats with ostrich feathers twisted round them. There were about twenty of them, and half-a-dozen horses were in the punt, the rest swimming after it held by their reins. In midstream one of the horses in front became restive, and soon put all the rest into the same condition. As their masters tried to quiet them they all got to one end of the punt, and as it was much overloaded, the extra weight at that end caused it to sink below the level of the water. In an instant the other end started up, and shot the cargo into the stream, and then, after standing upright for a second, fell the other way, bottom up, right on top of the struggling lot of Boers and horses. Never was such a spluttering and splashing, but as the bank was not ten yards off, all got safely ashore, when the *verdoming* and *Alamagtiging* was enough to make one's hair stand on end. However, no harm was done, and the Boers got the only washing they had probably had for years. We had a tough job to right the punt and get our own trap over.

Shortly before we had started on this journey

the same cart was washed down the Mooi River.
We were going up to Harrismith by way of Weenen,
and found the Mooi River very full. As in those
days there were no habitations near, we determined
to attempt it, though, as I cannot swim, I did
not half like it. Before we had got far the water
was well over the bottom of the cart and half-way
up to the seat, and the horses were swimming.
In the middle the stream proved too strong,
and we were washed clean away broadside on.
Fifty yards down was a long narrow tree-covered
island, and we were fortunate enough to strike
it, and get fairly on its shores. I advocated waiting
here until the stream ran down a bit, but my friend
would not hear of it. Stripping his clothes off
he entered the stream and led the horses, while
I took the reins, and after a hard fight we gained
the opposite bank. These Natal rivers were
regular terrors at that time, for South Africa was
a much damper country in the sixties and seventies
than it is now.

South African horses in those days had few
vices. They seldom shied, and I never owned
a kicker or a rearer. Jibbing in harness was
the commonest fault, but occasionally one came
across a good bucker. One reads a good deal
about the bucking of horses in the States, in
Australia, New Zealand, Mexico, and other places ;
but I have come to the conclusion that much
of it is pure imagination. I lived five years in

New Zealand, and the same time in Australia, and
I never saw a single case of really bad bucking.
It is true that in Australia I lived chiefly in
Sydney; still, besides the larger places like Melbourne, Ballarat, Geelong, Sandhurst, Bathurst,
Goulbourn, Maryborough, and many others, I
have been to what were then mere out-of-the-way
districts as Echuca, Deneliquin, Hay, and others.
In New Zealand I have been all over the North
Island in every direction, and a good deal over
the Middle Island, living at farms, stations, Maori
wharrys, and small villages, besides the larger
centres of population. No doubt a good many
horses could be made to buck for a show-off, if badly
broken, or if ill-treated; but I am of opinion that
there is much less spontaneous bucking than the
reader of Australian romances would suppose. In
South Africa, in my day, bucking was unusual,
and in most cases was the result of bad breaking
in. Indeed, few horses were broken in at all, in
the proper sense of the term. Usually a saddle was
put on a colt, and somebody got into it as soon
as he could, and stuck there as long as he could.
The sjambok and spurs was almost the only nursing
a young horse got. A horse broken in by Boers
was a horse spoilt. They must be the very worst
horsemen in the world—long stirrup-leathers, with
the toes just in the irons, loose slovenly seat,
stolid, nerveless hands, and bits with long curbs
which were constantly roughly jabbed at. All their

horses had but two paces, a canter and a sort of jog, which, it must be admitted, enabled them to cover easily forty or fifty miles a day with very little fatigue to the rider. This applies especially to the Transvaal Boers; some of the younger Natal Boers, who had mixed more with English, had much better seats. This suggests the question: Are the Australians such wonderfully good riders? My experience, such as it is, leads me to believe them not a bit better horsemen than any others of our race. No doubt a man who has been stock-riding all his life is more at home than another who has done nothing more than hacking it; but, other things being equal, the Australian is no better than any of his cousins. I well remember an Australian who came to Natal with a great re-putation as a horseman, but he was not in it at all with many of the young Natalians. Colonists of thirty years ago will remember G. M. H. I believe myself that Natalians are, or were before the days of railways, in reality the best of all horsemen. One reason why they should be is to be found in the roughness of the country. I should say that a horseman bred in the plains of Australia would natually not have so many resources in the saddle as another used to the country where even a cricket-field is difficult to find, and where no ride of 50 miles could be accomplished, except along the coast, without ascending and descending at least one range of hills of 3,000 feet, and often three, or without crossing a good many rivers. A ride from Durban to Maritzburg, or from Maritzburg to Estcourt, or from Grey Town to the Biggarsberg (especially in the rainy season), would, I should say, take more horsemanship than a month's overlanding in the salt bush. In fact, there is no comparing the two things, and I know of no such ticklish riding as cantering down a greasy unmacadamised road 3,000 feet into the valley below. Canter one must, for one cannot canter up, and there is nothing but up or down. If the horse was walked all the way the journey would take two days instead of one.

But to return to the bucking. The worst case I ever saw was a really extraordinary one. The friend before mentioned had a grey mare and foal which he wished to sell. Some Boers came to look at it, and putting the foal in a kraal, he saddled her, and proceeded to show off her paces. The mare wished to get back to her foal, and he had some difficulty in getting her away from the kraal. After a while he succeeded, but when she had been trotted and cantered about a little, the mare started bucking. My friend sat a good many bucks, but at last he went flying, saddle and all. Of course I thought that the girths had given way, but when I went to pick up the saddle, to my astonishment the girths were intact, and still buckled. I could not make it out, but it was clear that by placing her head between her forelegs,

and then giving a kick out behind, she had jerked
the whole over her withers, and then down her
neck and forelegs. I had heard of such a thing
before, but never believed it. I was once bucked
off a horse in the main street of a village to such
a height that my head seemed on a level with the
thatch of the "hotel" opposite which I was, and
then I came down on my feet as though I had
jumped off a wall. It is said that some men can
sit a bucking horse all day without holding the
saddle with their hands. I do not believe it; at
all events it depends on what is called bucking. I
do not believe that the man was ever born that
could sit a real determined bucker which had made
up its mind to get rid of its rider, and knew how.
Of course, if you put a long-legged scarecrow on
a twelve-hand pony, that man can sit there for
ever unless he goes to sleep; but put an ordinary-
built man on a fifteen- or sixteen-hand horse, and
if that horse wants to get rid of him and knows how,
I don't care where that man came from, but I know
he'll *go*.

In my day, there were few well-bred horses
in South Africa, except in the Cape Colony; still,
I have seen many good runners, and most young
Natalians owned a bit of stuff that could hold
its own, either on the flat or over hurdles. I once
won in a shooting match a bright chestnut that
had a rare turn of speed, and served me a pretty
trick with it. I ran it in one of the races at a Grey

Town meeting, and, after coming in a long way in front of the rest, it bolted with me, left the course, galloped at top speed through the main street of the village, and then for a mile along the road to where its stable was, and then, stopping suddenly, shot me over its head into the rose fence that enclosed the grounds, from which I had some difficulty in extricating myself.

Colonial post-carts in the old days were, under some circumstances, not unpleasant vehicles for travelling in. How many hundred (indeed, thousand) miles I have been jolted over in them, to be sure! In 1863 I went all round the Cape Colony in these vehicles, but the journey was without much adventure. The post-cart journey that is most impressed on my mind took place in 1869. I was on my way to England, and the coasting steamer *Natal* put into Mossel Bay to pick up the mails. On board were two or three grass widows, whose husbands were at work in Natal, while they went home to recruit and refill their dress-trunks. These ladies were of a vivacious disposition, and agreed among themselves to take a rise out of me. I took them on shore after breakfast, but at eleven o'clock they said it was too hot, and they would go on board again. I put them in the boat, and as I had forgotten to ask at what time the steamer would resume her voyage I asked them if they knew, when I was told at three o'clock. I therefore determined to remain on shore and walk up to the lighthouse. When I was in the lantern, to my astonishment I saw the *Natal* beginning to move, and at once perceived that I had been sold. I walked back to the town, and learnt that in a few hours a post-cart would leave for Riversdale, Heidelberg, and Swellendam, and thence on to Cape Town by Sir Lowry's Pass. I had very little money, but the steamer agents lent me £5 more, and I started. These carts are so built that two passengers are required to balance them; if there is only one he must sit crossways in the middle, and I sat, or reclined, with my legs dangling over one iron bar and another under my neck. Under any circumstances this would not be a pleasant method of travelling, but over a rough Colonial road it was just awful. As there was a strong head wind, and the *Natal* was a slow steamer, I had some hopes of reaching Cape Town first, and therefore bribed the driver to go his best pace. How we did tear along all through the night! It was pitch dark, and I could not understand how the driver kept the road, for I could not see it. For more than forty hours the pace was kept up, only broken by changes, and when we arrived at Cape Town the third morning the *Natal* was being signalled as coming in. The distance, I think, is about 300 miles, and we had three carts, five drivers, and about fifty horses.

As it was Friday, when a military band played
in the gardens, I knew my friends would put in
an appearance, so I had a good nap, and in the
afternoon repaired to the gardens. I watched
behind some bushes until I saw the three
ladies approaching with the captain in their
midst, when I sauntered down towards them in
a nonchalant way, not so much as glancing at
them. People more astonished I never saw.
They thought they saw a ghost, so that I had
much the best of that deal, after all. There had
been no fear of my losing my passage, because
we were not in a hurry in those days, and the
detention in Cape Town often reached a fortnight.

Another post-cart journey that is impressed on
my mind was one from Wakkerstroom to Heidelberg in 1866, and the reason of its being so
clearly impressed is the fact that we met with a
troop of no less than sixteen lions. This is far
the largest number I ever saw together. At
first I took them to be vlakvarks, and was about
to take a shot, when the driver advised me not
to. They were only about 200 yards off the road,
and the driver made a short *détour* to avoid
them. He said that he had never seen so many
before, but often saw three or four. Owing to
the immense herds of game that inhabited these
districts in those days, the lions were never
hungry, and were therefore not dangerous.

A funny, and perhaps not very creditable, incident occurred in a post-cart on the road from Harrismith to Bloemfontein, *en route* to the Diamond Fields. It was a bitterly cold night, and I had provided myself with a bottle of "square face" to keep the blood in circulation. I shared this with the driver, a well-known white man, and by and by its contents made me sleepy, and I rolled up on the mail-bags and went to sleep. I was awakened by the jolting of the cart, and sitting up found that I was alone in it. The driver had evidently tumbled off somewhere, and I found that the horses had left the road and were trotting over the veld among the ant-hills. It was very dark, and I did not know where to look for the road, but from the appearance of the stars I was sure the horses were going back to Harrismith; so I turned them, and in a few miles struck the road. I still did not know where to look for the driver, but seeing what appeared to be a light a good way ahead, I made for it, and found him sitting on an ant-hill smoking his pipe.

The most wonderful post-carting probably ever seen was when Murray and Collins held the mail contract between Durban and Maritzburg. The distance is about 58 miles, and a rougher country could hardly be made, for it is nothing but hills and valleys, streams and swamps. The greatest height attained is about 3,400 feet, and Maritzburg itself is about 2,600 feet. The roads were not macadamised, and after rain were as greasy as ice ; but Murray, who generally drove, used to do it in six hours, and I believe never had an accident. Before his time a queer old card of the name of Welch had the contract, and that to Pretoria *viâ* Harrismith as well. Welch had a rare stock of yarns, and when well primed they used to be real startlers. I remember going with him to Pretoria once when we got stuck in a horrible stretch of black mud on the further side of the Town Hill, known, if I remember rightly, as Reit Spruit. He told us that once when he was crossing this same place he saw a hatless man probing the mud with the butt end of a wagon-whip. He had seen an old hat lying on the road a little way back, so he called out : " Say, chum, your hat's not there, it's behind." The fellow looked up and said : " —— the —— hat ; 'taint that I'm looking for. I've lost a —— wagon and span of oxen somewhere hereabouts, and I'm —— if I can find them." The story is exaggerated ; but it illustrates the difficulties of South African travel in the rainy season.

Talking of Murray makes me wonder whether he was not the best driver I ever saw. The only one I can call to mind whom I should be disposed to place in front of him was a man named George Jones, who drove a Cobb's coach from Napier to Taupo and back, in the North

Island of New Zealand. Cobb's coaches, with their leather springs, are too well known the world over to require description, and at the best are awkward things to drive. This particular bit of country is in some respects even rougher than Murray's road, for some of the ranges to be crossed are nearly 5,000 feet in height, and the angles of the cuttings in some of the ravines very sharp. In addition to this, the River Petane has to be crossed no fewer than fifty-four times in twelve miles. But against this the road is macadamised, and not greasy like the Natal one. Jones used to come down those mountain cuttings at full split, and turn corners on the way down almost as sharp as a V without slackening much of his pace. How he prevented the old ramshackle coach from capsizing I never could understand. As the cuttings were on the sides of precipices two or three thousand feet in depth, it was exhilarating work. I have seen strong men, fit for anything, crush their fingers into the edges of the seats as he came down. Jones used to do this each way every week, the distance being, if I remember right, about 120 miles. He told me that he dare not drink any spirits while working; but, instead, went on a week's "bust" two or three times a year, which set him up until he began to get hipped again.

I have never seen it remarked in print that colonial whips do not hold their reins as the

English do. Some bring the reins over their thumbs, as we do in riding; others have the near- and off-side reins on the outside of the hand, and not between the fingers at all, and then crossed over inside the palm—this gives a very firm grip; others again hold the offside reins on top between the two first fingers, and the near side between the two last; some I have seen holding the palm downwards, with a rein between each finger; while others hold the leaders' reins respectively between the two first and two last fingers, and the polers' together between the middle fingers. I am not sure that this exhausts the different methods I have seen.

Cobb's coaches, in spite of their cumbersomeness, are comfortable and safe vehicles, the leather springs taking off a good deal of the jolting, though once on a corduroy road in the Forty Mile Bush in New Zealand I got as fine a shaking up as man need desire; but then no vehicle on wheels can stand a corduroy road. But for sheer discomfort commend me to the passenger wagons that ran from Cape Town to the Diamond Fields soon after the Dry Diggings were first discovered. I made this journey in May, 1871. The vehicle was a long light wagon, with a number of iron pens inside in which the passengers sat looking forwards. At the back was a seat facing the other way, which was occupied by the guard and one passenger. I was that unfortunate passenger, having neglected the precaution of secur--

ing an inside seat. At first I thought I had got the best of it, but soon found out my mistake. The seat was nearly over the hind axle, and of course received the full benefit of every stone or irregularity the wheel passed over, and as the road contained nothing else but stones and irregularities it was lively work. The footboard was only about a foot deep, and there was no strap to keep us from tumbling out. The distance by the road then used was reckoned at 750 miles, and, with the exception of six hours allowed for sleep at Beaufort West, I occupied that seat for eleven days and ten nights. In my present decrepit and debilitated state I sometimes find myself wondering how people stand the amount of rushing about I see; but a second's flash of thought back into the old days soon dispels that. But of all my adventures in the way of roughing it I think my occupancy of that back seat was about the toughest job. It was holding on like grim death all the way, and only on the sandy road beyond Victoria West was any sleep possible, and then only by tying myself to the back with a bit of rope. I was only thrown out three times, in which I bested the guard, who had five pitches off; but it seemed a wonder to me that every bone in my body was not broken. Nevertheless, except that my feet were rather swollen from sitting so long, I arrived at Pniel perfectly fresh and fit. Two years later I did the same journey in the opposite direction, and by a road a

THE COACH IN WHICH I SPENT ELEVEN DAYS AND TEN NIGHTS, FROM CAPE TOWN TO ENIEL (800 MILES), EARLY IN 1871.

28

little more to the east, in six days and nights.
These wagons were drawn by eight or ten horses
or mules, and driven by two Hottentots or half-
castes, one of whom held the reins and the other
a long bamboo whip, and were frequently changed.

Nearly all my big-game hunting—and by big
game I mean elephants, rhinos, buffaloes, giraffes,
hippos, elands, sable and roan antelopes, gemsboks,
and lions—has been done on foot, and I know little
personally of the behaviour of horses in such work ;
but the little I did learn did not prepossess me in
favour of hunting in the saddle. No doubt I was
unfortunate in my mounts ; but my horses always
seemed timid when opposed to very large animals,
and when I dismounted to fire they generally left
me in the lurch. On one occasion a hard-mouthed
brute very nearly settled me. It was in the
Mangwato country, and I was in pursuit of a
gemsbok. The bush was pretty open, with good-
sized trees, and as we went along I noticed one
with low spreading branches right in our route. I
tried to turn the nag, but the brute took no notice,
and kept his line at a hard gallop. I levelled
myself to the horse's neck and we got under all
right with only some slight scratching ; but directly
I raised myself again a branch of another tree
struck me full in the chest, and knocked me back
as though hit by a cannon-ball. My head struck
the horse's rump, and the animal, realising that
something strange had happened, stopped short.

It was fortunate that he did so, for I rolled out of the saddle, and for many minutes was so dazed that I did not know what had happened. It was a long time before I fully recovered from that blow. Many of the most successful elephant-hunters, notably F. Green, C. J. Andersson, and Selous, probably the three very best, have been foot-hunters. In the flat country hunting wildebeestes, blesbuck, spring-buck, hartebeestes, ostriches, and other flat game is, of course, best done in the saddle. It is some-times ticklish work from the number of colonies of meercats. These elegant little creatures will often make a colony extending over two or three hundred square yards. All this ground will be honeycombed with their holes, and if your horse gets on to it while in pursuit of game there is nothing for it but to shut your eyes and wait for the catastrophe. I was once shot I am afraid to say how many yards, but it was certainly more that ten, coming down a slope over one of these awful places when trying to run down some blesbuck.

UNWIN BROTHERS, THE GRESHAM PRESS, WOKING AND LONDON.